The Secrets of Supervillainy

by

C. T. Phipps

Copyright © 2016 by Charles T. Phipps

Published by

Amber Cove Publishing

PO Box 9605

Chesapeake, VA 23321

Cover design by Raffaele Marinetti

Visit his online gallery at http://www.raffaelemarinetti.it/

Cover lettering by Terry Stewart

Editing by Valerie Kann

Book design by Jim Bernheimer

All rights reserved.

This is a work of fiction. No part of this book may be reproduced in any form or by any electronic or mechanical means including information storage and retrieval systems, without permission in writing from the author. The only exception is by a reviewer, who may quote short excerpts in a review.

Visit the author's website at
http://unitedfederationofcharles.blogspot.com/

Printed by Createspace

First Publication: August 2016

ISBN-13: 978-1537052533

ISBN-10: 1537052535

Dedication and Acknowledgements

This novel is dedicated to my lovely wife, Kat, and the many other wonderful people who made this book possible. Special thanks to Jim, Shana, Rakie, Matthew, Sonja, Bobbie, Devan, Tim, Joe, Thom, and everyone else.

C.T. Phipps

Table of Contents

Chapter One 1

Chapter Two 9

Chapter Three 17

Chapter Four 25

Chapter Five 33

Chapter Six 41

Chapter Seven 49

Chapter Eight 57

Chapter Nine 65

Chapter Ten 73

Chapter Eleven 81

Chapter Twelve 89

Chapter Thirteen 99

Chapter Fourteen 107

Chapter Fifteen 115

Chapter Sixteen 123

Chapter Seventeen **131**

Chapter Eighteen **139**

Chapter Nineteen **147**

Chapter Twenty **155**

Chapter Twenty-One **163**

Chapter Twenty-Two **171**

Chapter Twenty-Three **177**

Chapter Twenty-Four **183**

Chapter Twenty-Five **189**

About the Author **197**

The Secrets of Supervillainy

Foreword

The *Rules of Supervillainy* and *The Games of Supervillainy* followed would-be supervillain Gary Karkofsky, a.k.a Merciless: The Supervillain Without Mercy™, on a journey that showed him the ups and downs of being the bad guy. If he learned nothing else, it was that genuine evil took effort and was something he wanted nothing to do with. It also cost him significantly as his heroic wife, Mandy, was transformed into a vampire while he put aside his dastardly ways to save Falconcrest City from destruction.

When I wrote my first two novels, it was with the desire to explore the darker side of comic books in a humorous and intelligent fashion. Falconcrest City was every dark corner in graphic fiction from Batman's Gotham City to Robert Kirkman's The Walking Dead. It was easy to be the lesser of two evils in that place because everything was draped in one form of shadow or another.

The decision to "kill" (I use quotation marks since she's still around as a vampire and Gary hasn't given up on saving her) Mandy was a highly controversial one with a lot of fans. A lot of readers complained, asking why it wasn't possible to have a happily married couple in superhero fiction. Believe me, I understand this sentiment completely and am still hoping for Gary to be able to have his happily ever onward. A marriage should be the start of all your main couple's best adventures, not the end.

But the story took me there.

Mandy chose to give her life so Cindy would survive, and because Gary's did not respect that choice, a monster is walking around wearing her face. Mandy's choice to make the ultimate sacrifice has also farther reaching consequences than her husband's grief—especially for the person she chose to save.

The Supervillainy Saga world has taken on a life of its own, and I love each of the myriad characters I've created. The Secrets of Supervillainy marks a new phase in Gary's story as we move from gloomy Falconcrest City to explore some of the other locations in the setting as well as the consequences of his actions.

The world is changing in ways both big and small, a process which was begun by the death of the Nightwalker and will continue until the dust settles. In a very real way, Gary has become a supervillain at the twilight of the superheroic age—something he's going to fight tooth and nail.

Also, unlike in comic books, we don't have to hit the reset button after changing things up.

C. T. Phipps

Chapter One

Always Open with a Big Fight Scene

Sister Christian's eyes glowed and she laughed before shooting a column of flame at my head. Her attempt to kill me with fire didn't work out quite the way she expected. Instead, it resulted in her flames striking against my own conjured snowstorm.

Dropping my briefcase full of stolen diamonds, I held up my arm and used it as a shield while throwing every bit of magic I could into producing an icy defense. The results were a massive cloud of steam that blanketed the entirety of the room.

If you're wondering why I was having a fight with a woman who owed royalties to Night Ranger for the misuse of their song in the middle of an abandoned cathedral, it was part of a much larger story that can be summarized as me trying to buy a magic rock which could resurrect my late wife Mandy. I am Gary Karkofsky, a.k.a. Merciless: The Supervillain without MercyTM, and I am not going to let a silly thing like death stop me from bringing my wife back, especially since I was Death's number one minion.

"Gary, look out!" Cindy called as she threw the London Werewolf over her shoulder with a judo throw.

Cindy Wakowski, a.k.a Red Riding Hood a.k.a my favorite henchwench, had cleaned up her act tremendously since Mandy's death. Cindy had returned to medicine and now spent a lot of her time treating the destitute in a free clinic. She'd also given up all (okay some) of her ill-gotten gains to help disadvantaged students complete their degrees in medicine. Perhaps the craziest part is she'd taken to fighting crime as well, serving as a semi-noble superheroine in-between helping me in my various schemes against the city's rich. I didn't know how she managed to find time for it all.

"*That woman loves you, I hope you realize that*," Cloak, my, well, magic cloak, said. He was the ghost of the superhero known as the Nightwalker and the only source of sanity in my otherwise insane life. Not that I listened to him much.

"We're not like that," I said, feeling the steam burn the side of my face.

"*Perhaps you could be, if you were willing to give it a chance.*"

I sighed, shaking my head and wiping some water from my wife. "I'm a married man."

"*I see.*"

I could tell Cloak didn't. He seemed to think this was my going through the various stages of grief. That Mandy was someone I would eventually accept the death of, that I'd move on to someone else. I loved Cindy, maybe as much as I'd loved my ex-fiancé Gabrielle, but Mandy was my life. I'd gotten her killed and I couldn't stop until I made this right. If I couldn't, if she really was gone forever, then I didn't deserve to be happy.

"*Oh Gary,*" Cloak said, hearing my thoughts.

"Forget you heard that," I said, dodging behind a pew as Sister Christian, dressed up today as a fetish-ware version of a nun's attire, flew over the steam cloud and threw a storm of fireballs down at me. I barely managed to stay ahead of them, feeling like someone dodging out of the way of a WW2 plane's gunfire in an Indiana Jones pastiche.

"The Stone of Elderrah is mine, Merciless!" the Left-Handed Bokor laughed, his zombie-henchmen moaning despite their mouths being sewn shut. He was the guy responsible for Sister Christian, the London Werewolf, and all the other guys trying to kill us right now. He was also the guy I'd been trying to buy the magic rock from. "No force on Earth or the Heavens will separate it from my power."

The Left-Handed Bokor defied stereotype for a voodoo-practicing wizard by looking more like Jay-Z than Baron Samedi. He wore a ten-thousand-dollar white suit and shoes with a panama hat that seemed to shine every bit as much as the diamonds on his twelve or so rings. All of them contained imprisoned souls he drained for energy. One of the downsides of my ghost-themed powers was I could hear them moaning from here.

"You offered to sell the stone to me, numbnuts!" I shouted, not really up to my usual game insult-wise. "We've all been hurting since the Fall!"

"I got a better offer!" the Bokor shouted.

It had been a year since the Fall when Falconcrest City was overrun by zombies, the Great Beast Zul-Barbas killed, and the Brotherhood of Infamy destroyed. None of it mattered because it had come at the cost of what I treasured most in the world. Mandy Karkofsky, my wife, had died sacrificing herself to save my best friend Cindy. I hadn't taken it lying down and it had resulted in her resurrection.

Of sorts.

"*Despite what comic books and television have portrayed, death is not as easy a thing to recover from in our world,*" Cloak continued to speak. "*It may be time to let Mandy go.*"

"Never," I hissed under my breath, throwing a blast of ice up into Sister Christian's face which blinded her and send her flying backwards against the stone walls behind me. "Also, stop distracting me."

"*Oh, you can take a second-stringer like the Bokor out easily enough,*" Cloak said. "*It's more important we discuss your love life.*"

"Ha-ha, very funny!" I snapped.

"I am not a second-stringer!" the Bokor shouted, firing hex-bolts of green energy from his hands at my head. I ducked under them and they slammed into the altar behind me, transforming it into a hideously misshapen lump of rock.

"You heard that, huh?" I said, preparing a fireball to burn him to ashes. If I couldn't buy the Stone of Elderrah from him then I guessed I'd have to take it from his cold dead body.

"Roar!" The London Werewolf tried again to go after Cindy, only to have a fire axe buried into its shoulder as she dodged out of the way of zombie gunfire, shooting them up one after the other with bullets that tore through the spells keeping them animated.

"Feel the power of the Loa!" the Bokor chuckled, pulling out a wand and sending a glowing death beam at me, which I turned insubstantial and ducked under the floor to avoid before coming back up.

"Voodoo doesn't work that way!" I shouted. "You're making fun of a real-life religion, asshole!"

That was when Sister Christian fully recovered and landed in front of me, her eyes and hands glowing with hellish energy. She then blasted me with every ounce of power she had, which was considerable.

I had to use all of my concentration to keep up the resulting contest of powers, and I was terrified of their cutting out at any moment. My abilities had been erratic since defeating Zul-Barbas, sometimes allowing me to defeat gods and other times leaving me vulnerable to has-beens and never-weres. Today, at least, I was operating at a mid-range capacity and just barely holding my own against the pyrokinetic's attack.

"*It's actually telepyrotic. Pyrokinetic is a creation of Stephen King in his book Firestarter and he bungled the Latin.*"

"I don't give a shit!" I shouted, turning insubstantial and going down through the floor of the cathedral. It was time to use one of my classic tricks.

"He's going to come up behind us!" the Bokor shouted to his zombie goons. "That's one of his favorite tricks!"

In fact, I came right back up to where I was, taking advantage of the steam cloud to come up behind one of the zombie goons and then pull on his trigger finger from behind. He shot another of his fellows and was subject to the retaliatory strike by everyone else's gunfire. The bullets were enchanted like Cindy's Uzis, so the zombie instantly disintegrated into a pile of bones.

Emerging once more into the cathedral, I levitated up to the rafters and tried to figure out how to take down the Bokor without damaging the stone. Assuming he had it at all. Arranging this deal hadn't been my finest hour.

"*No kidding*," Cloak muttered.

"No need to give me any 'I told you so's.'"

"*On the contrary, those are the high point of my day.*"

Seeing there was a heavy set of wooden beams over the Bokor, I moved my hands to freeze them and cause them to fall on his head. Nothing happened. Apparently, my earlier assessment about my powers working at mid-range capacity today had been overly generous. Something was interfering with them and had been doing so since I'd cast the spell to bring Mandy back.

"Fuck!" I shouted, which was about the absolute worst thing I could do when trying to remain stealthy.

Sister Christian responded by throwing a series of fireballs up towards me, some landing against the rafters and others passing me by. The wooden beams proceeded to catch fire and I was soon surrounded by a magical inferno which would probably hurt me even when turned intangible. Magic was funny like that. The others just started shooting at me, which I did turn intangible to avoid.

"Shit! Shit! Shit!" I said, running along the beam despite my intangibility. Shouting into my carefully-hidden earpiece, I said, "Diabloman, where the hell are you?"

Diabloman was my second-in-command and the heaviest hitter I had on my payroll. During the late eighties/early nineties, he'd been one of the most feared killers in the world. He'd possessed an army of Satanic cultist followers, unimaginable resources, and the respect of his peers. He'd killed heroes and nearly destroyed the world on several occasions. Hell, there was even a rumor he'd succeeded in destroying the universe once (obviously, it got better). Then he'd killed his superhero sister, fell in love, had a child, and decided being a complete monster sucked.

"I am trying to get to your position, Boss!" Diabloman shouted, the sounds of moans and grunts accompanying him along with the sound of gunfire. "The spot where you had me waiting to ambush the Bokor's men is overrun with ghouls! The Bokor has re-animated the entire church graveyard to come after me!"

I grimaced. Animating the dead in Falconcrest City was about as crass as sinking ships at Pearl Harbor or threatening to nuke Japan. The Bokor didn't care about anything like that. Honor amongst supervillains was a joke, but we were supposed to have rules, at least, and it was clear he didn't have anything of the sort.

"Just stay alive!" I said, running out of space to flee. I was on a cross of two wooden beams underneath a gigantic circular stained glass window of Saint Kirby, Patron Saint of Superheroes.

A terrible screeching noise was heard over my head and I looked up to see that we were being joined by yet another supervillain: the Fruitbat. Contrary to their depiction in media, it wasn't the vampire bat which was the scariest of flying rodents. No, it was the vitamin-C-munching motherfuckers, the ginormous monster-bats that could tear shit up.

Frederic Fledermaus, a relatively okay guy when he wasn't a seven-foot-tall monster, was a modern-day alchemist who helped henchmen who wanted to make the transition to supervillainy with various strains of lycanthropy. Last year, Cindy had briefly become a werefox and I'd been tempted to get in touch with my inner furry. Apparently, whoever was paying the Bokor to go back on our deal was really shelling out the big bucks tonight.

"*Lycanthropy only refers to werewolves,*" Cloak corrected me again. "*Theriomorphy is also a condition, not a source of superpowers.*"

"That's just bigotry!" I said, turning insubstantial along with the beam underneath me. That resulted in the Fruitbat passing through us both and plastering himself on the ground. "Shapeshifters are people too!"

"*You did not just say that,*" Cloak said. "*Especially since you're curing your wife of vampirism.*"

"Not curing her, just getting her soul back! There's a difference, okay!"

"*Whatever.*"

Cindy had already taken care of the vast majority of the Bokor's zombie goons as well as proven she was in a different class than the London Werewolf. The latter wasn't terribly surprising since werewolves seemed to seek her out from some sort of twisted need for verisimilitude. At last count, I thought she was up to a dozen or so dead homicidal werewolves. It was doubly-weird since her best friend at the hospital was one.

"Kill them, you idiots!" the Bokor shouted, trembling with rage. "We don't get the bounty and pardon if we don't get them all!"

Bounty and pardon? Hello. That was an interesting twist. Who had the kind of connections to pull that sort of thing off?

"*Too many, I'm sorry to say,*" Cloak said, sounding regretful rather than truly upset. "*Supervillains with connections to the government are a sad reality. Politicians are too easily bought in this day and age.*"

"They were always easily bought," I said, knocking away one of the Bokor's hex-blasts with a wave of my hand. I wasn't much in the way of a wizard but it turned out the Bokor wasn't either. "Besides, it could be a superhero paying for this hit rather than someone on my side."

"*You think a superhero would do this?*" Cloak said.

"You don't?"

"*I didn't used to,*" Cloak said, sighing. "*Today? I'm not so sure. Many of my former associates have shown darker sides I didn't think they were capable of.*"

"Only Ultragod is completely clean," I muttered. "Okay, let's kill these jackasses."

"*Any ideas?*" Cloak asked.

"Not a one," I muttered.

"I've got this fool!" The London Werewolf said, salivating as he talked. It was kind of disgusting really.

The London Werewolf growled as it slammed itself up against the side of the wall, climbing toward me by smashing its claws into the stonework. It had grown twice as large as its previous self and looked to be weighing in at around six-hundred pounds of muscle and fur. *Angry* muscle and fur. The Bokor, meanwhile, was casting some sort of enchantment I suspected was designed to remove my powers or, at the very least, do me no good. I was out of rational options. So it was time for some irrational ones.

"Geronimo!" I shouted before leaping off the burning beam right as the London Werewolf jumped at me. I slammed right into the creature, feeling like I'd jumped into a brick wall, but successfully redirecting his momentum downward. The two of us fell down toward Sister Christian, three stories of muscle and weight coming down on her.

"What the—" the London Werewolf hissed, too confused to use that moment to rip my head off.

"Burn!" Sister Christian hissed, turning up to fire against me. I used my levitation to push myself to the right, throwing me to the ground where I landed with a thud against the cobblestones. Above my head, the

London Werewolf screamed as he was consumed utterly in the fireball generated by Sister Christian. Only a few scattered charred bones and a burnt-out lupine's skull remained to clatter against the floor.

"One down, three to go," I muttered through pained breaths. I was partially invulnerable but that didn't keep me from getting my ass kicked.

The heavy body of the Fruitbat was thrown in front of me, its muscular frame covered in small cuts and showing signs of being burned with an industrial strength Taser. The beast, despite possessing low-level super-strength had well and truly gotten its ass kicked.

"Two down," Cindy said, stepping forward.

The Bokor, between us, was suddenly aware of how the odds had shifted.

"I love an unfair fight," I said, grinning.

Chapter Two

Where We Meet My Vampire Wife

Cindy Wakowski a.k.a Red Riding Hood was, in my opinion, one of the most beautiful women I'd ever known. With porcelain white skin, wide blue eyes, and strawberry blonde hair tied in bunches, she managed to combine a girl-next-door vibe with the kind of slutty punk girl you dated in college (or maybe that was just me since Cindy had lived next door while being the slutty punk girl I'd dated in college).

I was perhaps being overly generous on her looks since Diabloman and others considered her pretty rather than beautiful, but Cindy had started getting lovelier in my eye over the past year. I even loved the little scar on the lower side of her chin and her badly-healed broken nose, from her battles against zombies during the Fall.

Cindy had altered her costume from last year. Previously, she'd gone for style over function, wearing a sexy version of her namesake's attire. There were still elements of that, but she'd added pants under her dress, a gadget belt, and anti-ballistic mystic runes woven into her hood, and incorporated her extra-dimensional picnic basket into a satchel on her side. Cindy still wielded a fire axe but had enchanted it to be non-lethal against anything but monsters. She was less Sexy Red Riding Hood and more Red Riding Hood, Werewolf Hunter. Ironic, given I'd just killed the werewolf. Oh well, I'm sure her fans would give her half credit for the assist.

"Are you okay?" I asked, watching the confused group turn around.

"Five-by-five, chief. How about you?"

"A little singed, but okay. Sorry for bringing you into this."

"Eh, I love Mandy too," Cindy said. "I'll do anything to bring her back."

For some reason, that made me sad. "Alright, we should—"

"I will burn you in the name of the one true God!" Sister Christian hissed, charging with enough psychic power to level the entire block. Unfortunately, I was about out of juice. There was no way in hell I was going to be able to stand against that kind of firepower. "The Dark Christ empowers me to strike you down with a furious vengeance that—"

Cindy lifted up her left arm as a miniature crossbow popped out from her wrist and shot a bolt into Sister Christian's chest. A set of bolas popped out and wrapped themselves around the deranged nun before electrocuting her and sending her to the ground.

"We're Jewish," Cindy said.

"Ooo, good one," I said, standing up.

The few remaining zombie goons aimed their guns at us and unleashed a hail of bullets. I turned insubstantial while Cindy just stood there, unafraid. Half of them passed through me harmlessly while the others bounced against Cindy like raindrops.

"Enough!" the Bokor shouted. "Destroy him my minions!"

The zombies looked at him, taking note of the fact they were all that was left of the dozen or so undead gangbangers he'd brought to join him in this little fracas. I snapped my fingers and caused both of them to burst into flame. The zombies fell to the ground, sounding almost grateful in their dying gurgles for being released. That was, among other duties, part of what my job for Death entailed. Really, if the dead refused to stay dead, where would the living stay? I just wanted one person to come back.

My wife.

Was that too much to ask?

"You should have dealt fairly with me, Bokor," I said, debating whether or not to just kill him right now. Doing so had seemed like a good idea a few minutes ago, but I really didn't want to damage the stone. Also, despite what recent events implied, I wasn't a mad dog killer. I only killed when I had to, or when it was in the defense of someone I liked, or when I wanted to.

"*Smooth*," Cloak said. "*A real ringing endorsement.*"

"Shuddap," I whispered to my cloak.

I was pretty sure the actual fight portion of our conflict was over. The Bokor's henchmen had been brought on because the mid-level wizard wasn't exactly known for his serious punching power. He was more a "curse 'em from a distance" sort of guy. I suspected he was planning on running, but honestly, that would just mean he'd die tired. His only option now was to negotiate, and that gave me a moment to catch my breath and appreciate what a loyal wonderful henchwoman I had beside me. Also, what kind of horrible things I was going to do to this bastard. You did *not* screw with me when I was trying to bring back my wife.

"The Stone of Elderrah is priceless," the Bokor said, taking a few steps back. "I couldn't bear to part with it, even for the money you were offering. It would diminish my power too much, and with the recent rash of supervillain deaths, I had a chance of becoming a real power in the city."

I clenched my fists, wondering if he really didn't *get* why I wanted it. "I don't want it forever; I just want it to restore my wife's soul."

The Bokor paused, clearly rethinking his situation and realizing he might not walk out of this alive. It did wonders for his attitude. "I see. Perhaps we can come to an accommodation then."

"First, tell me why you betrayed me," I said, wanting specifics more than money and power. Those were the typical motivations for supervillainous betrayal and things I was accustomed to.

"I was offered twice as much as you were willing to pay me for the Stone of Elderrah to kill you and your associates." The Boker looked over to his fallen thugs. "I was also offered a pardon if I could kill you, Red Riding Hood, and Diabloman. I told my associates they would all be pardoned if they helped."

I'd say there was no honor among thieves, but that was self-evident these days. Also, the amount of money he was talking about was huge. There was over ten million dollars' worth of diamonds in my briefcase. Who hated me enough to pony up that kind of cash? Also, who was that stupid? I could name five or six top-tier assassins who'd work for a twentieth of that. Someone wanted me bad, but didn't care enough to purchase a quality assassin. It meant someone who had money to burn and was kinda dumb—which pointed to the government as the party responsible.

"I'm not hearing a name, Bokor. Also, it's hard to spend money when you're dead. Think on that," I said, deciding to take a different track. "How about you tell me who hired you and put my wife's soul back into her body. Then I'll pay you the ten million in diamonds I owe you and they can find someone else to do their dirty work."

"You're not going to kill me," the Bokor sneered. It was clear he was thinking of trying something else. His employer must have really put the scare in him, or I wasn't putting nearly enough of one. "Even your crazy girlfriend there isn't a killer anymore. She's one of the good guys now."

"I ain't that good," Cindy said, chuckling. An evil, almost insane grin appeared on her face and I was reminded why I loved her in a strictly platonic boss-to-henchwench way.

"*Keep telling yourself that,*" Cloak said.

Cindy smiled and then pulled out and tapped the side of her crossbow, causing the electrical charge on Sister Christian to return, only much stronger. A brief strangled cry filled the air before all that was left was a melted corpse.

"Where do you get those wonderful toys?" I asked, smiling at Cindy.

"Heistbay.com," Cindy said. "You can get some really amazing deals there."

"I saw you sold your old costume there. It's a shame, I really liked it," I said, crossing my arms and waiting for the Bokor's reaction.

"If you like Halloween-themed strippers," Cindy snorted.

"Who doesn't?" I said, stopping myself only when I realized I was flirting.

Cindy grinned. She then laughed and turned back to the Bokor, clearly ready to murder the criminal if he tried anything.

"Stand down, Cindy. Here's my new offer, Bokor. Help me and you get the diamonds and the Stone back." I was decent at necromancy but by no means an expert. "Don't help me and I'll look for another sorcerer. Oh, and I'll kill you. I want to know everything about who paid you to double-cross me. Someone is rich and stupid if they're throwing that kind of cash around just to take a hit out on me."

The Bokor raised his hands in surrender, thus proving he was smarter than the majority of supervillains out there. As the immortal Marcellus Wallace said in *Pulp Fiction*: Pride never helps it only hurts. In the fifth your ass goes down. "Very well, Merciless, it's a deal," he said. "I'll help you with your wife and tell you everything I know."

That was when the stained glass window above his head shattered and flaming debris fell from the ceiling. A motorcycle on the rooftop of a neighboring building had made the leap through and landed with a thump on the ground in front of us before spinning around and charging at the Bokor.

A woman in a long dark coat, form-fitting catsuit, and black helmet was riding on the back. The motorcycle was heavily modified with alien, magical, and unusual properties tech with the word *Nighthuntress* on the side.

Oh shit.

"No!" the Bokor shouted before the woman lifted up a sawed-up shotgun with her right hand and spewed hellfire from it, causing him to dodge or explode in flames. She then knocked her motorcycle to the ground, spun it across the ground and used it to knock the Bokor down while leaping off the top to tackle him.

The Bokor let forth a brief scream before the woman ripped off her helmet and buried her fangs into the side of his neck. It was my vampire wife, Mandy. She was the reason the already-diminished supervillain population of Falconcrest City had taken a dramatic downswing over the past twelve months.

"Fuck!" I shouted, feeling a dozen conflicting emotions at once. "He was about tell to us who hired him!"

"What the hell kind of entrance is that!?" Cindy shouted. "This isn't a music video!"

"Kind of missing the point, isn't it?" I asked, looking at Cindy.

"Not really," Cindy said. "He's still got the stone and we've got Mandy right here."

She had a point.

Mandy looked up from the Bokor's still form, her mouth soaked with gore and her eyes a predatory shade of yellow. A once-beautiful brown-haired Eurasian woman in her thirties, all of the gentleness and sweetness was gone from her features, leaving only a feral hunger. Her skin had lost its previous shine and was now the texture of dried paper and her fingernails were grown to the length of animal claws. Even her hair was stringy and dirty, looking like it hadn't been washed in days.

Those individuals who spoke of vampires as naturally beautiful had obviously never met one in person. They were monsters, and seeing one wearing the face of someone you loved was like someone kicking you in the gut until you were ready to vomit.

"Hello, Mandy," I said, trying to hold back the all-consuming sense of loss that filled me. Seeing her filled me with dozens of memories: laughing around the breakfast table, sex, playing Xbox games, walking our dogs, and every joyous moment of our marriage. This, this was just a mockery of the person I'd loved. Mandy had been a hero, not a murderer.

"That's not Mandy, Gary," Cindy said, reloading her wrist crossbow with a wooden bolt. "That's just the thing we need to put her soul back in."

Mandy responded by wiping her mouth off on the Bokor's sleeve, using his limp arm like a napkin, then licking her mouth clean. "Are you two still at this 'cure me' thing? I would have thought you would have gone off to do something else with your lives."

"Mandy died for me," Cindy said, staring. "It leaves an impression. I now only kill assholes who deserve it, rob people who have it coming, and beat up police officers who are trying to stop Insane Clown Posse concerts. Because those guys are awesome."

"I could have gone my entire life without knowing you were a juggalo," I said, keeping my eyes squarely on Mandy.

"Give em a chance!" Cindy said.

"No." I was trying to distract myself from the pain but couldn't. "Mandy, give us the stone. We can use it to fix this and be together again. You, me, the dogs, and everyone else we love."

Mandy reached into the Bokor's jacket and removed the crystal ball I'd come here looking for. The object wasn't terribly impressive, looking little different from a glass trinket you could buy at any New Age store. The kind of power it radiated, though, if you know what you were looking for, was the kind Terry Brooks wrote about in his *Elfstone* books. "You mean this stone?"

"Yes." I nodded, stepping forward. The ball was mesmerizing, but not nearly so much as the prospect of getting back my wife. "Remember who you are. Remember what you used to feel. Do you really want to live like this? Killing people, living in the darkness, and sleeping in filth? You only kill people who deserve it, so there's still something of the old you inside what you've become. Vampires only think about hunger, fear, and hate. Think of all you're missing and what you could feel again."

Mandy looked at the crystal ball, holding it up to the moonlight coming in through the shattered window above. "You have such an idealized view of our marriage, Gary. The old me always hated that. You put her on a pedestal and adored her, never bothering to think about all the very real problems you faced. You wanted kids, she didn't. You hated living a normal life, Mandy pretended she wanted one. You were mismatched from the day you walked down the aisle and broke the glass."

I was about halfway across the cathedral floor now. I just needed to get the stone from her and then it wouldn't matter what happened. "I don't care about any of that."

"You were never happier than when you were a supervillain, knowing she would never approve. Mandy was never happier when she was a superhero, away from you."

"I was happy in our relationship and she was too. You're not going to convince me otherwise. We loved each other."

Mandy stared into the crystal orb and held it in front of me, offering it back. "Love? Yeah, I supposed you did love each other. Warts and all."

I was close enough to grab it. All I needed to do was take the stone to an appropriately spooky spot, summon Mandy's spirit with it, and then bind it to her walking, talking corpse here. It would be as good as any resurrection spell—better even, as she would have all of the powers of a vampire but none of the weaknesses. The fact I had gotten this plan from *Buffy the Vampire Slayer* didn't mean it wasn't a good one.

"But it isn't enough," Mandy said, pulling the stone out of my reach and hurling it at the wall beside the doors.

"No!" I shouted.

The Stone of Elderrah shattered against the masonry, sending sparks of crystal in every direction.

I fell to my knees, staring.

Chapter Three

Where Mandy Becomes My Ex-Wife

"No," I whispered, gazing down at the Stone of Elderrah's ruined fragments. The stone had been my last lead after almost a year of research.

I'd poured over the entirety of the Nightwalker's collection of magical books and codices. I'd researched like a madman on vampires, the Great Beasts, curses, Death, necromancy, magical artifacts, and resurrection. I'd stored time in bottles and used his time machine to give myself extra days when my attempts to prevent Mandy's vampirism failed.

I'd trained myself through trial and error in the rudiments of sorcery. I'd learned to use the Reaper's Cloak as a focus to compensate for the fact I had the magical potential of a newt. All of that had failed until I'd been informed by Adonis that my best chance had been in Falconcrest City the whole time.

And now Mandy had destroyed it.

Goddammit!

Why?

Cindy picked up a piece of the shattered stone. "Wow, J.R.R. Tolkien really overstated the durability of magical artifacts."

"This is no time for jokes!" I snapped at her.

Cindy looked down at him. "It's always time for jokes, Gary. That's the only thing you can do when you're too sad to cry."

I opened my mouth, then closed it.

She was right.

"I like what I am," Mandy said, shaking her head. "The sooner you realize that, the better. Mandy Anne Karkofsky was a weakling and a loser. She never got the chance to be the secret agent she was born to be so she settled for being a housewife. It wasn't until you were locked up in prison that she got the chance to explore what she wanted to be—a superhero. Even then, she could never be the kind she wanted to be as long as you were around playing villain. Face it, Gary—you were holding her back."

I trembled with rage. "You are the antithesis of everything my wife stood for. You are a hollow mockery of a woman you are unworthy of speaking the name of. She was the heir to the Nightwalker and you are a mistake made from my grief. I correct my mistakes."

Mandy's expression then changed and for a moment I saw something pass her face that I didn't expect to see—shame and guilt. I couldn't help but wonder how much of the taunting she'd done was an act. That was when she drove it from her face and growled at me. "I don't think you have the stones for it, especially since I broke yours. A pity—if you did, we might be able to have some fun. I could make you and Cindy like me. You two could finally have that perverted little threesome you've always wanted."

I summoned every bit of my fury and created a fireball in my hand.

"Gary, I don't think—" Cindy started to say.

I threw it at Mandy. It sailed over her shoulder. I'd deliberately chosen to miss. I couldn't kill her. I slumped over.

Dammit.

Mandy looked behind her to the car that had been incinerated across the street. For a moment, she looked unsettled, then returned back to her contemptuous look. "See? I told you. Face it, Gary, we're bound together. Perhaps it—"

That was when Cindy shot her in the chest with a wooden crossbow bolt. The bolt missed her heart but came perilously close.

Mandy's mouth began to drip black fluid. "You...bitch."

"The alpha bitchiest." Cindy proceeded to pull out an old-fashioned Super-Soaker water pistol from her picnic basket and started spraying Mandy with its contents. "I had my rabbi bless this. I was told they don't usually do this sort of thing, but they were willing to make an exception once I told them it was for one of the Children of Lilith."

The water burned the vampire's face like acid. Mandy screamed and smoked, transforming herself into a bat before flying out the shattered window she'd come in through. It left us alone in the ruined cathedral, surrounded by corpses.

"Thank you," I said, watching her depart.

"No sweat," Cindy said, reloading her super-soaker.

"Where's Buffy when you need her?" I said, sighing.

"I kind of look like Sarah Michelle Gellar and Alyson Hannigan's lesbian science baby."

I gave her a sideways look.

"Or not." Cindy put away her super-soaker. "You realize she was trying to get in your head, right?"

"Yeah. She succeeded too. Whatever the case, I think I've finally accepted there's nothing left of Mandy in that thing. She's the ex-wife now."

Cindy paused. "Does this mean you're giving up?"

I stared down at the broken crystal. "No, I'm a fucking supervillain who is the chosen champion of Death. I live in a world where people are cloned, resurrected, reincarnated, and brought from alternate timelines all the time. If it takes another year, if it takes ten or a hundred years, I'm going to get Mandy back."

"Good," Cindy said, her voice determined. "I'll be with you every step of the way."

I looked over at her. "I'm going to start living my life like it's not going to happen tomorrow, though. I have other people counting on me and you've shown me the best way to honor my wife is to do good in her name."

Cindy brightened considerably. "I think that's a very healthy attitude. Your wife wouldn't want you to be miserable forever."

"I agree."

"You're lying to Cindy to make her feel better, aren't you?" Cloak said.

"You're damn right I am. This is the third worst day of my life. Cindy is the most important in the world left to me, outside of immediate family, though."

"Then maybe you should let her know that."

"Shut up, Cloak."

Cindy picked up her fire ax where she'd left it. "So, you want to go blow up something to make ourselves feel better?"

"We should probably check on Diabloman first."

As if on cue, which was happening a lot tonight, a hole in the East wall of the cathedral exploded outward and Diabloman stepped through. He was a huge man, almost seven-feet-tall, with a body built like the bricks he'd just bashed through.

Diabloman was dressed in a crimson luchador wrestler's attire with a demon-themed mask, having traded away his usual business suit for something more practical. On his chest and arms were hundreds of tattoos that wiggled and writhed with magical power.

In the late eighties to the early nineties, Diabloman had been one of the greatest supervillains in the world. He'd killed the Guitarist and, by accident, his sister Spellbinder. Time and guilt hadn't been kind to him, and now he worked for me. I'd paid for his daughter's medical school as well as gotten jobs for his entire extended family in the Merciless Media Franchise. He was still an incredibly dangerous man but probably need a rest after going for more than ten minutes of fighting.

"I am here, Boss!" Diabloman shouted, shaking off the skeletal arm of a zombie which had wrapped itself around his ankle.

"You're a bit late," I said, staring at my second-in-command. "A for effort, though."

"Could you smash through the wall again and go 'Oh yeah!'?"

"Oh yeah?" Diabloman said.

"Louder and with a pitcher of Kool-Aid in hand," Cindy suggested.

Diabloman glared.

I tried not to snigger and failed. It was an empty gesture but one born from a desire to feel something other than utter desolation at this disaster. One more attempt to make up for my wife's death and unholy resurrection and all it had resulted in were more senseless deaths.

"I take it the meeting did not go well?" Diabloman said, walking through the battlefield's aftermath.

"Yeah, you could take it that way. You could also take it as things turning into a complete clusterfuck."

"Vamp-Mandy arrived to show the Bokor her particular brand of justice," Cindy said, kicking Sister Christian's corpse. "Someone is also offering twenty-million dollars to kill Gary."

"*Si*," Diabloman said. "I heard of that."

"You didn't think to mention that?"

"If I mentioned everyone who wanted to kill you, Boss, we'd never leave the house."

He had a point there. "Know who is making the offer?"

"No," Diabloman said, "which is part of the reason why very few of the professionals are interested in taking up the offer. No wants to deal with an open contract that doesn't go through channels that can be verified. It is just one of many contracts which have been forwarded, though, on important supervillains and key figures in the underworld."

"So why are they interested in Gary?" Cindy said, unintentionally insulting me.

"That is a very good question," Diabloman said. "Tom Terror's bounty is and has always remained a hundred million dollars dead or alive. Gary having one at a fifth of that is bizarre, especially since Falconcrest City considers him a hero."

"You shut your mouth," I said, pointing at him. "They do not."

Diabloman let out an audible sigh. "I will keep my ear to the ground, though. I suspect the parties responsible have ties to the government."

That made sense. Ever since President Charles Omega had taken office seven years ago, he'd done his absolute best to make life a living hell for supers in general and supervillains in particular. While being anti-supervillain wasn't a platform anyone could really object to, even amongst supervillains, he'd made a lot of questionable decisions which had gotten a lot of people killed. Omega's worst had been sealing off Falconcrest City and preventing superheroes from intervening during the Fall, almost like he'd wanted to get everyone killed. Worse, he'd managed to spin the whole thing so he'd become even more popular, blaming the Society of Superheroes for not intervening sooner. The bigger the lie, the more people were willing to believe it. Well, except if it was something stupid like the honesty of politicians or the moon being made of cheese. There were limits.

"So, I repeat, do you want to go blow up something to make us all feel better?" Cindy said.

"Not tonight. I'm all blowing up stuff-ed out. It's back to the drawing board on Mandy's resurrection. I also need to figure out if I should proof my house for black ops teams breaking in through the windows."

"Our organization's psychics haven't reported anything of that sort yet," Diabloman said.

"Because they did such a bang-up job here," I said.

"They said there was a forty-percent chance he'd betray you," Diabloman replied. "Precognition is not an exact science."

"Fine, fine. I still want to call it a night. Tomorrow, we can figure out if President Omega's people are behind this and what to do about it."

"I could seduce him and incriminate him by forcing him to lie about the affair under oath!" Cindy said.

"It's been done."

"We can replace him with a clone!"

"Even more done."

"Donate lots and lots of money to his opponent?"

"He's not up for re-election."

Cindy crossed her arms. "Let's see you come up with something suitably mayhem-ish involving the president."

I thought about my answer, then shrugged. "I'll think of something. Even by our standards, bringing down the President of the United States should be a Level-1 project."

"You really are archvillain material," Diabloman said.

The Fruitbat, meanwhile, moaned and slowly climbed to his feet. The seven-foot-tall batman spread out his wings and looked ready to pounce before he noticed all of his confederates were dead.

Cindy pulled out her fire ax. "Ready for round two?"

I raised my hand. "I don't think that will be necessary."

"Oh?" Cindy said, looking disappointed.

Doing my best Al Pacino impression, I said, "You want a job, Fruitbat?"

The Fruitbat nodded vigorously. It spoke in a hissing slavish tone. "Yesssssssssss, master, I would love job."

I pulled out my business card with the address of my villainous lair and handed it over. "Report here on Monday. The Cool Crew of Crooks offers medical coverage, a 401K, and legal fees, but we have a strict non-compete clause as well as rules against certain behaviors. Do not, I repeat do not, work on Saturdays or eat pork. It offends our more orthodox members."

The Fruitbat looked confused.

"Just take the card," I said.

The Fruitbat did so and flew out the window.

"Fewer and fewer supervillains understand my jokes these days," I muttered, watching him fly away.

"That was a joke? If so, I've been losing a lot of Saturday business," Cindy deadpanned.

"*I'm sorry about what happened tonight,*" Cloak said, sounding genuinely concerned. "*I know it must have hurt to see Mandy that way.*"

"You have no idea," I whispered.

"What do you want to do about the diamonds?" Diabloman said.

I looked at the Bokor's magical trinkets. "Gather them up, I guess. I'll work some magic over them and send their souls on their way to Death. She'll sort them into their various afterlives as appropriate."

"No, I meant the ten million dollars in diamonds you brought to buy the stone."

"Oh." I looked over at the briefcase, discarded in a corner.

You knew you'd made it as a supervillain when you ceased to worry about money. Once you were really good at your job, you could always steal more than you could ever hope to spend. Once money had been my chief motivation and why I'd become a supervillain, that and honoring my brother Keith. Now? Now I really didn't give a shit about it, despite events making me richer than God. I'd give away everything for one more moment with Mandy.

Not that money wasn't good.

Very good.

"Do you want it?" I asked my henchmen. I didn't want to look like I still cared about that sort of thing with my henchmen.

Diabloman shrugged. "You have been generous to me beyond belief."

"Cindy?"

Cindy grimaced at the prospect of turning down wealth, then said through the fakest smile possible, "The hospital is paid up through the year. I also live with you and use your credit cards."

She was trying to be good. Trying to be a hero. She was just terrible at it.

I shrugged. "I dunno, we'll give it to charity or something then."

"Great!" Cindy said, looking in positive agony.

I decided I'd tell her she didn't have to be charitable as well as heroic. Someday.

Chapter Four

Awkward Confessions

Falconcrest City was a different place now. Once it had been a crime-ridden hellhole full of freaks, weirdoes, and murderers. It still was, but it once had included a thriving nightlife, prosperous businesses, and a populace unafraid to travel the streets even when they probably shouldn't have been. Those things were gone. The streets were now empty at night and many of the local businesses were now boarded up.

I'd ended up buying much of Downtown Falconcrest with the money I'd stolen from the Brotherhood of Infamy and was doing my best to rebuild the place. Ironically, it meant I was probably the richest asshole in town and the target of plenty of attempted thefts by supervillains. There were some benefits, though, of being the absolute biggest dog in a now much-smaller pond. I'd managed to pick up the Old Warren Estate for a song, and it was now my stately country home.

"*I can't believe what you did to my family home,*" Cloak grumbled as the Mercilessmobile (formerly known as the Nightcar) pulled up in front of the mansion gates.

The Warren Estate was a three-hundred room, three-building mansion that resembled a palace with over a mile of gardens surrounding it. A single large hill was directly behind the main house with its own observatory and a secret entrance to the massive bunker Arthur Warren had commissioned as the first headquarters for the Society of Superheroes. The site now sported a gigantic flashing set of neon letters that spelled out "Mercilessland." The house had also been painted in a rather garish shade of red with a huge statue of me in marble adorning the driveway fountain. There were similar statues of all my henchmen and colleagues spread throughout the garden now.

"Oh, come on," I said, turning the car keys off. "I think it's an improvement in several ways."

"*You've ruined a place of great historical significance.*"

"Ruined or *made better?*"

"*Ruined.*"

The roof of the Merciless Mobile slid open in lieu of a car door opening and I stepped out alongside Cindy. Diabloman was in the backseat, still holding the handle for the briefcase of diamonds.

"Have you considered your additions to the house might be dangerous?" Diabloman asked.

I looked over my shoulder at Diabloman. "Dangerous? How?"

"I'd say it was a big neon sign pointing out where your hideout is but that's kind of redundant," Cindy said.

It was logical thinking that had no place in my world. "*Au contraire*, real-estate developer and supervillain rap mogul Gary Karkofsky is the only man who absolutely cannot be Merciless."

Cindy crossed her arms. "This I've gotta hear."

"You'll be very pleased at my astoundingly genius method of preserving my secret identity."

Cloak sighed in my head.

"Android, time-travel, or body doubles?" Diabloman asked.

"You've started wearing glasses as Gary?" Cindy suggested.

I shook my head. "I pay taxes as both Gary and Merciless. No one who does any investigation will believe I would give up an extra-portion of my loot to the government."

They both stared at me.

I paused. "Okay, that sounded better in my head. Seriously, though, no one in town suspects I'm anything more than a collector of Falconcrest City's signature supervillain memorabilia."

A black and white police car pulled up beside the Mercilessmobile. The black police officer inside the driver's seat rolled down his window and waved at the three of us. "Hey, Mister Karkofsky! Enjoyable night supervillain-ing?"

Okay, maybe some people suspected my identity. "Uhm, yes. I went to a costume party with my friends here, as the Cool Crooks Crew."

"So you went as yourselves? Awesome." The cop gave a friendly wave then pulled off.

A moment passed in silence.

"All right, it's entirely possible my identity has been compromised," I said, giving a dismissive wave. "The house is still protected by the best magic and mad science money can buy. What's the worst that could happen?"

"Drone strikes," Diabloman said. "Exterminator-robots, special ops commando units, and snipers."

"*Seizing your assets, turning the public against you, and bringing down the wrath of the Society of Superheroes.*"

Cindy started counting out reasons on her fingers. "Kidnapping your loved ones, a gypsy curse—"

"It's *Romani* curse," I corrected her. "Gypsy is a racist slur."

Cindy glared at me.

"Okay, okay." I raised my hands in surrender. "I get the point. I'll see if I can get Adonis to magically 'oomph' away people noticing my identity."

"I'm not sure it's that easy," Diabloman said. "You will have to remove the giant sign at the least."

"Can't I just have people not notice it?" I said, wincing. I loved the sign.

"No."

"Shit." Still, as long as my family was living here, I needed to take precautions. I might be cavalier with my own life but I wasn't going to risk Kerri or Lisa.

Especially not if the government was after me.

"*Truth be told, I do not believe it is the government who is responsible for the twenty-million dollar bounty on your head,*" Cloak said.

"Why's that?" I asked.

Cindy sighed. "I wish you'd learn not to talk to Cloak aloud."

"Eh, I've gotten used to it," Diabloman said.

Cloak continued as if they hadn't spoken. "*If the government wanted you dead then they would undoubtedly do so through means far less circumspect than this. They could just arrest you for your many, many crimes. This strikes me as a private contract instead. Perhaps Tom Terror or the Brotherhood's remnants.*"

"If Tom Terror wanted me dead, he'd just nuke Falconcrest City." He was the world's worst supervillain and I'd foiled one of his schemes when it had come within inches of killing Ultragod. As far as I knew, he was still locked up, though. He was still recovering from having every bone in his body broken in our last encounter.

Cloak sounded unconvinced. "*I cannot think the government has degenerated to the point of taking hits out on its own citizens.*"

It was comments like that which reminded me Cloak had grown up in the Pre-Great Depression Era of the US of A.

"Truth be told, I think the government would love to come after me and a bunch of other figures, but they've been holding back."

"*Why's that?*"

"I kind of saved the world last year and a couple of times since then."

"*I can't imagine that would stop them from following the law.*"

"You'd be surprised. The Omega administration has been trying to frame superheroes as unnecessary awful idiots for the past eight years. As long as Ultragod is around, though, any traction he gets against the Society is minimal. He's bigger than Jesus. Maybe as big as the Beatles. The last thing they need is a public relations fiasco like all my good deeds becoming public or Ultragod coming to bat for me."

"*And you think Ultragod would protect you.*"

"I did kind of save his life. His daughter also is fond of me." Hell, we'd been engaged for about a minute in college.

"Is that what you call it?" Cindy said, making some porno music noises.

"Hush you," I said. "Gabrielle and I are just friends. I hear she's dating the Golden Scarab now too."

"Oh please, you're like her supervillain love-interest! It can't be more cliché," Cindy said.

I sighed, not in the mood to banter. I hadn't been for much of the past year. "Do you really think I'm interested in that?"

Cindy straightened and frowned. "Not really. I think there's one woman on your mind and only one."

Not really, but I did a good job of hiding it. "Anyway, while I do think Ultragod would run interference for me, I think he's more likely to protect me for another reason."

"*And why's that?*" Cloak asked.

"You're in my head. The Nightwalker. He'd do anything to protect his best buddy and prison would make you vulnerable."

"*...*" Cloak clearly hadn't thought of that. "*I don't think my friend would compromise his ethics to make sure I was safe.*"

"Then you may think too much of Ultragod or too little."

Cloak was silent.

Turning back to the Mercilessmobile, I hit the remote control on my keys and the vehicle lowered into a secret alcove beneath the streets. I then headed through the front gates that opened automatically at my presence and walked to the front door. Diabloman headed off to his unmarked white van.

"See those diamonds get to the children's relief fund!" I called out to Diabloman.

"I would not steal from children's mouths!" Diabloman called back. "Everyone else? Yes."

I chuckled.

"Do you think he's going to take any?" Cindy asked.

"Nah," I said. "He's skimming off the top from all the other businesses. Just like you."

"Only for good causes," Cindy said, putting her hand over her breasts. "I being a very good cause."

It was a weird feeling being one of the one percent who held the majority of the world's wealth, and not an entirely pleasant one. I'd railed against them my entire life and becoming one felt like a betrayal of my principles. I'd considered just giving away my entire fortune or burning the cash portion like the band KLF had done to a million pounds sterling. The only thing stopping me, aside from the fact that Cindy would literally kill me, was I'd unwittingly become a wealth generator. As one of the last three billionaires in the city aside from Amanda Douglas and Mordred Warren, I had a responsibility to—ugh—employ the people underneath my care. Ironically, I still gave away so much of my fortune I was constantly on the verge of bankruptcy and in need of stealing stuff to keep everything afloat.

Capitalism was an ugly system.

"Just following that train of logic was so horrifying, I feel a sudden urge to convert to communism."

"Excellent, another convert to theistic socialist anarchism."

"That doesn't even make any...ugh."

I banged on the door with the gigantic stone gargoyle knocker before pushing the doorbell, which played the theme for *The Addam's Family*. Weirdly, neither of these had been additions to the house I'd made.

"Do you think Kerri is still up?" Cindy asked.

"She's a night owl," I said, shrugging. "Comes with being able to talk to ghosts. Believe me, I know."

My sister, Kerri Karkofsky, was a Natural Super. One of those rare individuals who had been born with super-powers due to magical lineage, exposure to other-dimensional energies, cosmic tampering, or other wackiness. They were the bottom of the barrel when it came to respect and prestige in the world, perhaps because so few of them chose to become superheroes. People trusted those individuals who decided to be heroes and they envied those who became villains but they just flat-out didn't like individuals with powers who decided to be like everyone else.

"Isn't it weird how her powers are like yours despite different origins?"

"Yeah, almost like destiny or someone writing it in."

Cindy looked at the door. "Gary, there's something I've been meaning to tell you for a while."

"Oh?"

"I think I should move out."

I did a double take. "What now? You want to leave my kickass secret lair?"

"First of all, you can't call a place with a giant neon-sign over it your *secret* lair. That's supposed to be hyperbole, Gary. Second of all, well…"

Cindy looked into my eyes. They were a beautiful shade of blue and reminded me we'd been through a lot together.

"What?" I said, blinking.

"It's been getting uncomfortable between us."

I jolted and took a step back. "I'm sorry, if I've been giving you the wrong impression and—"

"Gary, I never stopped loving you."

Okay.

Floored.

"Pardon?"

"*Finally*," Cloak muttered.

"You shut up!" I snapped.

"What?" Cindy blinked.

"Not you!" I said, raising my hands in surprise. "I don't know what to say."

Cindy slumped her dainty shoulders. "That's the problem. You don't feel the same. You love Mandy and I love Mandy and I owe her everything and she's coming back. We dated in high school and college and I always thought you were going to be a part of my life. I took you for granted and….God, this is annoying. I just think it'd be better if we….stopped being henchperson and villain together."

"Cindy…"

I…I…

God, this was so hard.

That was when the door opened and my sister stood on the other side. She was an ash-blonde woman with looks suspiciously similar to Christina Ricci. She was wearing a plain black dress and vest over a white blouse with a little silver ankh pendant around her neck. Her eyes were a bit wider than normal and she had an earring stud in her right nostril.

"Welcome home you two! Did your criminal necromancy thing go well?" Kerri asked, cheerfully.

Cindy marched past her, feeling her face.

"Did I miss something?" Kerri asked.

I sighed and walked upstairs. "Now's not the time, Kerri. I'll talk to you about it tomorrow."

"Uhm, okay. Are you sure?"

"Please. Just let me be." I reached the top floor and sought out my bedroom. It was just one of the veritable barracks of them up here.

Cloak let loose a growl of frustration. *"You're being a fool."*

"Can it, Cyrano."

I should have gone after Cindy, I should have stopped her and told her I was having those kind of feelings as well. But every time I thought about saying I was falling for her, even more than I'd felt for her before, I ran into the fact that Mandy was my wife.

My one true love.

Cindy was my best friend, and I, against my will, was starting to see her as something more. She'd been there for me throughout my time of crisis and the only way I hadn't gone insane was because of her. I couldn't betray Mandy that way, though.

Especially since I was determined to see her come back.

Instead, I walked into the bedroom, plopped myself down on the king-sized mattress, and stared at the ceiling. Closing my eyes and wishing to God I wasn't a coward. I heard Cindy packing her things in the adjoining room but didn't go to speak with her.

Sleep, eventually, took me.

Chapter Five

Death is the High Cost of Living – Because She's Cheap

Sleep came quickly enough but didn't serve as a source of rest. Since the Fall, I'd been having a steady stream of nightmares that only ended when I woke up. They came in roughly three flavors. The first, the easiest to deal with, simply were of horrible things that had happened to me. Mandy and my brother's death, zombies, and the horrible violence I'd witnessed were all things I could deal with. Badly. But deal with. The second were worse. They were dreams where Mandy was still alive and at my side. It made the experience of waking up and finding out she wasn't all the more horrible. They were getting progressively less common and, perversely, I was starting to miss them. I'm glad those weren't tonight's dreams since given what Cindy had said, I imagined they would have broken me completely. The third? They were visits from Death.

Like tonight.

I found myself standing in the middle of Restland Cemetery, a lengthy green field just outside of Falconcrest City that had once been a prosperous suburb. The city had demolished it and made it a memorial site for all the victims of the Fall. It wasn't as big as Arlington, but it was amongst the singularly most depressing places I'd ever visited in my life. It was now a collection of tombstones, crosses, stars, weeping angels, and mausoleums as far as the eye could see. The sun was hanging in the air and there were no visitors, which gave the place an eerie sense of tranquility that was not quite wholesome. I didn't see Death in any of her avatars but I could feel her sickly-sweet presence, like being sick on too much chocolate. I'd wanted Death's help with Mandy, but despite how much I'd done for her, she hadn't been willing to even give me a reason why she wouldn't help.

"*You should not be so flippant,*" Cloak said, his voice low and troubled. "*Death has been a generous patron and she has the power to take away all the gifts she'd bestowed.*"

"She gave me enough power to deal with Magog and Zul-Barbas, a pair of big ass demons who were as much a threat to her as they were to humanity. I also remind you I've been paying her back ever since, with interest."

"*Gods do not see their favor in monetary terms, Gary. They do not bargain, as much as you try to, and disrespect is often severely punished.*"

"Yeah, well, I'm tired of being her personal shit-shoveller. If I wanted a new god, I would convert to Astaru. I'd at least I'd get a free hammer and a Valkyrie."

"Hello, Gary." A cold, feminine voice spoke.

"I meant for you to hear that."

"Of course you did."

I spun around and saw the figure of Death waiting for me. Today, Death looked identical to Mandy with her hair tied in bunches like Cindy's. Somehow she made it look elegant. Death was wearing a wide-brimmed black hat with a funeral veil and an elegant white dress. Her shining black stiletto high heels raised her slightly above my head. Death looked like a cover model for a "what to wear when you're attending a funeral and want to look your best" fashion magazine issue.

Death was one of the Primals, the cosmological constants of the universe that were just short of God in the grand scheme of things. Well, if you believed in God. The funny thing about gods, lower case g, was they loved taking the forms of mythological figures in order to deal with humanity. I believed in God and thought of Death as the archangel Samael but other people saw Hel, Thanatos, Hades, the Grim Reaper, and plenty of other people. It made theological discussions kind of tricky.

"Hello, Sammy," I said, using my nickname for her. "What's shaking?"

"We need to talk."

"That's never good."

Death narrowed her eyes.

"Err," I started to ramble. "I mean, that is, it's rarely, uhm...uh." I pointed over her shoulder. "Is that Osiris?"

Death gave a low chuckle. "Cute. Just for that you won't die of cancer in twenty years."

"What?"

"We need to discuss your next assignment," Death said, confidently striding across the graveyard to an unknown destination.

I followed her, keeping my head low. "I'm kind of busy right now. Personal stuff. Things like resurrecting my wife and dealing with the fact my best friend is in love with me."

"Would you like me to raise your wife from the dead?"

"Yeah," I said, suspecting it wouldn't be that easy. "It would be really nice if you helped with that."

"No."

I sighed. "Why am I not surprised?"

Death answered my thought. "Because you know me better than any other mortal. Your wife made the choice of her own free will and accord to take a blow meant for Cindy Wakowski. You, promptly, made a similar choice to use black magic in order to restore her—knowing it came from an unclean source. It's not my place to clean up your mistakes."

"I think you owe—"

"Careful," Death interrupted.

"Her," I said, simply, "more."

"I don't owe anyone anything, Gary, but complete fairness. I kill the rich, poor, greedy, and charitable alike. I strike children, the elderly, the sick, and the healthy. I am the Great Equalizer you always are talking about when you preach your anarchist philosophy. I was here when the universe began and will be here when the universe ends."

"Please."

Death stopped walking. "Gary, do you know where your wife is?"

"No."

"A better place. People say that a lot and sometimes they mean it, sometimes they don't. She is with her Goddess. Do you really want to rip her from that?"

I was silent and looked over the gravesites around. "Is it so wrong to say the answer is yes? I want to be with her. Hell, knowing there's an afterlife, don't think I didn't contemplate suicide. The only thing that stayed my hand is I don't think we'd go to the same place."

"More than that stayed your hand," Death said, her eyes seeming to look right through me. "You love life even if you loved your wife every bit as much."

I looked down at my feet. "There's nothing I wouldn't do to bring her back."

"Kill Cindy and Mandy's soul will return to her body."

"What?" I said.

"*What?*" Cloak joined me.

Death's voice became almost contemptuous. "You're pestering me for a cure for Mandy's condition, well, there's your cure. Mandy died for Cindy. Give up Cindy and Mandy will become human again. It may or may not be her soul anymore but it'll be as close as you're likely to get. Make your choice between them now."

I stared at her, horrified. "You evil—"

"Careful."

"I..." I looked down at my hands then turned away. "No, not Cindy. Anyone else."

"A baby then."

"What?" I snapped back.

Death sighed. "You use a lot of hyperbole but I think you're less of an unfettered force of nature than you think."

"Why are you doing this?"

"To simply illustrate the consequences of her choice are not wholly negative. Mandy's death has made you a better person. You, Cindy, and others. One act of heroism serving as a domino to others. You should take that into account and respect her choice."

I looked away. "Fine, I'll find another way to do this. With or without you, I'm bringing her back."

Death shook her head. "Then that, too, will be of your own free-will and accord."

I almost said "Thanks for nothing" but decided to bite my tongue. "Is there anything else?"

"A nexus has died."

"A what now?"

Cloak explained. "*A nexus is an individual who, by some quirk of their nature or events, is one of the single most important individuals in the history of everything.*"

"I, generally, don't hold with the 'one great man of history' thing," I said, shrugging. "Individuals don't make history, people."

"And you would be wrong," Death explained. "This individual has saved the universe on numerous occasions, rescued countless worlds, inspired billions, and done more good than the collected histories of several civilizations."

I blinked. "So, one of the big players in the superhero world."

"Yes," Death said.

"Someone I know?"

"Yeah."

I tried to think of the various people it could be. The Nightwalker was at the top of the list but he'd died and became Cloak. Then there's Ultragod but I couldn't believe that would ever happen. He was the symbol of everything good in the world, not to mention the father of my ex-girlfriend Gabrielle.

I couldn't see him dying.

Ever.

"That is a poor way to view the world. As great as Moses Anders is, at the end of the day, he is only human. Eventually, someday, he will go out into one of those many million-to-one odd fights and never return. It is the fate of all superheroes and one we have to accept if we are to face the sort of enemies we do."

"Is it Ultragod?" I was afraid of the answer. I was surprised how little I cared about losing my protection. Instead, all I could think about was how his loss would devastate the superhero world and Gabrielle in particular. He'd been a symbol of hope and freedom for the entirety of the world.

No, it couldn't be him.

Impossible.

"That is not my place to tell."

"Just give vague, somewhat annoying clues to, huh?"

"That is the prerogative of gods, yes."

I rolled my eyes. "So what exactly is it you want with his death? Assuming it's already happened."

"I want you to help solve it."

I raised an eyebrow. "This seems a little out of your wheel-house. Since when has Death ever cared about justice?"

"Not justice, pride."

"Eh?"

"The man who died had an appointed hour of death far from now, at a moment of epic cosmological importance. I am taking steps to rectify the situation so the destiny of the universe is not disrupted but this is against the rules. People are not supposed to go off-script."

"I thought you said we had free-will and accord."

"You do, but only within the lines."

Of course. One thing I'd found to be true in this reality and every other one was there was never pure freedom. No matter where you went, there were the haves and the have nots. The haves were always trying to make sure the have nots didn't become the gotta-gets too.

"So, someone broke destiny and you want me to whack em?"

"Essentially, yes."

"What do I get in return?"

"My continued good will."

"Keep going."

Storm clouds slowly moved over the horizon and the sun disappeared. I conjured a beach umbrella made of ice above both me and Death, letting it catch the dark drizzle that poured down.

I wasn't fazed in the slightest. "Looks like rain."

Death narrowed her eyes and I guessed she was debating obliterating me or torturing me for a thousand years. Instead, she said. "I'll owe you a favor."

"What sort of favor?" I decided to continue to risk her disfavor. After all, I had nothing to live for and Mandy worshiped different gods so what did it matter? If I couldn't have her, it didn't matter what happened to me.

Death's offer, though, changed my mind. "You can ask me for anything within my power to grant once this occasion is over."

It was too good to be true.

"*Of course it is.*"

I couldn't say no, though. "*Including* Mandy's return?"

"Yes."

I struggled to control my emotions, trying not to freak out. "No funny business?"

"No funny business."

This was going to end badly, I just knew it. "Alright, I'll be your hitman. Who do you want me to kill?"

"I can't tell you."

"Where is he?"

"I can't tell you that either."

"Can you give me *any clues, whatsoever?*"

"You will have all you need to find them."

I paused. "Are you just fucking me with now?"

"To answer that would cancel the favor."

"So, yes."

Death laughed. It was not a pleasant sounding chuckle but a full-on belly laugh. "This is the reason I keep you around, Gary. You are an endless source of amusement to a truly jaded soul. In any case, that is all I wanted to talk with you about."

I wasn't quite done yet. "One more thing. My powers have been acting up lately. I'll need them in tip-top shape to do this mission, assuming it's not just some random guy on the street I have to shiv."

"It's not and yes, your powers have been affected by recent events," Death said, nodding.

"You tainted yourself with Zul-Barbas' magic when you tried to resurrect Mandy and used the majority of your reserves destroying him. Since that time, you've also been training yourself with foreign magical sources in hopes of finding ways to restore your wife. These diminish your capacity to serve as my avatar."

"Speak English, Doc."

"You fucked up and aren't as powerful as you used to be."

"Ah."

"No more teleporting with the Reaper's scythe or killing gods. You also have a limited supply of necromantic energy again."

"That's definitely going to hurt my ability to take out your target." I paused. "Hint, hint, drops a suggestion, hint, hint."

"Fine. Take this," Death said, conjuring a forty-thousand-dollar Louis Vuitton purse. Opening it up, she produced an ivory-handled hair brush and presented it to me.

I took the brush and stared at it. "A brush with Death, ha-ha. Funny."

"Take out the scythe with your other hand."

Confused, I produced the tiny pen which could transform into the Reaper's scythe. I was now holding a pen and brush in my hands. "Okay."

Death waved her hand over both and they became a pair of silver-plated Desert Eagle pistols. The two pistols seemed to connect with the magical energy inside me and then disappeared into the folds of my cloak.

"They're made from swords wielded by Greek soldiers during the Maccabean revolt. They will channel your power through them and shoot out bullets made of hellfire. It will compensate, a little, for your reduced power."

"Will they also allow me to shoot like Chow Yun Fat?"

"No, you will probably miss everything you shoot at if you fire them at the same time."

"Figures."

Beggars couldn't be choosers, though, and if I was going to find and kill someone Death wanted dead, then I needed every advantage I could get. I knew enough magicians I could also probably get the weapons blessed so they could fire themselves. Which was good since I wasn't exactly trained in how to use firearms.

At all.

"*I hate guns. The superhero that uses them has shown he is incapable of fighting in a non-lethal manner and thus does not deserve the title.*"

"Thankfully, I'm not a superhero. So, anything else, Death?"

Death looked honestly concerned for a moment. It was an expression that didn't sit well on her face. "Good luck, Gary. If it's any consolation, your wife would want you to be happy."

I stared down at the guns in my hand. "That's not really her decision to make."

I woke up seconds later.

Chapter Six

Where I Meet with the Family

I woke up from my dream with a pounding headache. The encounter with Death was fresh in my mind and I had mixed emotions about the whole thing. If anyone in the world could bring Mandy back, it was Death, but I'd been burned before dealing with such a being.

I had to believe this would be the secret to my salvation.

But if it cost me Cindy, I didn't know what to think.

"*You should go speak to her,*" Cloak said. "*Try to resolve this before it is unfixable.*"

"Why do you care?"

"*I could say it is because I pushed away my own family and loved ones. Because I know what it is like to die alone because an obsession dominated my life. But, in truth, it is because I care for you both. You are like the son and daughter I never had.*"

"Who you're trying to set up together."

"*...alright, that metaphor went in an odd direction.*"

"I'll go talk to her after I'm decent."

"*So, never?*"

"Ha-ha."

"*Honesty is the best policy,*" Cloak suggested.

"I've never found that to be the case."

"*How do you feel about her?*"

I was silent. "I'm not sure that matters."

"*I can't imagine that's the case.*"

I slipped out of bed, took a shower, and got dressed in a pair of shorts and a Hawaiian shirt with a pair of sandals. A reminder to do the laundry since I was down to vacation apparel. Taking a look in the mirror, I gave myself an appreciative glance. I was a handsome man, a quality that separated me from many of my fellow geeks. My body had seemingly gotten more and more buff the longer I wore the Reaper's cloak.

I kept my head shaved since becoming a supervillain, a quality that just seemed right. Also, it concealed the fact I had hair as golden as Jaime Lannister. No one took a blond supervillain seriously. Putting on a pair of sunglasses, I headed down the hallway to Cindy's room, trying to figure out what I wanted to say to her.

"Do you know how I met Cindy?"

"*You met her in a seedy hotel serving as a makeshift brothel. There, she was an underaged prostitute and was witness to your murdering the anti-hero Shoot-Em-Up. She recognized you from school and agreed to keep your secret. You were both fourteen. Later, you befriended her to keep her quiet and became partners-in-crime until your college years when she went on to study medicine while you became a history major.*"

"Yeah," I said. "I've been manipulating Cindy since the first time we met. Even if I did love her, how would I know it wasn't just to keep someone useful by my side?"

"*I think you'd know.*"

"Well, I don't."

The door to Cindy's room was slightly ajar and heading on in, I saw it had been cleaned out. Gone were weapons, explosives, her stuffed animal collection, and her collection of sexy theme costumes. The only thing left was a framed selfie of me, Mandy, Diabloman, and herself. It had been taken during the night of the Fall with all of us in costume. The picture was lying on the bed.

"Well, shit."

"*So what now?*" Cloak asked.

"If you love something, set it free. If it comes back, it's yours. If it doesn't come back, it was never yours."

"*I've always found that an immensely stupid saying.*"

"I'll bear that in mind. In the meantime, I'm going to work on solving Death's case."

"*I'll lend my aid to you. I was, at one point, the world's second greatest detective.*"

"Who was the first?"

"*Detective Duck.*"

I shook my head. "Only in this world."

Heading downstairs, I was struck how lonely the mansion was. Truly, it should have been populated with a horde of servants waiting at my beck and call but I wasn't comfortable with that sort of life. I had no interest in the Downton Abbey existence and preferred to look after myself. Still, right now, being in a gigantic house with only my immediate family wasn't improving my mood.

Seeing a couple of ghosts hanging around my kitchen, I decided to go speak with my sister. The mansion kitchen was larger than my first apartment with a checkerboard floor, a walk-in freezer we barely used, and a table in the center where both my sister and my niece sat. Sunlight was streaming through the windows and it looked to be about seven or eight in the morning.

Kerri wore a black bath-robe with a little spider-motif on her label. My niece, Lisa, was a pink-haired girl with pigtails wearing a pair of hot pants and an Ultragoddess T-shirt. They were having breakfast and coffee with a trio of newspapers on the table.

Kerri was my younger sister by a few years and had been the baby of the family. As a result, she'd never really gotten to know my brother Keith the way I did and had been immunized to his supervillainous influences. Lisa, by contrast, was his daughter, and had the same level of hero worship for me I'd once had for her father.

After Lisa's mother had abandoned her, marrying the publisher of her book *I Was a Supervillain's Sex Slave*, Lisa had come to live with Kerri instead. Now both of them had decided living in my mansion was better than trying to scrape out a living in New Angeles. It had its downsides, though, like the fact ghosts followed my sister faster than I could dispel them.

There were also a half-dozen ghosts present right now, in fact, the most recognizable one being an overweight middle-aged man in a sequin jumpsuit with a cape. He had an epic pair of sideburns and was wearing a pair of mirrored sunglasses that did nothing to disguise his identity.

"Shouldn't he be in Graceland?" I asked, pointing to the King.

"Tourists were bad enough when they were alive," the King said. "They've gotten worse after death."

"Ah," I said.

"I noticed Cindy left," Kerri said, buttering some toast for me. "What happened last night?"

"Stuff," I said, wondering just how badly I'd screwed up. "How serious did she look?"

"*In my experience, women do not move out on a whim.*"

"Cindy sang a variation of 'Do You Want To Build a Snowman' called 'Do You Want To Rob a Jewelry Store' outside your door before you woke up," Kerri said. "When you didn't answer, she took the Ferrari and drove off in a funk."

I blinked. "She went Disney on our break-up? *That is* serious."

"Are you breaking up?"

"Are you even dating?" Lisa said, looking at me sideways. "I thought you were a supervillain-henchwoman, shared lunacy sort of thing."

"It's complicated."

Kerri buttered some toast for the King. "Cindy loves Gary, Gary is in mourning for his dead wife, but he kind of likes her as well."

"Okay, perhaps not so complicated."

"What's the problem then?" Lisa asked.

"Gary resurrected Mandy badly with necromancy and is trying to fix his mistake so she's not zombie Mandy anymore," Kerri said, handing the toast to the King.

"Thank ya, thank ya very much," the King said, taking it.

"*Vampire* Mandy, not zombie Mandy," I corrected, "albeit not the sexy kind of vampire. Less Anne Rice and more *Near Dark*."

"It's all very tragic and *Dark Shadows*," Kerri said.

"I'm sorry I asked," Lisa said, watching the toast free-float to her eyes. "No, seriously, I really am sorry I did."

I sat down at the table and picked up my copy of the Falconcrest City Herald. "Yeah, well, it's my problem and I'll deal with it."

"Like you've been dealing with everything else since Mandy's death?" Kerri asked.

I glared at my sister. "Like you have so much to complain about."

"The city is finally starting to recover," Kerri said. "I think you should focus on helping with that. Don't let obsession cloud your judgment and just let time work things out. Maybe Mandy's spook will show up sometime."

"Death said she's at peace." I ignored the rest of her statement.

"Oh, how is she?"

"Fine," I said, checking the newspaper headlines one by one. "Did any major heroes or villains die last night?"

"No," Kerri said. "Not that's been reported, why?"

"Just a feeling," I said, putting the reports down. "Listen, things may be getting hairy in the next few days because of a bounty on my head. As a result, there are going to be some safety precautions—"

"You're finally going to train me to be Mercilass?" Lisa said, suddenly paying attention.

I frowned at her. "No."

"I don't have to be Mercilass. I could be Dangergirl, Lil' Lisa, the Pink-Haired Killer, The Bubblegum Bandit—"

"The Bubblegum Bandit, really?" I asked.

Lisa shrugged her shoulders. "I saw this great deal on Crime Bay for a glue gun. I figured I could use hot pink ammo."

"While not a bad idea, I have to ask: Don't you have superpowers?" Lisa was every bit the Natural Super as Kerri.

"Little light sparks. That barely qualifies."

"Any superpower is better than none at all. Be that as it may, you're not going to be a supervillain."

"Is this one of those 'do as I say, not as I do' things?" Lisa asked, crossing her arms and leaning back in her chair.

"No, it's me telling you you're not going to be a supervillain because I say so. One of the benefits of actually being a supervillain is I don't have to worry about hypocrisy."

During the Fall, I'd found out from Keith's ghost he'd never wanted me to follow in his footsteps as a supervillain. I'd idolized my brother the same way Lisa now idolized me, and it had been a sobering revelation to discover that Keith was not only horrified by my life choices but also genuinely remorseful for his actions committed as Stingray.

It was too late for me, and by too late I meant I liked being a supervillain and had no intention of stopping, but I wasn't about to let Lisa go down the same road. I'd explained to Lisa about Keith's desires, that crime didn't pay, and both the mental and physical consequences of the supervillain lifestyle. Unfortunately, my living in a gigantic mansion with a sexy supervillainess had given her mixed signals.

"You are the worst supervillain uncle ever!" Lisa said, pulling out her cellphone. "I'm texting my friends to tell them how lame you are."

"You do that," I said, taking a glass of orange juice from a small twelve-year-old ghost I'd nicknamed Casper. "Either way, I'm going to try and make sure you're protected from the consequences of my actions."

"How's that?" Kerri asked, looking at the child ghost. "Thank you, Robert."

"I'm going to give you my billion and a half dollars."

Lisa stopped texting.

Every ghost looked at me.

Kerri, instead, took a sip of her milk. "That's nice."

"You are the best supervillain uncle ever!" Lisa said, rushing over to my side and hugging me ecstatically. "I'm going to buy a car today. No, three cars! Fuck, I'll buy the entire dealership and then blow it up!"

I shook my head. "While I respect your enthusiasm for destruction and mayhem, I'm actually putting it all in Kerri's control until you're thirty."

"What the hell!?" Lisa shouted before making a strangling gesture with her right hand.

"Sorry, the Darth Vader throat crush doesn't work in real life. Believe me, I've tried on many an occasion."

Lisa threw out her hands and left the kitchen in disgust.

"What brought on this sudden burst of generosity?" Kerri asked.

"Last night, when I failed to get what I wanted from the Left-Handed Bokor, I ended up finding out someone has put a substantial price on my head. I'm not sure if it's the government but if it is, I'd rather you guys were taken care of. You know, in case something were to happen to me."

"That's sweet of you, Gary, but Lisa and I don't need your money. You've been too generous as is."

"Speak for yourself!" Lisa called from outside the door. "We definitely need his money!"

Kerri felt her temple. "She is way too much like you."

"That's what I'm afraid of." I proceeded to conjure an iphone from the shadows. The Reaper's Cloak's extradimensional pockets were available even when it wasn't technically in existence. Typing into the phone, I summoned a holographic interface that listed the entirety of my assets.

The Brotherhood of Infamy had included some of the wealthiest citizens of Falconcrest City and they'd contributed a massive amount of their fortunes to their operating budget. I'd done my best to give it back to the city but I'd stumbled in a few places, ending up keeping perhaps a bit more than my fair share.

"You mean, stealing billions of it and using it to become even richer."

"Job creator!" I snapped back.

Several keystrokes latter, all of my bank accounts emptied out and I was once more a penniless supervillain.

"There we go," I said, sighing. "I don't have Mandy's gift with computers, but I learned something about covering electronic transfers. Everything I've stolen looks like it's been earned through legitimate business transfers, and it's all yours rather than mine. Indeed, it should look like it's always been yours."

Kerri stopped eating and looked at me. "Are you really in that much danger, Gary?"

"I'm a supervillain, I'm always in danger."

"Maybe you should reconsider that, then. I have enough ghostly friends."

A young woman who was friends with Kerri in high school, I believe her name was Zoe, gave Kerri a glare.

"Not that there's anything wrong with being a spook!" Kerri lifted her hands up defensively.

I paused. "You do realize I intend to borrow ten or twelve million every month from this, right? And by 'borrow' I mean 'spend and never pay you back.'"

"Of course, Gary."

"Just checking." I thought about Kerri's words. "Being a supervillain cost me Keith, Mandy, and may have cost me Cindy. I, honestly, don't know if I should hang it up or not. I do know it's all I've ever wanted to be, though, and I don't know what I'd do with my life if I wasn't."

"Maybe you should think on that and see if there's anything you'd like to be as Gary rather than Merciless."

It was a thought.

Before I could respond, a glowing white streak of light fell from the sky and landed with a thud against the ground outside the kitchen. It caused the garden there to explode, sending up piles of dirt and shattering the windows.

"Oh dear," Kerri said, rising from her chair and immediately going for the dust pan and broom. With a furious devotion, she began cleaning up the broken glass and kitchen like a woman possessed.

Lisa popped her head in. "Did something cool happen?"

"Stay inside!" I said, getting up from my chair and rubbing my ears. They were still ringing from the miniature explosion.

"Like hell!" Lisa shouted.

"Is where I'm going to send you if you don't stay inside!" I shouted back.

"*That doesn't actually make sense*," Cloak said.

"Hush, you," I said.

Heading through the kitchen door to the site of the explosion, I saw a fifteen-foot-long and two-foot-deep hole in the ground from where the white light had struck. On the ground, in a gold and white uniform was the brown-skinned and black-haired form of Gabrielle Anders a.k.a Ultragoddess. My ex-girlfriend from college.

Her uniform consisted of a white bodysuit with a golden miniskirt and golden thigh-high boots with no insignia on the front like so many other heroes. Her golden cape was tattered and there were cuts all across her face. This, despite the fact that she was indestructible. Walking over to her, I slid down into the hole to touch her, only to draw my hand away from her like she was a hot iron skillet.

Please, please don't let her be the superhero who was murdered. I didn't feel the same way for Gabrielle I did in college but I still cared for her.

There was a lot of that going around lately.

Gabrielle opened her eyes and slowly climbed to her feet, staring at me. "You better be the real Gary."

"What?"

Chapter Seven

Back When I was Dating the Lady of Light

I remember the first time Ultragoddess saved my life. I'd been sitting across from Gabrielle at a little outdoors cafe done in a deliberately 1950s retro style, the bright sun and brilliant colors of Atlas City visible around us. It was, in every conceivable way, the opposite of my adopted hometown. There were brilliant white-glass skyscrapers, ultra-modern architecture, clean streets, and people who looked genuinely happy to be there.

Gabrielle sat across from me, wearing a white sports jersey with a short gold skirt, and glasses, her hair back in a ponytail. The fashions of Atlas City tended toward the old-fashioned, but this somehow helped with the wholesome atmosphere. Even so, it was one of the most progressive cities in the country, with its civil rights attorney Polly Pratchett constantly moving to help the disadvantaged.

She slurped on her milkshake, looking over at me while I tried to choose where we'd head next on our visit to the city. "You've been staring at that thing all day."

"There's just so much to see. The first Earth-based transstellar spaceport for alien-human interaction. The submarine residential area inhabited by Atlanteans and Merrow. The world's first clean-energy fusion plant."

"So, an airport, the suburbs, and the power plant?" Gabrielle said, smiling.

I looked down from my map. "I know this is all old hat for you but I've never been in a city like Atlas City. I mean, the air is clean downtown. That's just... wrong."

Gabrielle chuckled. "You can blame Ultragod for the majority of this. You can't have a superhero in a city for eighty years without it impacting things."

"Yeah," I paused, putting down my map. "Ultragod."

"You're not a big fan of superheroes," Gabrielle said. It was a statement of fact. She'd known it for years.

"No," I said, looking down. "I don't like superheroes. You know about what happened to Keith."

"Yeah," Gabrielle said, sighing. "Shoot-Em-Up was the first superhero to start killing criminals. He served as judge, jury, and executioner before inspiring a generation of copycats. Your brother was his second kill out of fifty-seven, before someone killed Shoot-Em-Up in a dirty hotel in Falconcrest City."

I was silent. "Yeah."

"I know, Gary."

I looked up. "You do?"

Gabrielle reached over and put her hand on mine. "How long have we been living together?"

"Three months," I said, smirking. It was a smile without happiness.

"I know you," Gabrielle said. "You are a good person. What you did is something that weighs on your soul every day. You torture yourself because of what happened and I can see how it warps you. Makes you want to be someone you're not. I see it. I also know you can rise above that."

Gabrielle suspected, even if she didn't know, that I was planning on becoming a supervillain. My brother, Keith, had been Stingray the Underwater Assassin. He'd been one of the Nefarious Nine and had tried to take over Atlantis. The archnemesis of both the Silver Lightning and Aquarius. She was right. I had killed Shoot-Em-Up and had been thinking about following in my brother's path.

To honor him.

I loved my brother's memory more than anything on Earth.

Or I thought I did.

I looked at Gabrielle and squeezed her hand. "As long as I have you in my life, the light will drown out the dark. I will never follow in my brother's path as long as I have you."

"You always will." Gabrielle smiled.

"Ugh," Cindy said from about three feet away. "Must you two be so disgustingly saccharine?"

I turned around to look at my best friend, who was standing behind us. She was dressed in a red football jersey and black sweatpants. She had a tray with a fountain drink, burger, and fries on it. Her hair was kept in place with a headband with a little skull pattern on the top.

"Yes," I answered her automatically. "Yes we do."

"What do you suggest we do, Cindy?" Gabrielle said, smiling.

Cindy smiled like a Cheshire cat. "I say we hit the bars, score some Z, get utterly blitzed and have a threesome back at the hotel room."

A customer looked up at her.

"What?" Cindy said, looking back at him.

"Uh-huh," Gabrielle said, looking back at her. "Gary, is your bestie always like this?"

I sighed. "Only when she's sober."

"What's she like when drunk?"

I started to answer only to be interrupted by a glowing orange fireball falling from the sky and landing in the middle of the crowded city street just a dozen yards away. A few of the customers screamed and got up, running away, while others just looked on with a curious indifference.

"Aw, man, not on my lunch break," Gabrielle muttered, turning to look at the object from space.

The glowing meteorite was roughly twelve feet in diameter and cracked open like an egg. This revealed an eight-foot-tall square-bodied figure with rock-like orange skin and bone protrusions jutting out of his joints and chest. It was twice as large as any muscle-bound bodybuilder, with a craggy face and stringy long white hair coming from the back of its skull.

The monster had a big bone protrusion coming out of its chin, almost like a beard. Strangely, it was also wearing a pair of scarlet swim trunks were unharmed by the fact he'd just fallen from space. A huge battle axe was attached to its back via a harness, glowing with little black energy dots surrounding it.

"I am Akuma the Accursed!" the figure bellowed. "The Harbinger of Pyronnus the Destroyer, Master of a Dozen Worlds, and Slayer of a Thousand Heroes! I come here to challenge Ultragod to a duel to the death and claim his daughter as my bride."

Gabrielle narrowed her eyes at that last bit, frowning deeply.

"Is this common around here?" I asked, looking at the sudden appearance of an alien warlord amongst us.

"You have no idea," Gabrielle muttered, growling. "They're always here to challenge my fat...Ultragod. Never Ultragoddess. This despite the fact she was trained from birth to be the greatest warrior on Earth."

"It's a man's galaxy, huh?" Cindy said.

"Ain't that the truth." Gabrielle shook her head.

Akuma removed his battle axe from his harness and started shaking it. "My ship's sensors detected an Ultraforce energy signature in this area!

Someone who has been touched with the power of the First Ones! Show yourself, Ultragod or I will begin destroying these people!"

"Should we get out of here?" Cindy asked.

"That'd just draw its attention," Gabrielle grumbled. "Moron doesn't even know Ultragod is off in the dimension of Mister Imagination."

"So we should just wait here?" I said, not sure if we should help evacuate the surrounding citizenry or just wait for the authorities. I wasn't used to being inactive in the face of a threat and hated feeling powerless.

"Take some pictures," Gabrielle said, smiling. "The paper would pay big bucks for these. In the meantime, I need to use the bathroom."

"Wait, what?" I said, watching Gabrielle duck from her table to the interior of the restaurant.

"When you gotta go, you gotta go," Cindy said, shrugging. "Someone should tell her she needs to go see a doctor, though, since that's the third time today."

I was about to speak when Akuma pointed at me. "You, puny mortal."

"Hmm?" I said, having pulled out my cellphone to take a picture.

"You have had sexual contact with an Ultra-force tainted being!" Akuma shouted, pointing his axe in my direction.

"Gary, you're cheating on Gabby with Ultragoddess!" Cindy said, horrified.

"I'm not!" I said, stunned.

Akuma was serious, though. "If you have defiled my bride, your pain will be endless."

I stared at him, fully aware your average alien could obliterate me with a thought. "I don't know about you, bub, but where I'm from women can have sex with whoever they want. So fuck off."

Cindy grimaced then sighed. "Well, it was a nice life. I only regret it wasn't longer."

Akuma lifted his glowing axe at me and there was a humming noise, as if it was charging up to do something unpleasant. I didn't bother to move. Instead, I just stared at him, knowing that I would never be someone like him.

A predator on the weak.

Scum.

A murderer of the innocent.

Or close to it, in my case, at least back then.

I was spared from obliteration by the sound of a mighty THWACK as Akuma went flying through the air with the force of a hundred speeding locomotives.

Ultragoddess had arrived. She moved faster than the Harbinger by a significant amount, catching him in the air before he slammed into a building and then punching him out over the bay. It was a well-known fact the biggest number of deaths from supervillains wasn't their actual murders—well, at least until the Big Disaster—but the aftermath of their attacks.

That was why every Society of Superhero member was trained in controlling the direction of a battle. Even so, I couldn't help but notice Akuma was trying to direct the battle back into the center of the city, perhaps in hopes of breaking Ultragoddess's spirit.

"Ever wonder what you'd do with those sort of powers?" Cindy asked, watching the resulting ballet of punches and cosmic energy blasts.

"Every day," I said, keeping my eyes squarely on Ultragoddess. There was something familiar about her that I couldn't place.

Little did I know, Gabrielle used her Ultra-mesmerism in order to make sure my brain, along with the brains of countless other civilians, couldn't put together the fact she was Ultragoddess. It was a personal betrayal, one I still struggled with, but one I understood at least.

Superheroes had revealed their identities to boyfriends and girlfriends, even spouses, only for them to let them slip or sell them to the media in exchange for immense amounts of cash. Several of these occasions had resulted in tragedy, either the superhero being forced into retirement or their family getting targeted by criminals.

People who didn't understand the secret identity thing, who thought of being a superhero as something more or less like being a celebrity, mistook what it was all about. The mob targeted witnesses and investigators in order to prevent them from testifying. What lengths did people think they'd go to avenge themselves on people who threatened their operations every day?

What lengths did they think madmen who could build a-bombs in their basement would go to? I'd been on the receiving end of a hero taking advantage of the fact my brother's identity had been open.

Cindy kept watching, unable or unwilling to take her eyes off the spectacle. "Yeah, but then you'd have to live a double life. You'd never be able to open up about who you were."

I shook my head. "Nah, I'd just live twenty-four/seven as my supervi...hero identity. No point in having a secret identity if you're Stingray or Merciful or Wrathful the entire time."

"Wouldn't that erode Gary Karkofsky? You're kind of cool as is."

"Am I?" I asked, sincerely.

"It'd be a shame to lose you."

I had no idea how to respond to that.

In the end, Akuma wasn't anything approaching a match for Gabrielle. He had fought Ultragod to a stand-still, even defeated him on a couple of occasions, but the Harbinger hadn't come prepared for someone trained by Guinevere of Avalon and the Nightwalker, in addition to her father.

His power-axe landed on an abandoned car a few blocks away from us, slicing it in half, before Gabrielle unleashed a hundred punching Ultra-force energy fists followed by a gigantic glowing energy hand that slapped him silly. Gabrielle had won the fight by that moment, but she continued for a few minutes more. She conjured an electric chair to shock him, battered him between a pair of gigantic ping pong paddles, and created a screen full of Tetris blocks she slammed down upon him.

Then she brought Akuma down a few yards away from us, smashing him a foot into the pavement, creating a pair of scissors around his neck. The look in Gabrielle's eyes was one of pure hatred and a willingness to kill. At the time I thought it was Akuma's threat to make her his bride, which was enough to justify his execution in my opinion, but I would later put together that she was just as angry he'd threatened me.

Yet as angry as Ultragodddess was, she held back. Not because Akuma didn't deserve to be killed or because she expected anything good to come from sparing him, but because she was a superhero. Heroes did their very best to inspire people to be better than they are, even if it meant not doing the smart or pragmatic thing. Chaining him up in Ultraforce bonds and sending him flying to the Society of Superheroes' base on the moon, she took a moment to look at me.

"Are you alright, citizen?" Gabrielle asked, disguising her voice and covering her face with a glowing white nimbus.

"Sure," I said, waving to her. "Thank you."

"Stay safe," Ultragoddess' voice cracked, letting loose a lot more affection and love than she should have.

She then took off into the air.

"Well, that was weird," I said, observing her disappear.

"No kidding," Cindy said.

Seconds later, Gabrielle emerged from the side of the restaurant, covered in sweat and looking like she'd been punched.

I got up. "What happened?"

Gabrielle said, "Someone hit me in the face while fleeing. Also, the bathroom has like *no* air conditioning."

I blinked, feeling an odd fuzziness in my thinking process. "Well, that's, uh, unfortunate. I'm glad you're all right, though."

Already, the forming bruise on the side of her face was starting to dissipate as the Ultraforce healed over her wounds. Her masquerade wasn't always this effective and there had been times she'd come home bloody and battered, leaving me to take care of her for the better part of a week. Those times I'd never questioned what she'd been up to had been one of the few reasons our relationships had survived. I'd speculated on her being involved in everything from underground female fight clubs to extreme sports. Even that she was a superhero.

Just not that she was Ultragoddess.

That she'd only been willing to tell me after I'd proposed to her.

Her response had to been to break up with me.

After saying yes.

Gabrielle was the mother of all mixed signals senders.

"Gary is sleeping with Ultragoddess," Cindy said, finally putting down her tray.

"I am not!" I said.

Gabrielle just burst out laughing.

Chapter Eight

Where the World Gets a Whole Lot Darker

Gabrielle continued to stare at me as I remembered that day and all the others we'd shared together. Gabrielle had been the woman I'd expected to spend my life with before Mandy and our lives just hadn't gone in that direction.

The strangest feeling I had looking at her now? I didn't feel the same way I used to.

I didn't love her the way I did Mandy.

Or Cindy.

Crap.

I was in love with Cindy.

"That's hardly a thing to go 'crap' about."

"Speak for yourself."

Noticing Ultragoddess looked like she was ready to punch me in the face, I said, "Wait, could you repeat that? You don't think I'm who I appear to be?"

Looking up in the sky, she turned back to me with wild eyes. "I *need* you to prove you're actually Gary Karkofsky. I mean, I can hear Cloak, and that's a point in your favor but this has been a very strange day."

"Excuse me?"

"Tell me something only you would know!" Gabrielle said, causing a white-green glow to appear around her right hand as she drew it into a fist.

I raised my hands, now alarmed. "I was motivated to become a supervillain by my brother's death."

"Not good enough!" Gabrielle shouted. It was clear she wasn't thinking clearly.

I took a step back. "When we used to do 'Opposites Attract' for karaoke night, I made you sing the cat verses."

Gabrielle deflated and caused the glow to fade from her hand. . "Okay, well, maybe you are—"

"For years, I thought Madonna's 'Like A Virgin' was about how the sex was awkward and unsatisfying."

"Gary!"

"Sorry! I tend to babble and make bad jokes whenever I'm upset." Being threatened by your ex-girlfriend, dumped by your henchwoman, and however the hell you'd describe the Mandy situation had made this a day perfect for bad jokes.

"It's you alright." Gabrielle pulled me close and wrapped her arms around me, embracing me. She pressed her face against my shoulder, holding me for comfort. It burned a little because she was still hot from the crater she'd fallen into.

I hugged her back. "What's wrong?"

Gabrielle continued to hold me. "It's awful. My father....is dead."

Oh...wow.

"*No,*" Cloak whispered. "*Not Moses. Not Ultragod.*"

I hated being right. Ultragod had been my first suspect when Death had suggested one of the great heroes had died but it hadn't felt real. Suspecting and knowing were two different things. Hearing it from the daughter of said individual and a close personal friend was something else entirely.

Ultragod had been the champion of the people for eighty years. He'd smashed slum lords, dismantled the KKK, brought down Hitler, humbled Stalin, and came within inches of making the world a paradise on several occasions. In the end, he'd always been prevented from fulfilling his dream by monsters like Tom Terror, Ultramind, the Great Beasts, Entropicus, and Pyronnus.

It was hard to believe he was gone.

"*The world is doomed without him,*" Cloak said, devastated. "*He was the bulwark against the darkness.*"

"*Ultragod was an inspiration to hundreds of other heroes, Cloak. Ultragoddess are every bit as skilled and talented as him,*" I thought back to him.

"*Moses was unique.*"

"*So is Gabrielle.*"

"Thank you," Gabrielle said, once again displaying her ability to hear the Reaper's Cloak. It was an ability she'd shared with her father.

"I'm sorry," I said, hugging her close. "What happened?"

Ultragoddess pulled away. "I don't know."

"You...don't..." I paused, not wanting to interrogate her. "Well, I'm sure we'll find out soon. There will be state funerals, national days of mourning, hundreds of examinations—"

"No one knows he's dead."

I blinked. "Did he die in space? Another dimension?"

"No. Everyone thinks he's still alive. He's currently heading up the Society of Superheroes Annual Conference to discuss their role for the year."

"Okay. Then how—"

"Moses Anders was found dead in Atlas City. He was shot with a gold ultranium bullet."

Oh. That would do it.

"So no one in the Society but you knows his secret identity?"

"My father's was known only to the Nightwalker, you, me, my mother, and Guinevere. Guinevere is currently in Fairyland, hunting down Morgana Le Fey and Balor. We don't expect her back this year."

"So...someone is impersonating your father as Ultragod."

"Yes."

"And when you tried to tell other people—"

"I was revealed to be a shape-shifting imposter or clone. I'm not sure which. I didn't really stop to ask when all of my friends and associates tried to kill me."

I stared at her. "Kill you? That doesn't seem like them."

Gabrielle took a deep breath. "It's not. I suspect whoever is behind the new Ultragod, they're exerting a subtle influence on the rest of the Society. They're meaner and more *definitive* than they should be."

"You mean they're killers."

"It sure looks that way."

My brother Keith had been a supervillain, albeit one who was never as successful as me at it. Known as Stingray: The Underwater Assassin™, despite never killing anyone, he had ended up beaten up and in jail more times than I could count. Eventually, he decided to go straight and try to salvage some form of normal life from the crooked path it had taken. That hadn't stopped a wannabe superhero calling himself Shoot-Em-Up from killing him and a number of other retired or unarmed supervillains. I had a very low opinion of them, for obvious reasons.

"*This nightmare grows,*" Cloak said. "*We need to get her inside. The magical wards on the house will muffle her presence, assuming she managed to cover her tracks.*"

I'd eventually tracked Shoot-Em-Up down and shot him the way Cloak described earlier, getting away with it thanks to the fact that Theodore Whitman had made the poor decision of having a minimum of security while he indulged in his passion for underaged prostitutes. Shoot-Em-Up had been lionized by the media during his short-lived career, though, and triggered an age of murderous anti-heroes that still reverberated through the system.

The Society of Superheroes had been torn over the past few years over whether these anti-heroes were to be condemned, embraced, or controlled. Unlike in comic books, most traditional superheroes would kill if it there were absolutely no other choice to save lives, but anti-heroes tended to embrace the role of judge, jury, and executioner. They didn't want to be superpowered police or rescue workers so much as soldiers.

I also had a very low opinion of them, for obvious reasons.

"Yes, because they're going to miss the big glowing comet that hit my backyard."

"We'll have to move quickly," Gabrielle muttered.

"I agree." I hated asking my next question but I had to be absolutely sure. "Are you sure he's dead and not, I dunno, kidnapped or in another dimension or something? This sort of thing has happened before."

If Ultragod was—and I hated using this comparison—really most sincerely dead, then it was the end of an age. He'd been the bedrock of superheroism since the thirties and the measure by which they all judged themselves. It just wouldn't be the same without him.

Gabrielle nodded. "I sensed his spirit joining the Ultraforce the same way so many other Ultraheroes of the past have done."

"I'll pretend I know what that means."

"I can feel him inside my soul like my other dead relatives."

"Oh."

"I know what that's like." I gave her another hug and started leading her to my kitchen door.

"You don't have to worry about the Society of Superheroes showing up on your doorstep, at least for a few hours. I managed to fake an Ultraforce explosion over the Himalayas with one of my constructs. It's not going to fool them for long, though, and when they start scanning the Earth then they're probably going to find me—even with my stealth suit."

I looked at her. "That's your stealth suit?"

Gabrielle looked down at her attire. "Yeah, I may need to cover it up with something a little less ostentatious."

"Just a little bit," I said, reaching the door and heading on in. Kerri was trying to keep Lisa away in the next room. Which was probably a good idea given our present circumstances. ""What can I do to help?"

"You're the only person I thought I could turn to."

"I understand."

It had been a smart idea coming here. My relationship with Gabrielle was a secret shared with precisely no one outside of our most trusted confidants: the Shadow Seven black ops team, Diabloman, Nightgirl, Cindy—okay, actually, it wasn't a very good secret. Still, if Ultragod's secret identity was secret, then so was Gabrielle's and that meant our relationship was secret. After all, who in the world would suspect the World's Most Beloved Kid-Heroine-Turned-Adult had dated one of the world's most infamous supervillains?

"*Most infamous would be stretching things.*"

"Not the time, Cloak."

"*I offer my decades of service and skills as a detective to this cause. We have to find out who was responsible and put a stop to this.*"

"No argument from me."

Gabrielle continued. "I need your help, yours and Cindy's and even your second-in-command Diabloman."

It must have pained Gabrielle to say that since Diabloman had been a dire enemy of her teenage years when she was leader of the Texas Guardians. "With the superhero world compromised by whatever thing is impersonating my father, you're the best hope I have for tracking down whoever killed my father. We need to find them, punish them, and foil whatever scheme they're planning."

I didn't say that whatever scheme they had planned had already taken a great step forward by killing Ultragod. People had been trying to kill him for the better part of a century and doing so altered the power balance of the world forever. I believed Gabrielle could pick up the slack and the rest of the superheroes, but that didn't mean the world wasn't a far darker and more unpleasant place thanks to this event.

"*Perhaps now is the time to consider becoming a hero for real.*"

"You shuddap," I said to Cloak.

"I agree with Cloak," Gabrielle said, taking a seat down to the damaged breakfast table. "Now is a time for heroism."

"Now is a time for friendship. Everyone on Earth will want to help you avenge Ultragod, I'm sure." It wasn't a good time to recruit Cindy but, really, I had faith she'd put aside her feelings to help deal with this.

"We should also try and talk with Tom Terror," Gabrielle suggested. "Get his input on all this."

"Okay, everyone on Earth but him." I blinked, not sure I heard that right. "You want to recruit the *Nazi scientist?*"

"He's done of a lot of evil since then. He's not really a Nazi scientist so much as a mad scientist in general."

"Jewish supervillain," I said, pointing to myself and explaining why any defense of a former Nazi was talking to a wall.

"Point taken."

"Tom Terror also has tried to kill you, your father, your mother, your father's best friend, your father's boss, and everyone even tangentially associated with your family. He is, as I know you know, a very bad person. Which, given who is speaking, is saying something. Why in the world would you want to speak with him? He's probably the one who killed Ultragod."

"Tom Terror is one of the few people I can confirm didn't kill Ultragod."

"Why's that?"

"Because if he did, he'd be announcing it to the entirety of the world," Gabrielle said, disgusted. "He might be able to provide some insight into the possible suspects, though. He's still imprisoned in Atlas City Penitentiary after his transfer from the moon. Whatever you did when you blasted him with the Power Nullifier has left him kind of batty."

"Or so he wants you to think."

This was a bad idea.

That was when Lisa managed to get past Kerri and walked through the King to get into the kitchen. Holding her cellphone, she started to take pictures of Gabrielle. "Holy crap, you really do know Ultragoddess! This is awesome! I can't wait to post this on—"

I grabbed her cellphone from her. "You can't share these on Insta-whatever or Facewho."

"What?" Lisa stared. "Why?"

I tried to figure out what would dissuade Lisa from social media and drew up a blank.

"Because a bunch of people will come and kill us," Gabrielle said, simply. "I'm in hiding and if people know where I am then there's nothing that will be able to prevent them from doing so. So, please, don't do that."

Lisa blinked then nodded. "Okay, I'll go upstairs and do my homework."

She then walked off, robotically.

I stared at her, confused, then glared. "Dammit, do NOT mesmerize my niece!"

"Sorry! It was just the first thing that came to mind!"

"Brainwashing should not be the first thing that comes to mind!"

Kerri proceeded to head into the kitchen and started cleaning up the mess on the floor. "I assume breakfast is over?"

"Yeah, sorry about that," I said, frowning. "Uh, Kerri, this is Ultragoddess, Ultragoddess, Kerri." I tried not to let there be any hints that Gabrielle my ex-girlfriend whom Kerri knew was also Ultragoddess, the world's greatest superheroine.

Kerri extended her hand to Gabrielle and shook it. "It's nice to meet you, again, Gabby. I'm sorry you and my brother didn't work out."

"Ah, you saw through her disguise, huh?" I said, grimacing.

"Not really," Kerri said, shrugging. "Whenever Gabby and I met while you were dating, she mesmerized me to not make the connection to her secret identity. However, my spooks just told me the truth."

Gabrielle frowned. "Ugh. Well, keep it to yourself would you? Secret identities are something some superheroes choose to be without but not something I intend to be without."

Looking up into the sky out the windows, I said, "Yeah, who knows what the consequences of being targeted by a bunch of sinister unknown people could do to your sense of security?"

"You're talking about the twenty-million bounty on your head?" Gabrielle asked.

I did a double take. "Yeah."

"Yeah, that was issued by President Omega last week. His Department of Superhuman Security contacts has been getting in touch with mercs left and right for it."

Well...crap.

"Why not just arrest me?"

"Well, you did kind of bankrupt his corporation. The one he'd intended to return to after his term ended. I think he wants you dead."

Chapter Nine

Yet Another Flashback

I knew the event she was referring to. It had been a few months ago, when Cindy had managed to persuade me to try and get back into the game of being a supervillain. The site of our prospective heist? The Falconcrest City Stock Exchange.

The floors were full of frantically-working traders. The walls were lit up with monitors depicting the ever-changing price of corn, seed, cloth, microchips, robots, and alien consumer goods. Business had been booming since the Fall. It was the biggest tragedy in decades, an event that had caused the rest of America to wake up and take notice of Falconcrest City's dire situation. Money had poured in to rebuild it from all corners. Some of which made it into the hands of its residents.

While I was rich enough to not hate the one percent with an instinctive fury, the corruption for Falconcrest City's rebuilding projects pushed one of my few remaining class-warrior berserk buttons and today was going to be a day when me and my crew took vengeance. I could have just held up the place with a gang of mercenaries like some supervillains, but I wasn't that sort of fellow. No, goddammit, if I was going to get back in the game then I was going to do it *in style*.

The side of the north wall exploded at exactly eleven o'clock, the prow of a sixteenth century pirate ship sailing through the concrete floors of the building and sending rubble forth in every direction. This monumental feat was accomplished through the force field generated around the vessel by my latest henchperson, Nicky Tesla, who was dressed in a mad scientist's overcoat with a pair of thick goggles on her face over a car battery-powered harness she was wearing with a dozen tentacles sticking from her back.

I was wearing my usual Sith robe-like attire, but I'd put a Long John Silver's paper pirate hat on my head as well as a fake stuffed parrot on my shoulder. It was held in place with Velcro. In my right hand was a plastic sword covered in very real blood.

"Ahoy there, Warner Street rapscallions, and prepare to be boarded! Tis Talk Like a Pirate Day and we've come here to seize your booty!"

"Seize your booty! Squawk!" my stuffed parrot added. My sister, Kerri, had a little microphone attached to it so I could get running data on whether the cops were responding or the local millionaire's private armies.

"Yes! The money kind of booty!" Cindy added, swinging her own sword. She, of course, had adopted the "Sexy Pirate" variant of a costume.

The countless jacketed brokerage firms employees, security guards, and a number of people who just appeared to be there for other reasons all started panicking before running in different directions. Those who managed to reach the doors slammed their faces into an invisible force-field, the same kind that had allowed my dramatic entrance.

"Great job, Nicky," I said, smiling.

"*Jawohl, Mein Kapitän*," Nicky said.

I glared at her. "Never say that again. Really."

"*Ja*," Nicky said.

I cleared my throat and walked over to the edge of the ship. "Ladies and gentlemen, consider yourself occupied!" I paused. "That's not too dated is it? Anyway, if you're all willing to cooperate then this will not take but a moment."

"There's nothing to steal here, though!" one stockbroker in the back said.

I made a tsk-tsk-tsk noise. "Oh please, we both know that's not true. Warner Street and its sister avenues are the place where the most theft in the United States goes on. A regular bank may be robbed, an ATM smashed up, or a purse snatched, but it is here where we encounter the big leagues of crime. Just last year, all of you helped prop up the Omega Corporation Rebuilding Initiative which along with fifty other corporations, received *forty* billion dollars to restore our great city. That's more than twice what was allocated to the rebuilding Iraq after we invaded it, folks, and do you know how much ended up in the hands of the people?"

There was a guilt-ridden oppressive silence.

"Two words, first one jack. Second one shit," I said, staring them down. "I'm not a Robin Hood figure. That superhero would consider the recovery of the funds to be the chief priority of my effort. No my friends, I am a supervillain, and I am quite content with exerting a limited amount of retribution on behalf of the good people of Falconcrest. People, I, alone, should be allowed to pilfer from. Cindy, would you be so kind and distribute to these good people their boxes?"

"Sure boss!" Cindy shouted, taking a selfie of herself with a terrified stockbroker. "Please note, I am not the reformed supervillain turned heroine Red Riding Hood but Pirate Girl, a wholly distinct and legally unknown supervillainess."

"Yes," I said, rolling my eyes. "That's a really brilliant piece of criminal misdirection, there."

"Says the neon-sign-over-his-house guy," Cindy snapped back.

"You're never going to let me live that down, are you?"

"No."

"You're going to force us to sell our stock?" an elderly man said, looking like he was torn between fear for his life and his fortune. "Bankrupt us?"

"Oh no," I said, looking over them. "I am much more devious than that. Diabloman?"

Diabloman was dressed in his spandex and luchador mask but had added a seventeenth-century greatcoat over his head and a patch over his left (masked) eye. As if accenting the gangland nature of pirates, he also was wearing a great deal of bling—gold necklaces, rings, and other bits of jewelry. Beside him, being held by a leash, was an elderly man who was the key to my current stratagem.

The man on a leash was white-haired and Caucasian, with a significant amount of work done and a twenty-thousand-dollar power suit. On his head was a Christmas tree-light-covered colander which Nicky Tesla insisted was a mind-control helmet. Given the man was drooling out of the right side of his mouth, I couldn't dismiss her statement out of hand. The man was also holding a computer tablet in his hands.

"This, folks, is John Wormwood, acting CEO of Omega Industries in lieu of President John Omega who not only prevented superheroes from intervening in Falconcrest City during the Big Disaster but also managed to secure himself a second term by proceeding to blame Congress as well as the Society of Superheroes for not doing enough. Wow. Since I can't get the president, yet, I'm going to settle for the person who personally made over a billion dollars from his cut of rebuilding contracts."

"He is a bad but entirely legal sort of person," Cindy said.

"Many of you have done business with him," Diabloman said. "For which you should all be ashamed."

"The police are not inbound yet," Kerri said via the parrot. "There's a hostage situation with the Chillingsworths nearby."

Taking note of that, I put my arm around my hostage. "Mister Wormwood, here, is going to sell a staggering amount of his stock in a few minutes. Which, bluntly, will cause a staggering number of other investors to sell their stock due to the large number of rumors the company isn't nearly as solvent as it appears to be. Which, given the way they make use of projected earnings and books more fictitious than *The Lord of the Rings*, may be true. You, my friends, are going to be purchasing stock in competing firms of my choice which will drive up their price substantially and make me a substantially wealthier man. Mostly, because I own a huge amount of stock in said firms."

That was when one of the asshats in the back raised his hand. He was a middle-aged black man with white tufts of hair on the sides of his head.

"This isn't kindergarten," I said, staring at him. "What do you want?"

"Stock fraud?" he said, as if I should be offended. "Isn't this a bit outside your bailiwick?"

"Okay, kudos for using the word bailiwick. What do you mean?"

"You're a world-famous supervillain," the man continued. "We saw you rescue the city last year during the Big Disaster but that was after you killed the Extreme and escaped the Society of Superheroes moon prison. Shouldn't you, I dunno, be trying to take over the world or something?"

Cindy looked over at me. "He's right, boss. This is kinda beneath you."

"I am having a very stressful year!" I said, snapping back. "It's stock fraud *with a pirate ship on land and mind-control*. This is very much not beneath me."

"I disagree," Diabloman said, backing up Cindy. "A year ago, you'd have a musical number plus a half-dozen-dead bodies."

"I disagree. Tis very good!" Nicky Tesla said. "Most avant-garde."

"You can speak real English, Nicky. The fake German is fooling nobody."

Nicky looked aside and muttered in perfect English. "Spoilsport."

I lifted my fingers and shot a fireball into the air, causing everyone but my henchmen to take a step back. "Silence! We're going to do this my way and I'm not going to hear any more—"

"Halt, evildoer! So says the Nightwalker!" a cheerful female voice shouted before a figure in a costume similar to mine swung from a window above, landing on the ground in front of me. She was a small Japanese-American woman with long dyed blonde hair sticking out from the side of her hood.

Amanda Douglas was the second Nightwalker, a billionaire hotel magnate and evil cultist's daughter who had taken up the mantle after the original's death. She was one of the city's two superheroes and pretty good at her job despite her relative inexperience. We'd helped each other end the Big Disaster and even hung out socially but didn't let that affect our working relationship.

"Your foul felonies have reached their finality!" Amanda shouted, producing an extendable staff which then produced an electrical charge on both end.

"Merciful Moses," I said, rubbing the bridge of my nose. "What is this, the sixties?"

"*Well, she was trained by my old partner,*" Cloak muttered. "*I'm going to assume the hostage situation is resolved.*"

"Well, good for them," I said, pointing at her. "I'm not in the mood for any interruptions. Get her."

"*You're not in the mood for many things lately,*" Cloak said.

Diabloman leapt off the side of the pirate ship and charged at her, my super-strong henchman immediately getting sent flying backwards by one of Amanda's uppercuts. A half-dozen black-sweater-wearing pirate crew charged out from the hole next, all of them with a stylized M on their attire.

Amanda displayed stunning gymnastics as she leapt over henchmen, spin-kicked others, zapped a few more, and hurled others into each other. I, meanwhile, levitated downward with Wormwood in my arms and pulled out a computer tablet to begin programming my plan. I couldn't bring myself to throw in some witty commentary.

God, they were right. I *was* phoning it in.

"*Perhaps supervillainy isn't for you since Mandy—*"

"Don't mention her name," I growled.

Cindy managed to backstab Amanda with an industrial-strength taser as Amanda knocked away the last of my goons. Amanda yowled, fell to her knees, and then grabbed Cindy in a judo throw, hurling her in the air. I levitated upwards, grabbed Cindy, and then hovered back down.

"Thanks for the save," Cindy said.

"You're welcome," I said, turning back to Amanda. I handed my tablet over to Cindy who finished programming it.

Diabloman was getting up for the next round but I shook my head to him.

This was my time to show off.

Amanda pointed at me. "The police will arrive any minute to finish off your scheme. Damn, I should have used finish in that earlier line. Anyway, you won't be able to—wait, is that John Wormood? The guy who got a bunch of people killed because the money for moving people to hospitals from refugee camps disappeared?"

I paused. "...Yes?"

Amanda narrowed her eyes, paused, then started to fake choking. "Oh, no, you...bastard! You're using your magic to drain away my supernatural power. I...can't move. I can't stop...whatever you're going to do to him."

I crossed my arms. "Really? Have you no pride?"

Amanda banged on the ground with her fist. "Oh woe, my inability to save this horrible person from his fate—whatever it may be."

"Oh for the love of King David," I muttered then looked at Wormwood. Cindy handed him the remote. "John, I command you to sell all of your stock."

The mind-controlled executive nodded and short-sold everything.

I addressed the crowd of stockbrokers. "Now, it's technically illegal for you to act on this information but—"

All of them were already taking advantage of the deal to make more money.

I sighed. "Why am I not surprised?"

"Because you've lived here more than a year?" Cindy said.

"Point taken."

I checked my remote and proceeded to transfer the resulting funds into my account, having made a quarter of a billion dollars and tripling my fortune. Sighing, I paid my henchmen their section and sent the vast majority of my wealth to various charities around the city before wiping out the records with a keystroke.

"*So much for not being Robin Hood,*" Cloak said.

"I have enough money to buy anything I want," I said, frowning. "Anything I can't afford, I steal. I'm just keeping myself motivated by giving the excess to those who could use a helping hand."

"*Sure.*"

Looking out the window of the stock exchange, I saw a couple of police cars with flashing lights. The department was still being rebuilt after having had a substantial amount of its ranks revealed to be insane death cultists.

Staring at them in disgust, I said, "Gather up my half-conscious goons and tie Amanda up. We're bringing her with us."

"You're taking her prisoner?" Diabloman said, surprised.

"Yep," I said, gesturing to a pair of magical chains I'd brought along for just this sort of occasion. "We'll let her out after a suitable period of time where, clearly, she'd been held hostage and was unable to stop this."

"Thanks...." Amanda said through faked strained breaths.

"Ooo, are we taking her back to the lair for a kinky sex game?" Cindy said, a broad grin on her face.

"That happened once," I said, staring at her. If by once when if you counted when I was really depressed and Cindy and I had slept together for a month. I still felt guilty about it but it was about the only thing that kept me alive when I thought I'd never see Mandy again. "We're not making that a regular part of our repertoire."

"It's good to see you again, Gary," Amanda said, right before Cindy lassoed her with the chains, the magic causing the bonds to move around her and squeeze. "The city hasn't been the same without the Supervillain without Mercy^{TM}."

"That's the problem."

I managed to get away scot-free, especially once attempts to locate the money had proven difficult because the majority of it wasn't supposed to be in Omega Corp's hands to begin with, but it left me feeling no better about myself.

Only one thing could do that. The one thing reality couldn't permit me. With that, I started to think back on the present.

And the fact President Omega was trying to kill me.

Chapter Ten

The Bad Guy for the Book is POTUS

"The president has *taken a hit* out on me?" I said, incredulous. "For robbing him?"

"Don't act so surprised," Gabrielle said, looking to one side. "President Omega is the most corrupt and bigoted United States president since William Henry Harrison. He hates supers, aliens, and mystery men. He also bought the election with his company's millions. You probably did more damage to his plans by destroying his company than we've done in eight years of fighting him through the legal process."

"Still, I'm more surprised I'm not dead than anything else."

Gabrielle paused. "There's rumors that he's sent several hit squads and assassins against you already. People who end up with their throats torn out and bodies drained of blood. Know anything about that?"

I looked away. "Err, maybe."

"Also, a bunch of ghosts dragged a wizard who tried to curse your family to hell."

Kerri started whistling "Whistle While You Work" as she continued to try and clean up the mess.

"Have you been attacked randomly by supervillains and anti-heroes trying to kill you this past year?" Gabrielle asked.

I blinked. "Isn't that normal?"

Gabrielle felt her face. "No, Gary. No it's not."

"Well, don't I have egg on my face."

"There's also rumors that President Omega has plans for something big in his final year of office. Something that he can try to use to change the balance of superhuman-baseline relationships forever."

I snorted at her description of the president's actions. "Like leaving everyone to die in Falconcrest City wasn't enough."

People often talked about the destructive nature of superhuman fights and the government's incompetence during a crisis, but usually, they were both pretty on the ball when it came to rebuilding things. The ideal superhero-government relationship had the former fighting the bad guy, the latter evacuating civilians, and the two of them cooperating to make sure everything was cleaned up thereafter.

The biggest good superheroes did wasn't actually punching out terrorists and bank-robbers, but using their powers for rescue work during disasters as well as lending themselves to relieve global crises. Things like oil spills, earthquakes, typhoons, and worse had been prevented with millions saved thanks to the efforts of heroes.

Recently, though, superheroes had started including more and more people uninterested in anything but punishment while the government had begun to act like they didn't need superheroes at all. President Omega was very good at making the latter seem like a flaw of the heroes rather than the reverse, especially when he preferred his heroes violent and jingoistic.

Could you tell I'd voted for the other guy?

Gabrielle nodded. "The legislation Omega drafted in response to the Fall has drastically increased his powers. Powers he intends to use to finally push through the changes he's long desired. Truth be told, this has been coming a long time. People are sick of supervillains, superheroes, useless police, technology they don't understand, alien invasion, colorful terrorist attacks they can't defend against, and constantly being in the shadows of gods."

"Superheroes are what people should aspire to," I said. "Not something people should bring down to their level."

Gabrielle and Kerri both looked at me, their thoughts obvious. After all, who was I to talk about superheroes when I'd chosen to go the exact opposite route with my powers?

"*It's a good point*," Cloak observed. "*You could do so much more.*"

"I could do worse too," I thought back. "You *got any theories as to who might have pulled this off?*"

"*Not without knowing the circumstances of his death, no. I do know this might be a cosmological shift-point in history, though. The historical records of the fortieth century speak of a Twilight of the Superheroes that occurs sometime in this era. A terrible conflict that results in the deaths of the majority of superhumans as well as much of the baseline population. It's an event that followed the deaths of the Nightwalker and Ultragod.*"

"You didn't think to mention this until now?" I thought to Cloak.

"*It's only one of many alternate pasts.*"

"Alternate pasts?"

"*There are an infinite number of pasts the way there are an infinite number of futures. Continuity in this reality is more like suggestions rather than hard facts. For example, there's a Gary Karkofsky, Teen Reporter who is Gabrielle's love-interest in the sixties. A Gary Karkofsky who is Mandy, Foundation Agent's husband in the* nineties. *There's also a grim and gritty Gary Karkofsky who is a cannibal pimp in a universe where superheroes just appeared last year and are all arrogant sociopaths."*

"A cannibal pimp?!"

"*Yeah, we don't like to talk about that universe.*"

"Do you think the government is responsible for Ultragod?" I asked, deciding to push all that to the back of my mind.

Gabrielle looked down. "I don't know."

There was a time when the idea of the government having the most powerful and beloved superhero in the world assassinated would have sounded like tinfoil hattery nonsense spouted by people like—well, me, but hearing Ultragoddess seriously contemplate that was like a punch to the gut.

Things had changed in the past two decades, becoming less and less fun. It was harder to trust the government and the government reacted by becoming less and less trustworthy. Then again, maybe it had always been that way and I just hadn't noticed until adulthood because I'd grown up a reasonably privileged white kid. Still, I hoped it wasn't President Omega.

I could deal with the president wanting to kill me. I wasn't sure I wanted to deal with a world where the president wanted to kill the Society of Superheroes. I was too much of an anarchist to believe in American democracy but still liked to think our leaders had some standards.

My mistake.

"Ultragod's dead?" Kerri asked, shocked. "He once came to our school to talk about how drugs were awful!"

"Yeah, I was dealing pot with Cindy that day so I missed it."

Gabrielle gave a half-hearted chuckle. "Thanks, Gary, I needed that."

"Yes, that was totally a joke and not at all; what actually happened."

"*A lot of those public relations visits were Ultraforce-construct doppelgangers anyway. It allowed him to do more good than any single man could accomplish.*"

"Keep it under wraps for the time being, Kerri," I said, taking a deep breath. "There's an imposter running about and he's after Gabrielle."

Kerri nodded. "Cross my heart and hope not to die because then I'd become a spook and I'd be surrounded by friends."

Sometimes, I had no words. "Okay. Sure."

Kerri and I had gotten into plenty of arguments about the fact that my job as the Reaper's Cloak-bearer was to serve as a psychopomp, i.e. a guy who sent spooks to their natural resting place. I'd sent onward literally thousands of ghosts since getting it, and some of them had been people Kerri had known.

The vast majority of them had been happy with it, though. It's just Kerri had difficulty telling the difference between alive and dead. Then again, I was the one who insisted Mandy could be healed no matter what. I made a mental note to also try and figure out a way to bring Ultragod back.

"Well, I suppose we can start to investigate your father's death once we've got the rest of the team joined. Cindy is likely to be at the hospital—"

"Are you sure she'll want to help?" Kerri asked.

I made a throat slit gesture across my neck. I didn't want to get into this around Gabrielle, especially given what she was suffering through right now.

"What's wrong with Cindy?" Gabrielle asked.

Kerri ignored my gesture. "She confessed her love to Gary and he fumbled the return because he's still in love with his vampire wife."

The King shook his head. "You've checked into the heartbreak hotel friend."

"I'm not in love with what is walking around in Mandy's corpse," I corrected her. "Also, please kindly avoid quoting your songs in everyday conversations."

The King shrugged. "People expect it."

"Ignoring the fact that you talk to far too many people I can't see," Gabrielle said, "I'd like for you to know I approve. Cindy is a good girl."

I stared at her. "No, she isn't."

Gabrielle paused. "Okay, no, she isn't. However. she might be good for you."

"How reassuring."

Kerri finished sweeping up all the debris from our windows into a pile. "You aren't jealous?"

"Putting aside the fact my father is dead, no. I long ago made a decision to put being a superheroine over any romantic considerations. Gary was when I chose that. I haven't changed my mind since."

"I thought you and the Golden Scarab—"

"Just sex and friendship."

That was the definition of my best relationships. "Well, I trust Cindy to want to help. Diabloman is just a phone call away too. Are you sure he's someone you want working on this? I know you two have history."

"History is putting it mildly. If I was going to assume any single supervillain was responsible for Ultragod's death, Diabloman would be high on the list. You didn't know him during the nineties. He was a terrifying monster who had all of the Nightwalker's intelligence, strength, and cunning combined with my father's leadership capabilities. He even destroyed the universe once."

Kerri paused in lifting a dust bin full of broken glass. "How do you destroy the universe?"

"Surprisingly easily it turns out," I said, remembering how Zul-Barbas had almost destroyed reality and remade it without any supers. I still had nightmares about a world where heroes only existed in fiction. "Thankfully, it can be rebooted."

"Ah," Kerri said. "I'm going to go hide under a pillow now."

I gave a dismissive wave. "Eh, it's not that bad."

"*Actually, it's much worse.*"

"Either way, Diabloman has changed. I'd stake my life on that."

"You do, every time you go out into the night with him. You hope and pray he doesn't revert to realizing you've given him access to millions in the way of funds he can use to rebuild his criminal organization, weapons he can use to take over the city, and powers that can be used to heal his crippling illness."

I looked over my shoulder. "Actually, I kind of healed Diabloman of that crippling black magic illness which ended his career awhile back. I stumbled over it when I was looking for a cure for Mandy."

Gabrielle closed her eyes. "Well, *that's good*."

"Hey, you believe in redemption, right?"

"Yes, it's just harder when the person is the person responsible for the death of friends."

I knew that feeling. "Yeah. Well....we don't have to call him."

"Do it." Gabrielle sighed. "We need all the criminal masterminds we can get on this."

"Kerri, could you go make sure Lisa isn't tweeting about all of this? If anyone can shake off Ultra-mesmerism, it's a teenage girl."

Kerri looked around. "But I'm not done cleaning!"

"You can afford to hire someone."

"But they might disturb our colony of sentient spiders from space in the basement!"

"We have a what now?"

Kerri looked guilty. "Yes, I will go deal with Lisa now. I will do that and hope you forget about what I just told you."

Kerri quickly rushed out the door to the lounge.

Gabrielle watched her leave. "Man, and I thought my family was weird."

"Are you sure you don't want to call in any of your Shadow Seven friends? Maybe the former Texas Guardians?" I asked, starting to make a phone call on my computer watch.

The Texas Guardians had been sort of a Pre-Team for younger or simply inexperienced superheroes. Texas was a state the size of a country with its own collection of myriad monsters, ruthless gangsters, supernaturals, and weirdness in constant need of dealing with.

With the supervision of local heroes, the Texas Guardians had managed to make it one of the safest places in the world. Diabloman had destroyed that safety with the aid of his cult and army of mercenaries, killing both the Guitarist and his sister, Spellbinder. It had triggered the Dark Age of Superheroes every bit as much as Shoot-Em-Up murdering my brother. There were still some of them around, though, like the Texas Twister and the El Paso Avenger. I'd heard they'd even reformed the team, recruiting a new generation of young heroes and former sidekicks eager to make a name for themselves.

The Shadow Seven were a different story, being something of a covert ops team of superheroes who didn't mind getting their hands dirty and supervillains looking for redemption. It included Mandy's ex-girlfriend Black Witch, the Red Schoolgirl, the Human Tank, the Bronze Medalist, ex-terrorist General Venom, and technically me. They did a lot of the work that people like President Omega tried to prevent, like protecting the people of Falconcrest City during the Fall and overthrowing dictators being propped up by the big nations.

"Not right now," Gabrielle said. "I don't know how many superheroes have been affected by the Ultra-imposter's powers and if he doesn't know about Shadow Seven, that leaves them as a possible ace in the hole. Besides, I don't have enough friends in the world to risk them against a threat that can kill my father."

"Just all the world-destroying threats we've already faced together."

"Later, Gary, please."

I nodded and dialed Diabloman. I heard the song, *Highway to Hell* by AC/DC before he picked it up. "I told you to not call me in the mornings. The shipments of weapons and robots will be ready for Operation Kingslayer."

"What was that?"

"Oh, hello, Gary!" Diabloman said, sounding chagrined. "I was just, uh, planning the overthrow of a government."

"Ours?"

"Yes." He sounded guilty.

"Super!" I said, disappointed in Diabloman. We were supposed to be a team. "However, I'm going to need you to take a break from that to help me and Gabrielle solve a murder."

"Who?"

"I'll tell you at Cindy's hospital. You never know who may be listening."

"Yet, you speak about where we're going to meet."

I hadn't thought of that. "....Just go there."

I then shut off my computer. "Okay, everything's prepped. Are you okay keeping your powers on the down low? We don't want anyone picking up on your presence until we're ready to reveal ourselves. I've got a couple of changes of clothes in your size upstairs."

"Have many women over or is Cindy cosplaying as me?"

I paused. "Yes and no. I'm not saying to which. Let's go...TO THE MERCILESS MOBILE!"

Gabrielle frowned. "Yeah, let's go play hero."

I gave her another hug.

And she broke down crying in my arms.

I cried too.

Chapter Eleven

Where We Discover Not to Screw Around with the US of A

"This isn't quite the vehicle I expected you to be driving us out in," Gabrielle said, now wearing a pair of khaki pants and a white sweater. She had a pair of glasses on and her hair in a ponytail, which without Ultramesmerism would have done little to disguise her identity as one of the world's most famous superheroines.

The two of us were driving around in a white minivan with the words "Carol's Floral Arrangements" on the side. I'd changed into a pair of black jeans and a black hoodie, which wasn't all that better disguise-wise. I looked like a hip new re-imagining of Merciless rather than a thirty-odd-year-old civilian.

"Incognito is not just a funny-sounding word. Even I know that, crazy house additions aside," I said from behind the wheel. "Besides, I never quite got the hang of driving around the Nightcar, so it's better to do this in case we get into any chase sequences."

"I thought the Nightcar, Mercilessmobile, or whatever was self-driving."

"Yeah, but that's cheating."

It was never really morning or afternoon in Falconcrest City. Rain clouds, snow, or the towering gargoyle-covered buildings always blotted out the sun. Still, I noticed more people out and about than in previous trips. The Fall had devastated the city, but almost two-thirds of the population had returned, with the remainder being replaced by new arrivals looking for cheap housing. There was something different about the city too. The people who had been trapped in dome had rallied together under Ultragoddess and Mandy, which left them closer than they'd been before. With the destruction of the Brotherhood of Infamy, the police force was far less corrupt too. I would never say the Fall was a good thing—you only had to wait until night for that to be rebutted—but I did believe my city was going to rise from the ashes.

Stronger than before.

"Or maybe I'm just kidding myself," I muttered.

"Thinking about your city?" Gabrielle asked.

"Yeah," I said, shaking my head. There was so much going on it was hard to process it all. "Superheroes have failed to stop big disasters before. Terrorist attacks, individual murders, and natural disasters but this somehow feels different. It was the worst."

"Superheroes aren't invincible. Sometimes we fail." That statement had a lot more weight to it since I knew that Ultragod was dead.

"You did your best, but a lot of people expect you to be immortal and perfect."

"I wish that were true."

We passed by a statue of Ultragoddess on the way to South Falconcrest City. The proverbial wrong-side of the tracks was one of the biggest changes in the area as Karkofsky Company Construction was tearing down the slums to build better housing. Better housing which, shockingly, all of the residents would be able to afford.

There was, hilariously, a billboard sign of Merciless endorsing SuperCola over one of the finished buildings, and another of Cindy in her Red Riding Hood attire, telling parents to get their kids vaccinated, "Or we're going to come and steal your stuff." I was pleased to say that little bit of fear-mongering had worked wonders.

"You're very popular here. The supervillain thing doesn't seem to have affected that."

I shrugged. "It seems if you kill a bunch of violent supervillains and psychotic superheroes before tossing around free money, people will start to like you."

"You underestimate the kind of good you've done."

"That was mostly you and Mandy. I'm still the supervillain without mercy."

"I still don't understand why you call yourself that. You do what you think is right and are one of the most merciful people I know."

"You don't know me as well as you think you do."

"I know you pretty well. Enough to know it's not the city taking a hit which is bothering you." Gabrielle looked out the window at a trio of black children playing with super-soakers. One of them had scars around his neck from a zombie bite. "I'm sorry about what happened with Mandy. I heard about her transformation into a vampire and considered trying to help with it. I decided I'd only end up doing more harm than good."

That got me curious. "Didn't you work with a vampire?"

"Yes, Bloodscream the Retributive— or as I liked to call him, John. He was a good man who struggled every day to fake feeling mercy, pity, love, remorse, and friendship. He struggled to regain the sense of empathy he'd lost. In the end, the hunger won and we had to put him down. He was my friend both before and after he died."

I suspected there was something more there as well, or perhaps there simply could have been.

"I'm not giving up on Mandy."

Gabrielle removed her glasses and looked at me. "Is that because you think you can succeed or because you blame yourself?"

"It's because I can bring her back. If a man can fly, a woman can be restored from the dead. This city was overrun by fucking zombies last year. The least it can do is restore its protector to life."

Gabrielle was silent. "If you figure out a way to reverse death, Gary, share it with the rest of us. You're not alone in feeling grief."

That was a real kick in the chest.

"Can't you just, I dunno, bring him back from the dead?" I asked. "I have a time machine."

"Those don't actually alter time Gary."

I sighed. "Yeah, that's true. They just take you to a parallel universe. After I failed to help Mandy, I started using it to attend Beatles concerts."

Also, to kill Nazis.

A lot of Nazis.

Gabrielle smiled. "How did that work?"

"Pretty well," I said, smiling. "I'm actually friends with a couple of John Lennons."

"I'm surprised you came back to the future."

I had considered, at one point, finding a Mandy and settling down with her. It wouldn't have been my Mandy, though. I would have been depriving another Gary of the opportunity to be with her as well. Even so, the temptation to look at her again had been overwhelming. I'd finally asked Diabloman to hide the machine so I could stop stalking my past self and wife on their happier days. "Yeah, it was hard at times."

"Thank you for helping with this, Gary. I don't know who else I could have turned to during all this."

"You have a lot of friends, Gabrielle."

"Not as many as you'd think. I was raised by superheroes and that means there's always layers between the real person and who they pretend to be. Plenty of people saw me as Ultragod's daughter instead of Gabrielle Anders."

"You're both."

"You get to see both. Not many people do."

"You should tell Cindy."

Gabrielle paused. "I think she knows but you're right. She's my friend too."

"We'd both kill for you." I noticeably avoided the word die. I was not a big fan of self-sacrifice and considered it to be a sign of insufficient planning. There were people I was willing to die for but I'd made a career of avoiding putting that to the test.

Gabrielle nodded. "You may have to do that in the future."

"You mean your father's killer."

"I'm not an executioner by nature but I also don't believe the legal system provides any greater sense of justification. We all have to do what we think is right in the end and whoever killed my father can't be allowed to get away with that."

It was a very un-superheroic sentiment but a very human one. "Do you have any suspects?"

"As I stated, I don't think it's any of my father's old foes. They would have been dancing on the rooftops, shouting about how they triumphed over Ultragod at last. They also need to be someone who can create a near perfect copy of my father or have access to one but are willing to use a gun to kill him. Your theory about the government is a viable one but there's only one problem I can see."

"Which is?"

"They actually succeeded."

"That was black humor. Very black."

Gabrielle gave me a nasty look.

"Oh, sorry," I said. "Not trying to be racial there."

Gabrielle gave another gallows' chuckle. "Any theories?"

"Have you considered P.H.A.N.T.O.M?"

"P.H.A.N.T.O.M?" Gabrielle said. "You're going all the way back to them?"

"It's a long shot but it's not impossible."

P.H.A.N.T.O.M was a bogeyman that a lot of people considered to be nothing more than a relic of a less-civilized age, something middle-aged men watched programs about on the History Channel and had ceased to be relevant as anything other than stock villains on spy shows. My father had fought in the Second Vietnam War against them and his speeches told me they were anything but a funny anachronism.

Decades ago, after Ultragod had brought both Hitler and Stalin to heel, everyone was ready to work toward a peaceful Europe. That had been when the P.H.A.N.T.O.M leader had arisen and started up World War 2 in earnest, conquering whole swaths of Europe and Russia before forcing other nations to ally with him at the point of a death-ray. P.H.A.N.T.O.M's operatives had aliens' technology, superpowers, magic, and worse. It had been a wakeup call for the world that not all Supers were going to be superheroes, and the worst sort of people they could face had powers on their own. A lot of people had died in their labor camps. I still remember my Polish grandmother screaming once when she found me and Kerri watching *Hogan's Heroes*.

"P.H.A.N.T.O.M hasn't really been a thing since the eighties when it fought America Force One and the Super Giant Robots," Gabrielle said, crossing her arms. "Older than dirt or immortal supervillains like Tom Terror, Doctor Thule, and Baroness Blitz use gangs armed with their own weaponry but the last serious effort by them was the Berlin Offensive in 1991. I don't think they're going to prove responsible."

I paused. "The Nightmaster had P.H.A.N.T.O.M stormtroopers accompanying her. Back during the Fall."

Gabrielle blinked. "That was the Brotherhood of Infamy, though."

"P.H.A.N.T.O.M made use of a lot of magic during WW2 and the Brotherhood had a Nazi robot. Maybe there's a connection."

The Brotherhood of Infamy had been motivated by a desire to destroy all Supers in the world. They saw the world of mechanical wonders, people who could fly, and miracles so they summoned a Great Beast to destroy it. They'd been richer than God and President Omega had devoted a substantial amount of effort to making sure the Fall wasn't prevented by superheroes. Maybe there was a connection between the Brotherhood and P.H.A.N.T.O.M. The terrorist organization's leaders often said the only way to bring Supers to heel was to destroy them, whether it employed them or not.

"You think the President of the United States is a member of a secret Nazi cult?" Cloak asked.

"It's possible?" I suggested. *"I mean, his last name is Omega. Have you ever noticed all the really bad guys have names like that?"*

"No, I haven't. Your theory is stupid."

"Fine," I said. "I was just hoping all of our problems were interrelated. I'll keep my theorizing to myself until we have something more concrete."

"Probably a good idea."

We were silent for the rest of the trip to the South Falconcrest Hospital, formerly the single largest ruined building in the city and home to such wonderful people as the Malt Shop Gang as well as a diverse collection of the city's drug dealers. Cindy had purchased the property, redeveloped it, hired on all manner of medical personnel, and then charged nothing for her help. It was, in simple terms, a gigantic money-pit and the center of countless acts of criminal activity to keep it running. It also had saved something like ten thousand lives since starting operation.

Entering through the sliding front doors, we were greeted by small crowds of people who were gathered around televisions spread throughout the main entrance way. They were holding each other, crying, and staring at the news announcement being shown on every channel. For a second, I thought they'd announced Ultragod's death and the imposter had been revealed. Then I noticed Sally Sutler, the local anchorwoman, was showing a black and white of Gabrielle in her Ultragoddess attire. It listed her birthdate, followed by today's date at the bottom of the picture.

"Oh those sons of bitches," Gabrielle whispered. "They've announced my death."

"That's going to be awkward when you show up again," I said.

"Not if they claim I'm an alien imposter," Gabrielle muttered.

I tried to figure out a way to reassure. "This stuff has happened before, right? Alien imposters, clones, and so on?"

"This is different," Gabrielle said, looking down the hall. "More final. Can we get to Cindy? I'm not really comfortable being this exposed."

"Sure."

We walked down the hallway and I couldn't help but notice people casting me nervous glances. I don't think any of them actually recognized me as Merciless but my attire reminded them of such and their reaction wasn't friendly like it used to be. Several people nervously tried to take cellphone pictures of me only for me to duck or move

Something was wrong.

I didn't get a chance to think too much on this fact before my cellphone started to play *Witchy Woman* by the Eagles. Kerri. Pulling it from my pocket, I lifted it up to my ear. "Hello."

"Um, hey, Gary?" my sister said.

"Yeah."

"We've got a wee bit of a problem."

"How's that?"

"Let me send you a picture."

Kerri hung up and seconds later a picture of my mansion—or more precisely, the remains of the mansion—appeared. There was a gigantic crater where the building once stood. Someone had dropped a missile on top of the place, something you didn't often see happening within the continental United States.

"I'd complain about my home being destroyed but I'm more curious why you think Hawaii, Alaska, Puerto Rico, and Guam are more likely to be bombed," Cloak said, surprisingly deadpan about the whole thing.

I tried to process just what had happened. The destruction of my house by a bomb wasn't just a minor inconvenience, stolen wealth or not. President Omega had taken the gloves off and with the entire United States behind him, he was all but invincible. It wasn't exactly like I could depend on due process after having flouted the law in astoundingly funny ways for the past year.

I ignored him. "Is Lisa alright?"

"Yeah, I was out walking the dogs with her when the place exploded. Minutes later, some men in dark suits tried to grab us only for my spooks to possess their car and crash it into them. I think they were trying to kidnap us."

The president was, officially, no longer fucking around. He'd also decided to go after my family. That settled that. Now I had to kill him. The very thought of it made me ill but I decided to steel myself. He was a monster, the highest office in the land or not, and I needed to protect my loved ones. Oh, who the hell was I kidding? There was no good ending to this. Even if I took him down, the USA would hunt me and my loved ones forever.

"It gets worse," Kerri said.

That wasn't good. "How?"

"They're saying you killed Ultragoddess. A bunch of superheroes showed up and demanded to know where you are so they could kill you."

Well shit.

Chapter Twelve

A Friendly Chat with Cindy About My Being and Idiot

"Gary. Are you all right?" Gabrielle asked, reaching over to touch my arm.

I took a deep breath. "Surprisingly, yes. At least, I'm no worse off than I was before finding out the government has framed me for killing America's sweetheart. Oh yes, and they blew up my house."

"*My house*," Cloak said, growling. "*Which has been in the Warren Family since the 18th century.*"

"Which would explain why it was a bitch to get updated with decent electricity and wi-fi," I said, talking aloud. "Seriously, though, Gabby, it's okay. No one I cared about was in the house when it went kaboom. If the events of the past year have taught me one thing, it's that the only real currency is those you love."

"I see," Gabrielle said, keeping her expression even. "Good."

"I mean, it was nice having a mansion I literally couldn't jog around before passing out. The heated underground grotto Cindy and I used to go skinny-dipping in. The massive comic book collection with its own personal vault. The conservatory with man-eating plants. The literal shark tank. I mean, Good God, you could play live-action Clue and pretend to be a Bond villain there."

Gabrielle kept patting me on the shoulder. "I'm more concerned about the fact that it's increasingly apparent our suspicions about the president are correct."

"Not necessarily. I am kind of an asshole, but given he's framing me for killing you, I suppose it's not a big step to think he's a bad guy too."

"Yes," Gabrielle said. "So, what we have to do next is clear."

"Yep, kill the President." I'd just have to figure out some person to blame it on who wasn't me and whom the courts could execute in my place.

"What? No!" Gabrielle said, appalled.

"Then we have different definitions of clear."

"We need to prove I'm still alive, that my father has been replaced, and that the president had Ultragod killed, and then have him impeached."

"Seems awfully complicated."

"Do you really want to go down in history with Lee Harvey Oswald and John Wilkes Booth?"

"Everyone forgets Leon Czolgosz and Charles Guiteau."

"Well, do you?"

I sighed. "No, I don't. As much as I don't think Diabloman would mind assaulting the White House and choking the first successful third-party candidate to death, that's the kind of heat I don't need. Also, I have a speck of a Grinch's heart three-sizes-two-small of patriotism left in my body."

Gabrielle rolled her eyes. "Your nobility moves me."

"Come on, let's go get Cindy as I try and think of a plan to get President Omega to confess on live television that doesn't involve torture."

"Torture doesn't work."

"Only if you're interrogating someone and expect truthful answers like on television. For hurting people it works fine."

"*I hate that you know that from experience*," Cloak said.

"Sometimes assholes have to be hurt."

The two of us managed to avoid any more media attention as we reached Cindy's office on the second floor, taking the stairs to avoid crowds and walking in without bothering to knock. That proved to be a mistake, as the two of us found ourselves surrounded by a hundreds of labeled plastic bags filled with Blitz, the most popular supervillain-produced street drug in Falconcrest City.

Cindy was sitting behind her desk in a surgery mask, cutting a pile of red dust into manageable packets of one hundred to put in each sack for distribution. She was in her civilian doctor's attire; her hair still in bunches, with a television on her desk showing the *Esoterrorism* movie. The one starring Karl Urban as Derek Hawthorne and Jessica Chastain as Shannon O'Reilly.

Despite our last encounter ending in literal tears, Cindy looked up without a care in the world. "Oh, hi guys."

"Cindy!" Gabrielle said, staring at the massive amount of narcotics around her. "This is horrifying!"

"Yeah, don't you have people to do this?" I asked, reaching over and taking a sniff of the red dust. The effects were an immediate sense of euphoria followed by a somewhat goofy feeling—how I normally felt as a supervillain, basically.

Gabrielle stared at me.

"What?" I said.

"Speaking as a doctor, it's important that I properly match the purity and size of each Blitz package with appropriate instructions printed on the side for usage. Otherwise, they might be misused by consumers."

"Yeah, because junkies are so well-known for following the warnings on printed labels," I said.

"Your prejudice against recreational drug use is terrible," Cindy said, shaking her head.

"Aren't you trying to reform?" Gabrielle said, feeling her face.

"Hey, I can be a good-girl vigilante in a slutty-sexy Halloween costume and a drug-dealing, free-hospital-running doctor. There are no laws against that."

"There are like thirty, actually," I said. "But who's equivocating?"

"God, Gary, spare me the lecture. This is like that time you tried to convince me *The Force Awakens* wasn't crap."

"How can you not like *The Force Awakens*?" It was more a statement than a question. My mind momentarily lost track of why I was here thanks to the Blitz.

"What?" Cindy said, pulling her surgery mask down around her neck. "It's just *A New Hope* with new characters and more lens flare."

"Heathen!" I said, appalled. "There's Kylo Ren, though, and Rey! And stuff! The thing with Han!"

"Guys—" Gabrielle started to speak.

"Adam Driver was hot in it, I admit," Cindy said, sighing. "But you don't think Rey was a Mary Sue? I mean, I like the fact a woman is headlining a *Star Wars* movie but we didn't see Luke pick up a lightsaber to fight Darth Vader after Obi-Wan died. Luke lost the fight in *The Empire Strikes Back*. Which was great because it's realistic."

"No, she's not a Mary Sue!" I said. "There's a high probability of prior Jedi training or being part of the Chosen One's bloodline! Maybe she's even Anakin reincarnated if you want to go with some crack internet theories."

"Guys," Gabrielle said, speaking louder.

"First of all, if it's not on screen then it doesn't count. Second, Luke and Leia are Vader's kids and didn't—"

"Where's your sense of loyalty?!" I shouted, appalled.

"The Prequels killed it! Kylo Ren is also Vader's grandson! That should also cancel out any advantage!"

"Guys!" Gabrielle said, getting our attention. "Focus, please."

"Alright," I said, then looked back at Cindy. "Poe Dameron is going to be the new Han."

"Poe Dameron should be dead! The TIE Fighter exploded!" Cindy snapped back.

"Are you done?" Gabrielle said. "Because, I never thought I'd say this, you guys may be too geeky for a girl who slept with her stuffed Ewok until she was thirty."

"I can steal you a replacement," Cindy offered. "In the original packaging no less."

Gabrielle felt her face, half-laughing and half-horrified but looking more amused than she'd been since the start of this crisis. "You two, are just so...bad...at not being supervillains."

"We're trying not to be?" I asked, genuinely confused.

"Eh, sort of?" Cindy said.

I took a deep breath, deciding to get down to business. "I suppose there's no use beating around the bush. I've got some terrible news: Ultragod is dead."

"Oh, wow," Cindy said, blinking as she took that in.

"I'm afraid so," I said, lowering my head.

"How long do you think that's going to last?" Cindy asked.

"Wait, what?" I looked up.

"He's the most popular, most successful superhero of all time. There's no way he's going to stay dead."

"Cindy!" I snapped.

"It doesn't work like that," Gabrielle said. "I'm sorry to say."

"Sure it does. This is like the third time he's died for real, let alone all the fake-outs with robots or shape-changers. I've read your historical comics. You and your dad have literally met GOD three or four times. Just dial him up and ask for a freebie."

I balled my fist, furious at how insensitive my partner was being. "It didn't exactly help Mandy, did it?"

"Have you talked to Death?" Cindy suggested.

"Yes," I muttered. "She's also offered to resurrect Mandy if I do her a favor."

"See!" Cindy said. "It's a matter of perseverance!"

Gabrielle blinked. "You don't think Death could—"

"Please don't put me in the awkward position of being forced to choose between resurrecting my wife and your father."

"Sorry," Gabrielle said. "Really."

"Thank you." Well, that was a mood-changer. "Oh, Ultragod has been replaced by an evil doppelganger and has turned the Society of Superheroes against Gabrielle by claiming she's the evil doppelganger. Also, they think I murdered the real Gabrielle, and the president had my house hit by a drone strike."

"And your first choice of action was to come to a hospital full of civilians," Cindy said. "Great thinking."

I paused. "When put like that, it's probably a good idea for me to depart this place."

"Probably a good idea," Cindy said.

"We need your help, Cindy. I don't know who I can trust." Gabrielle looked over her shoulder. "The government is deeply involved in this and watching our every move."

"Please tell me you have evidence and it's not because Gary has co-opted you into one of his right-wing conspiracy theories."

I glared at her. "I am a *left-wing* conspiracy theorist, thank you. Less the Illuminati, FEMA, and secret Nazi reptile men than the government is run by corporations as well as fascist imperialists."

"And the president is trying to kill you?" Cindy said.

"Yes," I said.

Cindy rubbed the bridge of her nose. "Okay, well, the Brotherhood of Infamy was secretly controlling Falconcrest City the entire time so I'm inclined to give this a fair shake. I also love Gary and consider you a close friend, Gabby, so let's do this."

"Wait, you love Gary?" Gabrielle said.

"Yeah, that's a new development. We're still sorting through that," I said.

"What's to sort out? You don't feel the same way. I'll just have to deal with that."

"I didn't say that!" I snapped back.

"So, you do love me?" Cindy asked, blinking.

"This is..."

Gabrielle paused. "As much as I love both of you, I'd like to state that we can talk about this outside of the hospital when we're not being hunted by the president's goon squad."

"Goon squad, really?" Cindy said, putting her elbows on the desk and resting her chin on her crossed hands. "Listen, guys, don't you think you're being a little bit paranoid. The government hasn't been able to do anything about the supervillain problem in the United States for, oh, seventy-five-years. I don't think we're going to have to worry about them tracking us down."

A nurse ran in through the door, ignoring the massive amount of drug paraphernalia. He looked oddly like Ben Stiller and I wonder if he was one of the shape-changers Cindy and I had recruited from the various exiled aliens leftover from the last failed invasion. "Doctor Wakowski, the hospital is surrounded by a bunch of giant robots and armed paramilitary forces led by cyborgs!"

I looked at the door. "Maybe we should have gotten out of here sooner."

"You think?" Cindy said, shooting me a nasty look before tapping a button underneath her desk and turning around her seat. Half of the wall in front of her slid away to reveal a complicated zeerust futuristic 1960s computer system and television set I remembered she'd bought from Doctor Dinosaur's estate sale.

Liver cancer. Poor bastard.

Cindy fiddled with the switches and knobs before it conjured up an image of the hospital's outside in glorious black and white. The hospital was indeed surrounded by twenty-foot-tall robots, mecha tanks, black jeeps, and armies of soldiers in power armor. They had a gear logo with a sword through it which put me in mind of *Fallout*'s Brotherhood of Steel, a reference you're only likely to get if you're a dedicated gamer. There were close to a hundred of them and they'd blocked off traffic as well as taken prisoners.

"Darklight," Gabrielle said. "Just when I thought things couldn't possibly get worse."

"Who?"

Cloak explained for me. "*After the civil war between Guinevere and Ultragod over the Superhuman Law manipulated by the space god Entropicus, the Foundation for World Harmony was briefly replaced with Darklight. It's a collection of mercenaries drawn from America's prisons and asylum, and those who failed in the actual military. All of them had portions of their brains removed and replaced with cybernetics, which was downloaded with obedience as well as martial training. They planned to arrest all Supers, depower them with Tom Terror's ray gun, and then execute them.*"

"That's...pretty damn evil."

"*Yes, it was all proven to be a plot by P.H.A.N.T.O.M and they were all arrested. They shouldn't be here.*"

"No shit, they shouldn't be here," I muttered.

That was when the video feed went frizzy and was replaced, ironically enough, with the plastic, blandly handsome features of President Omega. He was a tall Caucasian man with a good head of hair and a smile that was just a little too broad. He was standing in front of a podium with a dozen microphones, but the Presidential seal had been replaced with the Omega symbol from the Roman alphabet plus the motto "In Omega, we obey." Which, honestly, didn't even make sense.

President Omega had a goofy, almost psychotic grin on his face, exposing his too-many-teeth smile. "Hello, folks, I thought I'd address you personally. You know, before I kill you—and believe me, Gary, I've been looking forward to it for a long time."

"I knew I should have voted for the other guy," I muttered.

"This is why I voted for the other guy," I said.

"He does some redeeming qualities," Gabrielle said. "Like now I know who to punch to the moon."

"He is like...President Evil," Cindy said. "We should totally make that his codename."

"Versus President Omega?" I said, looking at her.

"What about it? It's his name," Cindy asked, confused.

"What do you want, Omega?" Gabrielle growled, staring at the black and white screen.

President Omega smiled. It was a plastic, almost inhuman look. "To conquer the world, exterminate all Supers, re-engineer humanity to become a race of cybernetic fascists, and then proceed to unleash a jihad on the rest of the universe where we exterminate all life different from ourselves. Oh, and to balance the budget."

"Well that's a shitty way of doing it," I said. "Unlimited military spending is how we got into this mess!"

Gabrielle shot a look at me rather than at him.

"How the hell did a psychopath like you get elected in the first place?" I said, at least glad my enemy had shown his true colors.

"Time travel," President Omega said, smiling. "I was born in the forty-ninth century, you see, where everything is peaceful and joyous. So, I built a time machine, travelled to the last century when people were interesting, and proceeded to manipulate the economy by causing financial crisis after financial crisis before eliminating all of my potential competition. Unfortunately, every time I tried to eliminate the various superheroes that stood in my way of making a really fun future, my plans failed. They have protection from higher authorities than even my Lord Entropicus is able to match. At least, until now."

Lord Entropicus was the immortal space god who ruled over the planet Abaddon at the end of time—I couldn't make this stuff up if I tried. He was also the force that P.H.A.N.T.O.M's soldiers worshiped and responsible for all manner of horrific universe-conquering plans. Tom Terror may have been Ultragod's archenemy, but Entropicus was probably his most dangerous foe. His being the patron of President Omega explained a lot.

"Cindy, are you recording this?" I asked, hoping his talking had given us some evidence against him. It wouldn't be rock solid in a world of shapeshifters, illusionists, alternate universe doppelgangers, and robot replacements, but it would be something we could use.

Cindy sighed. "Nope. I didn't buy the tape drives this thing uses. Shame, this would have been really convenient."

"You killed my father," Gabrielle said, balling her fists. "You monster."

"Oh, even better, I've *replaced* your father," President Omega said. "Just like I'm going to replace you and the rest of the Society of Superheroes with nasty, anti-hero versions of themselves from a reality so dark it might as well have been written by a British comic book writer. Your Society of Superheroes is so used to blindly following Ultragod, they'll do half my job for me before they realize it's leading to their graves."

"Nice plan," I said.

"You would know," President Omega said.

I looked at him confused. "Uh-huh."

Well, at least I knew whom I had to kill to get back Mandy now. Death had wanted me to find the person responsible for Ultragod's death and kill him. Honestly, I was kind of glad it turned out to be a time-wielding despot since that sort of removed any moral ambiguity from the situation. The fact he was a time-traveler also meant it was possible to fix all of the crap he'd pulled.

Because that's how it worked according to my understanding of temporal physics, which was derived primarily from *Star Trek* and *Back to the Future*. Then again, I remembered Omega Corp from my childhood on, and if he'd screwed up time that badly, then who knew what "fixing" things would entail. I didn't want to end up like the finale of *Continuum*, another work that Cindy and I disagreed on.

"One last question, dipshit," I said, staring at him.

"Oh, go ahead. I'm just taking a break from using *my mind-control satellites* to take over the world." President Omega spoke with a childish glee. It was like hearing myself talk about supervillainy.

First Lady Omega, wearing a replica of Jackie O's iconic pillbox hat and coat, chased a senator in front of the camera with a fire axe while cackling madly. Weirdly, she bore a suspicious similarity to Cindy now that she was covered in blood and laughing.

"Ah-ha-ha-ha-ha-ha-ha!" Constance Omega shouted.

I tried to ignore that. "Why me? Is this really all about ripping your company off? Why all the effort to blowing up my house and putting a bounty on my head?"

President Omega blinked then looked surprised. "Oh, you think I'm trying to kill you? No, no, no, Gary. Quite the opposite. All that is done by the Resistance aided by the Time Police. They're trying to get me through you. You see, you're my father."

My eyes widened.

Chapter Thirteen

Where We Choose to be Heroes and Villains

I stared at the screen, gobsmacked. So did Cindy and Gabrielle.

President Omega was my son? Who was his mother? What did this mean?

Omega stared back at us, meeting our gaze. He then struggled to suppress a grin before bursting out laughing. "Just kidding. I'm not your son. No, I just hate you for reasons that would involve revealing way too much of my evil plan."

"Oh, fuck you!" I said, appalled.

Cindy couldn't help but burst out laughing. "I'm sorry, Gary, but that's actually pretty damned funny."

President Omega snorted. "I mean how would that even make any sense? I'm older than you and from the fucking future. I mean, yes, time travel, but what are the odds?"

The nurse, who was still in the room, said, "Actually, assuming Gary has a child that lives to pass on their genes, then the statistical likelihood of being your ancestor by the forty-ninth century is actually pretty good."

"Get that guy out of here," I said, shaking my head.

"So, yeah, I actually am responsible for all of that horrible stuff that has happened to you," Omega said. "I even prevented the military from putting down the zombie apocalypse in your hometown less to discredit the Society of Superheroes than to ruin you personally. Not that the Society of Superheroes needs much discrediting with how little they change this world. I mean, forty super-scientists and they still haven't cured cancer? Doctor Aeon is useless."

"Again, why me?" I asked, wondering how Omega had disguised his insanity so long.

"Probably robot doppelgangers," Cloak said. *"Though the ability to reverse time means he really only has to disguise it once."*

I needed to get me some of that.

"You really don't," Cloak said.

Omega's smile became predatory. "You keep acting like this is some sort of personal vendetta. Oh, *it is*—but not the way you think. Do you know what the best part of time-travel is? The complete lack of consequences of being an asshole. I killed the girls who disliked me in high school. I had my mother banished to some hellish torture dimension for not catering to my every whim. Yesterday, I had the guy who screwed up my latte's entire family killed. Then I had them re-animated so they could eat him. I'm *that* much of an asshole. Why you, Gary? *Because I don't like you.* Your giving away all that money you stole from me really offended me. I also have had to listen to you *way* too many times these past few months planning this whole shebang."

Cindy and Gabrielle exchanged a look then gave one to me.

I shrugged my shoulders. I had no idea what he was talking about. "I'm confused."

"Get used to it," President Omega said. "Today, I'm going to kill a few million people and by the weekend, I hope to have slain an even billion."

A glassy-eyed Playboy Bunny-dressed woman whom I recognized as a prominent journalist brought Omega a martini, followed by similarly confused-looking man in a Chippendales outfit, who gave the president a napkin to stuff down his shirt.

"You're a monster," Gabrielle said.

"Exactamundo!" Omega said, drinking his martini and letting some spill on his shirt due to the way his mouth was shaped. "Now you're going to turn Gabrielle over to me so I can use her as the power source for a big Death Star-sized laser I'm building so I can blow up planets of peaceful aliens."

"Yeah, I don't think so." I looked at Cindy. "Is there an off switch for this thing?"

"Sure," Cindy said. "I'm tired of this channel anyway."

"You'll do it," Omega said, smiling. "Otherwise, Darklight has orders to kill every single man, woman, and child in the hospital."

Gabrielle said. "You'll never get away with this."

Omega made finger guns at me. "That's what they said destroying Patience, Delaware. It's amazing what you can get away with when you have sufficiently-advanced technology indistinguishable from magic— mostly because it runs on magic in the forty-ninth century. You have a minute to decide."

"And you'll kill us when we surrender," I said.

"Probably," Omega said. "Hell, I'll probably have everyone in the hospital killed anyway. *Adios!*"

He lifted his martini glass and disappeared. A test pattern on the screen replaced his image before going back to the Darklight unit which had now completely surrounded the hospital. They also had dozens of hostages lined up for execution in front of the building. Roadblocks and black helicopters kept other people from coming to the scene and I wouldn't be surprised if they were jamming all communication in or out. When this whole ordeal was done, the story would be anything they wanted it to be. I imagined it would be, "United States government avenges the death of Ultragoddess by killing terrorist Gary Karkofsky. Three-hundred hospital patients were killed in the ensuing firefight."

I looked at Cindy. "And to think you voted for him."

"He seemed so nice in his political ads!" Cindy said. "He promised to lower taxes and deal with the supervillain problem."

"We're the supervillain problem!" I shouted.

"I know that now!"

Gabrielle, meanwhile, was silent. A silence she broke for a second. "This is why."

"What?" I said, confused.

"This is why the world fucking sucks!" Gabrielle said, conjuring a giant Ultra-Force fist and smashing the table. "Do you want to know why world hunger, cancer, war, and worse haven't been solved by superheroes yet? BECAUSE OF ASSHOLES LIKE THAT! People who ruin other people's lives for shit and giggles and because it makes them feel like big men! The guys who think the only way they can be better is by making other people feel worse! This is the difference between superheroes and supervillains! This is..."

I gave her a hug.

Cindy got up and also hugged her.

The nurse started to join us before I growled at him.

"It's okay," I said. "We'll get through this."

"I have to try and save these people," Gabrielle said. "Even if it's a trap."

"Duh," Cindy said. "It's not unselfish to protect people while trying to save yourself. It's just sensible for maintaining enlightened interest."

"Uh, what?" Gabrielle said.

"I think she's suggesting we should just kill those bastards outside and leave," I said.

"I don't kill, Gary," Gabrielle said, looking down.

"You don't have to," I whispered. "I will. Starting with these guys out there and ending with President Omega."

Gabrielle looked down. "Thank you."

That was when I saw the figure of Ultragod, or Ultragod's impostor, settle down amongst the Darklight forces. He was an Olympian-proportioned African-American man in a skin-tight white and gold outfit (presumably, I couldn't tell over the black and white monitors) with a similarly-colored golden cape flowing behind him. Otherworldly electricity moved through and around his body, circling his eyes especially. Unlike most superheroes, he wore no crests or symbols, but everyone in the world knew who he was. The False Ultragod had come here to help Darklight slaughter us all.

Gabrielle narrowed her eyes. "I know what I'm going to be doing during this."

"Good," I muttered, not at all wanting to tangle with a man so far out of my weight class it might as well have been Little Mac versus Mike Tyson.

"*Was he a boxer?*" Cloak asked.

"Sort of," I explained. "Much the same way Mario was a plumber."

Gabrielle looked at me. "Are you ever going to be serious?"

"No," I said.

Cindy broke off her hug with me. "I've got a secret tunnel underneath the hospital leading behind these guys. We'll take it and then ambush them on the other side."

"Good idea," I said, sighing. "We'll call in all of our crew to help. I can use some of the weak first level magic I can do to send a message past the jammer technology they have here to our crew and get some reinforcements."

"Don't sell yourself short, Gary. That's at least third-level magic," Cindy said, smiling.

I wanted to say something more. That I loved her, that I cherished her, and that Cindy was the closest person to my heart aside from Mandy. Even over Gabrielle, who would always be special to me but would never know me the way Cindy did. I wanted to kiss her, honestly, and tell her that we'd figure this out because it was possible to love two people.

But I didn't want to betray my wife either.

So I kept silent.

Unfortunately, the jackass outside didn't stay silent. The Faux-Ultragod levitated a few feet off the ground and crossed his arms like M. Bison, his cape fluttering in the wind behind him before he spoke in a voice that projected itself into the minds of everyone inside the hospital, myself included.

"Feeble mortals, I, Ultradevil, ruler of the anti-matter universe of Htrae, command you to come out and pay with your lives for the perfidy of challenging my right to rule this world! I have made an alliance with President Omega and together we shall crush all the sub-beings of this reality! Your time to debate your surrender is up and I am not so weak as to care for the lives of insects!" Ultradevil raised his right hand and aimed it at a group of civilians trembling on the ground.

One of them had a baby.

"Oh shit," I said, realizing what he was about to do and powerless to stop it. I kept my eyes open, though, because atrocities like this deserved to be witnessed. Beside me, I felt a whooshing sensation followed by a sudden empty feeling in my arms.

Right as Gabrielle appeared in front of the blast, taking it against her costume and staring Ultradevil down.

"Halt, evil doer!" Gabrielle shouted at the top of her lungs.

Ultragoddess was back.

And we had to make use of her distraction.

"Ben-11," Cindy said, looking at the nurse. "Take care of all of the patients as best you can. See if they can be moved safely to the security ward. Anyone else, ask Melissa to teleport away. She likes to hide the fact she's a super from everyone else but we could really use that right now."

"And people think you're an awful doctor!" Ben-11 said.

"They what?" Cindy said. "Fuck them!"

Dragging Cindy out of her office, I said, "Come on, we need to get to that underground tunnel you mentioned."

"I bet it was Rosemary Floral a.k.a the Florist on floor seven. She's always had it out for me. See if I ever screw her in a closet again."

Briefly distracted by that mental image, the Florist being one of Maxim's Top Ten Hottest Supervillains (Cindy was seventh on the list), I reluctantly shook it away. "Gabrielle isn't going to be able to hold out against Ultradevil long."

"Why not? Isn't she always on about how she's more powerful than her dad?"

"Those cyborgs had Venusian anti-force cannons. I know because I used to date her and every one of her villains had their henchmen armed with them. They'll sap her strength until she can't fight him anymore."

"Dammit," Cindy said. "I hate smart villains who aren't us!"

"You and me both." I started muttering a spell invoking several Jewish spirits before sending them to speak to my closest associates. Honestly, if I'd known religious studies could grant you magic, I would have paid more attention during my rabbi's lessons.

Much to my surprise, Diabloman responded by contacting me mentally. I sometimes forgot he knew magic too. *"Boss, are you there?"*

"Yeah, just currently under siege by cyborg mercenary goons and Ultragod's mirror universe counterpart. Shouldn't he have a goatee?"

"I'll pretend any of that makes sense to me," Diabloman said. *"I have transported your niece and sister to a cabin on an island in Lake Falconcrest. They should be safe from the President's forces."*

"Yeah, about that," I said. "The President is an insane time-travelling despot from the future and killed Ultragod. He's also outside."

"I see," Diabloman said. *"Well, that would explain a few things. You need reinforcements."*

"Just a wee bit."

"Then you are lucky I have been assembling a task force for just such an occasion," Diabloman said. *"You can thank me with a bonus."*

"Like the case of diamonds I gave you last night?"

"Point taken. We shall be there in ten minutes."

"Ten minutes may be too late!" I broke contact with him.

Cindy and I headed down the stairs into the hospital basement. The place still had graffiti on the walls and there was an unclean feeling in the air. No matter how much good Cindy had done in this place, it was still one where hundreds of people had been massacred by gangs and zombies both.

Good didn't erase evil.

But then again, maybe the reverse was true as well.

Or neither mattered.

"How can you say that, Gary? With everything President Omega and Ultradevil are doing? What Gabrielle is doing to oppose them? Good and evil are very real."

"Omega isn't complex," I replied, gritting my teeth. "He's a bully who gets his rocks off with petty displays of power. Ultradevil is probably the same. There's nothing terribly complex about them. Most people aren't so single-minded and devoted, though. What's going to happen when the president is killed by a Super? What will they demand as punishment? Who will have to pay the piper? Will it matter one way or the other that Omega was an asshole or will they just string me up? I think we both know the answer. I'm not going to let that happen, though."

"I see," Cloak said. *"You're thinking this through further than I thought."*

"Heroes and villains depend on who is telling the story," I said. "I choose to reject that argument. I'm the villain because I do what I want and tell the rest of society to fuck off for it. I forgot that because Mandy died. I thought, maybe, if I'd had an ounce of forethought that she might still be alive. No, it's not. It's the fault of this reality and not being smart or hard enough to get what I want. In that respect, Omega and I aren't so different."

"You two are **nothing** alike," Cloak insisted.

"We'll see when I come down on the White House with a couple of pipe-hittin' Supers to go to work on Omega with a pair of pliers and a blowtorch. I intend to get medieval on his ass."

"Down here!" Cindy said, gesturing to a janitor's closet door. Heading down inside it, Cindy pushed on a shelf which caused a door to open to a dark water-filled hallway. The interior of the hallway contained her Red Riding Hood cloak and a picnic basket. Tossing off her doctor's smock, she put on both. She didn't have time to change into the bustier or dress, which was probably for the best.

"Cindy, there's some things I should probably tell you—"

"Now is really not the time, Gary."

I took a deep breath. "You've made my life incredibly fucking complicated and I don't want you gone from it. Ever. You also know I find you hot as hell. You're my best friend I want to have sex with. I'm not sure that qualifies as love but it's probably close enough for government work."

Cindy turned around and looked at me. "Gary?"

We didn't get to speak further because the end of the tunnel collapsed. Gabrielle smashed through the ceiling and created a crater around her. Ultradevil proceeded to strike her with a gigantic Ultra-force Morningstar. Thankfully, the weapon didn't crush her outright, as she knocked it away with an Ultra-force hand the size of a car, then conjured a bullet train, which she smashed Ultradevil in the face with.

"I'm not sure we're going to be able to do much out there," Cindy said, watching the battle between Titans as it spilled out onto the streets.

"We have to try," I said.

"Because we're heroes now?"

"Because Gabrielle is our friend," I said. "Also, because we hate the people outside."

"Good," Cindy said, taking a deep breath. "I'd hate to think we were getting soft."

"Yeah."

"Try not to get killed, Gary."

"You too."
The two of us ran down the hall to join the battle.

Chapter Fourteen

The Big Epic Brawl that Gets Bigger

In what would be a surprise to many of my detractors (and quite a few of my supporters), I don't actually like hurting people.

I was very good at it, I didn't particularly mind it, and I'd gotten a lot of practice at it in the past year, but it wasn't something I enjoyed. If someone were to cut me open and examine the reptile portions of my brain, they'd find I exist somewhere in the spectrum between "is a killer when he needs to be" and "Murder is the best solution to any problem."

Knowing these facts about me, you should take note that when I said, "I am looking forward to killing each and every one of these bastards," I wasn't saying it on a whim. No, I was saying it because I was really looking forward to killing each and every one of these bastards.

The sight which greeted me and Cindy upon our emergence from the ruins of her tunnel was a bloody battlefield full of explosions, energy-blasts, black helicopters, building-sized suits of power-armor, armored cars, giant robots, and guys who looked like they'd come from a movie casting call for 'Space Nazis: The Oppressing.' Ultragoddess and Ultradevil were battling it over the hospital, but true to my predictions, the former was battling at a handicap thanks to everyone cherry-tapping her while she punched out the fake Ultragod's lights.

Gabrielle was also forced to take a hit every time she had to get in the way of Ultradevil firing his energy blasts at the hospital or the groups of civilians nearby. Given how powerful the Ultras were, the entire city was endangered by Ultradevil's complete disregard for any life but his own.

One thing I should mention: Movies and television don't actually convey how frigging *loud* battles between superheroes and armies actually are. The amount of gunfire and worse going on made my ears ring just entering the battle. Plugging my ears with shadow-stuff, I conjured forth my Reaper's pistols and said to Cindy, "Okay, we just need to find cover and pick off as many targets as we can."

"What?" Cindy shouted, right beside me.

"Let's kill these bastards!" I shouted back.

"No need to shout!" Cindy said.

Cindy reached into her picnic basket and pulled out a set of jacks and a rubber ball. They were slightly larger than normal, sized for adults to throw rather than small children, and shinier than the plastic ones I'd played with as a kindergartener. Cindy proceeded to throw them all into the air.

The jacks formed a cloud above Cindy's head, hovered, made beeping noises, and then zipped across the battlefield. A single jack attached itself to a dozen Darklight soldiers before exploding in a series of grenade-sized detonations. The rubber ball, by contrast, slammed into one of the mecha walking around and knocked the tank-sized machine over before smashing into a car and sending it into a roll, before banging into a helicopter's cockpit and causing it to explode.

I just looked at Cindy, stunned. "Where the hell—"

"Toymistress made these for the hospital's Hanukkah charity drive. I told her these were probably unsafe for anyone under eleven."

"Probably."

Unfortunately, Cindy's little opening shot had also gotten the attention of the rest of the paramilitary force surrounding us. Cindy slipped on a Star Knights energy shield ring which protected her from the initial barrage while I turned intangible.

"Okay, it's time to go John Woo on these guys' asses," I said, staring all at them.

"Gary, have you ever even shot a gun before?" Cindy asked.

I looked at her. "You know, just the once."

"Great," Cindy muttered.

"Death wouldn't steer me wrong."

"She's frigging Death!"

"Yeah, well..." I realized for the first time in my life I was out of funny rejoinders. I compromised by shouting out my battle cry: "Witticism and clever comeback!"

"What?" Cindy said.

I charged out into the attacking goon squad, firing both guns randomly because I was pretty sure it would be just as effective as my aiming. Much to my surprise, as I pulled the trigger, I saw the bullets and energy beams of the Darklight soldiers slow down to an easily avoidable crawl. I then realized what Death had done for me.

"Bullet time, jackasses!" I shouted, giving a whoop and firing dozens of shots while skipping over the attacks of my enemies. I even took time to aim at the mecha, giant robots, and armored cars around me since I hoped they would explode. After all, if we were running on movie logic, then we should have plenty of gratuitous explosions, right?

"*Death is far too good to you,*" Cloak muttered. "*All I ever got was vague threats and promises of damnation.*"

"You just don't know how to treat a lady," I said, cheerfully.

That was when I felt I'd reached the sum total of all my magical energy reserves and, just like that, time reverted to normal. Which, unfortunately, had the effect of causing a pair of bullets to graze my shoulder and leg.

"Ah, come on!" I said, falling to the ground. "It's on a timer? Really?"

I didn't have much reason to complain, though, because my earlier thought about explosions was right. Dozens more Darklight soldiers fell backwards as my hellfire bullets passed through their armor like it was paper. Even more so, the mechs and robots detonated like it was less a John Woo movie and more Michael Bay. Enough, really, that I was almost willing to forgive Bay for the Transformers movies.

Almost.

Unfortunately, all of that didn't mean a damned thing, as there was still a whole frigging army of Darklighters surrounding us. Which was the purpose of an army, really, to make sure that no matter how good a fighter you were, you still got your ass kicked in the end. Worse, it looked like Gabrielle was starting to lose against Ultradevil. He was hitting her with pretty powerful strikes and she was only barely able to fend them off. My only consolation was half his face was horribly burned, and there were several bloody strikes on his costume from where Gabrielle had overwhelmed his protective aura.

I managed to turn intangible, just barely able to hold myself in said state, as another round of blasts and gunfire headed my way. Looking over the wreckage and battlefield, I saw the bodies of the prisoners the Darklight mercenaries had taken. Despite Gabrielle's best efforts to protect the bystanders, the psychopaths had executed them during her brawl with Ultradevil. President Omega had gotten himself a real set of headcases.

Which gave me the strength to continue fighting.

Managing my output of necromantic power, which I never thought would be a concept I'd have to master, I levitated with my jumps to leap on the top of cars and mecha before firing down at the Darklight soldiers below. The bullet-time effect and my intangibility powers could be used at once but only for a few seconds at time given how draining they were.

I conjured walls of fire and hid behind armored wreckage whenever possible as they were some of the few things capable of withstanding their attacks. Contrary to what decades of cover-based shooters had taught me, it turned out that you needed really solid places to hide behind unless you wanted to be cut to ribbons.

I had no idea what Cindy's state was or if Gabrielle could keep fighting given the fact that we still hadn't managed to take down even half of the Darklight soldiers. Struggling to get up, I found I couldn't. I managed to get barely an inch off the crushed car hood before collapsing back down on it. The pain was intense, but I couldn't draw from it to move. Worse, my magical reserves were not just really spent but really most sincerely spent. I doubted I could conjure a candle with my mind let alone continue fighting.

But I had to.

For Cindy's sake.

For Gabby's.

For everyone's.

Unfortunately, while in most stories that would have given me the adrenaline rush to pull myself up, it seemed heroic willpower wasn't actually a cure for getting blown up and I found myself unable to do a damned thing. I was a sitting duck for whatever psycho, cyborg, or head of state that decided to kill me.

As much as I'd managed to fight my way around them, I didn't have the kind of skills that many other superheroes relentlessly trained themselves to possess, and as much as my powers confused them, it didn't take long for one of the giant robots to fire a pair of rockets from its hands that blew up the armored truck I was standing on. I turned intangible just a wee bit too late, and the force of the explosion sent me spiraling through the air and slamming into the top of a Cadillac in the staff parking lot.

If not for the fact that I was partially invulnerable, I would have been killed outright, but that didn't prevent me from feeling like I'd had ten guys beat the hell out of me. I also had a couple of bullets lodged into my costume. It was also possible they'd buried themselves into the surface layer of my skin and I'd have to pry them out with a screwdriver. Some of the magics I'd traded my extra power for had been protection spells woven into my skin, and while they didn't quite make me bulletproof, they certainly lowered my armor class a bit. Increased my armor-class? Which was better? I couldn't remember which edition of *Dungeons and Dragons* real life worked on.

Ah crap, did I have a concussion? Because I wasn't quite sure what I was thinking anymore. My ears were ringing and I could only vaguely hear the sounds of the battle outside. Kirk or Picard? Sisko. Luke or Han? Leia. *The Expanse* was the best thing the Syfy Channel had shown in years. The ninth and tenth Doctors were awesome. Eleven was okay but loved the companions. Don't much care for twelve. Okay, cool, still conscious and thinking clearly.

Which was appropriate, since all three in one grabbed me off the car roof and then proceeded to slam me up against the ruined car's side. The figure assaulting me was a hulking cyborg with gigantic metal arms and legs, excessively large shoulder pads, ammo belts across his exaggerated chest, and literally dozens of guns strapped to every part of his body. He was in his mid-sixties, biracial, with a cybernetic eyepiece that looked like the end of a microscope. I recognized the freakish-looking man as one of my first foes. Something I found more than a little unsettling, since I'd killed him and his team.

"Captain Disaster?" I said, wondering if I'd hit my head harder than I thought.

"That's Colonel Disaster now!" Colonel Disaster growled.

"How the fuck are you alive!?" I said, wondering if it was just the good people who stayed dead in this world.

"Nanomachines, son!" Colonel Disaster shouted in my face like a drill sergeant. "They transferred the memories and personality of my team into clone bodies waiting for us back at Extreme HQ!"

I blinked, processing that. "Okay, that would mean you're not actually Captain Disaster but his duplicate."

"What's the difference?"

"Well, for me, very little but for Captain Disaster it means he's still dead and you're walking around with his face and job."

That was when Colonel Disaster slapped me across the face with his steel hand. It loosened some teeth.

"You have no idea how long I've waited to avenge myself on you and your disgusting band of miscreants!" Colonel Disaster said, sending spittle in my face as he frothed with rage. "President Omega, God Bless his Soul, recreated the Extreme! and re-empowered it to lead his Darklight Initiative for the glorious purpose of protecting humanity from the evils of Supers."

I decided not to argue with the cyborg about what constituted a Super and lifted both of my pistols, which seemed to cling to my hands when I wanted them, putting them right in front of Colonel Disaster's face before pulling their triggers.

Nothing happened.

"Out of ammo?" Colonel Disaster said, chuckling. "Ain't that a shame."

I caused the two weapons to disappear into the folds of my cloak. I was exhausted and couldn't put up any fight but if I delayed, even for a few seconds, maybe I could come up with something. I needed to keep this asshole talking. "I don't need them to deal with the likes of a wannabe Space Marine like you."

"I was a Marine," Colonel Disaster said, throwing me over his shoulder onto the parking lot in front of me. It was clear he wanted to beat the hell out of me before killing me, unnecessary as that was. "My father thought I needed the experience to teach me some humility before I decided to follow in his footsteps and slaughter the mutated freaks of humanity."

"Sounds like a wonderful role model."

"He was." Colonel Disaster pulled out a gun with a sword on the top and held it by its barrel—possibly the dumbest thing I'd ever seen in my life. "But all my time in the Corps taught me was that every pissant dictatorship, hellhole, and slum in this world is ruled by the guy with the biggest gun. You should have joined me, Karkofsky. We could have saved humanity. You get your powers from magic. You're still human, kind of."

I stared at him, shaking my head. "Please don't tell me you buy into the bullshit you spew."

Colonel Disaster advanced, keeping his sword squarely aimed at me. "Why not? It's evolution. *Homo sapiens* are the dominant species on this planet because we're the toughest, meanest, vilest sonsabitches there are. *Homo eximus* has every bit of our viciousness, intelligence, and strength with the addition of superpowers. Ditto thinking machines and aliens. We have to exterminate all three before they destroy us."

He was almost in striking distance before I lifted a hand. "Hold the fuck up."

Colonel Disaster paused, raising his left eyebrow. "Yes?"

I was probably going to die now but some things needed to be said. "Look dumbass, that's not how evolution works. There's no straight line forward of bigger, stronger, meaner. Random mutations occur, and carriers who successfully procreate pass them onto the next generation. You know what the most successfully evolved organism in the world is? Bacteria. Why? Because it's still around and procreating after billions of years. Not because it's especially awesome. Humankind managed to survive because of its ability to socialize, build tools, and fuck its way through most of its problems. We're actually kind of squishy."

Colonel Disaster started to speak.

"Not done yet," I said, interrupting him. "The whole fear we're going to be eradicated by Supers thing is even more stupid because Supers *are* human beings. They just have a useful mutated ability. Being afraid of them replacing *homo sapiens* is ridiculous because it's going to be our children that replaces the current generation. That's the destiny of all parents. God, assholes like you piss me off. The biggest fuck-you to my people came from a guy who didn't understand Aryan meant from India."

"Oh, I didn't know you were Jewish. You don't look—"

"Which would mean the Romani are part of the so-called Master Race! Ugh, I'm so glad I have a time machine so I can keep killing Hitler over and over again."

"Hold on—"

"I'm up to thirty-six. It's the only therapy after Mandy's death that worked."

"Are you done?" Colonel Disaster said, surprising me by letting me finish. "Because I'd really like to kill you now."

I thought if there was anything else to say. I still hadn't gained back any of my magical strength. "Nah, that was about it."

"Time to die." Colonel Disaster moved his hand away from the barrel and onto the gun's grip before aiming it at my head.

He fired.

Chapter Fifteen

Where the Cavalry (of Sorts) Arrives

Closing my eyes, I briefly wondered what sort of awful punishments lay in store for me once I ended up in the hands of Death. I didn't believe in the Devil, per se, since I was of the "Samael is God's hatchet man" inclination but my boss wasn't exactly the forgiving type.

A second later, I realized I wasn't dead and opened my eyes. That was when I saw the bullet stop in mid-air, spinning as Colonel Disaster look confused. Blinking, I looked to the side and saw a breathtakingly beautiful raven-haired woman with ivory skin and a sexy witch's costume that clung to her rather generous curves propped up by a corset.

Selena Darkchylde a.k.a The Black Witch.

My ex-wife's ex-girlfriend.

"Hello, Gary," Selena said, waving her hand in a circle at the bullet's general direction. "Diabloman said you might be in trouble."

"Oh no," I said looking back at Colonel Disaster. "I've got this covered. Don't worry about me."

"You sure?" Selena said. "Because I can let it go."

"Whore!" Colonel Disaster growled, pointing his gun at her head and firing a half-dozen bullets at her.

All of them stopped in midair.

I, meanwhile, moved out of the way of the current bullet in front of me before it resumed its natural course and plowed into the ground behind me.

"Why does everyone always insult my sexuality? Is it because of the way I dress?" Selena said, making a tsk-tsk noise. "I like the way it makes me feel and that really shouldn't be any of your business."

"Rowr!" Colonel Disaster pulled out an electrified Bowie knife before charging at her.

Selena proceeded to flip the car he'd held me up against and land it on his face. It didn't kill Colonel Disaster; cyborgs were tough like that. It did, however, slow him down and give me enough time to recover a smidgen of my former power.

"Thanks, Selena. I take back roughly half of the horrible things I've ever said about you."

"I, in turn, intend to lord this over you for the rest of your natural life." Selena smiled. "It's good to see you."

"You too."

Freezing Colonel Disaster's arms against the ground because, honestly, I didn't want to kill the guy, I decided I needed to return to the battle. The thought of Cindy being hurt was enough to make me feel sick, horrified, and worried beyond measure.

"*Why do you think she's out there fighting?*" Cloak said. "*She's there to try and protect you.*"

I'd never thought of it like that.

Picking myself off the ground, I stepped forward before falling to one knee, then getting up anyway. The number of explosions and bullet noises had decreased dramatically. Looking to the sky, I saw Gabrielle smash Ultradevil with an uppercut before the diabolical doppelganger fled through a wormhole. Gabrielle looked exhausted but had proven, once more, that she was more powerful than Ultragod.

Selena helped me stand up and walked me toward the ruins of the battlefield, where the remains of the Darklight troopers had been handily mopped up. Getting a look at the cavalry that had shown up, I wasn't surprised why.

There was the Shadow Seven's other four members: General Venom, the Human Tank, the Red Schoolgirl, and Bronze Medalist. Nightgirl was present, having joined the fight with non-lethal weapons as well as EMP grenades.

Much to my surprise, my less-than-favorite person in the world, Adonis, had chosen to come with a winged eighteen-year-old man I recognized as the superhero Icarus. There were even a few supervillains I occasionally worked with who didn't consider me a category traitor: Nicky Tesla, the Florist (who'd been upstairs at the hospital after all), and my newly recruited henchman the Fruitbat. Gabrielle's boyfriend, the Golden Scarab, was there too and looking every bit like a white-and-gold Power Ranger.

Diabloman was wearing power-armor retrieved from one of our earlier capers, which gave the already super-strong villain even more enhanced strength, immunity to most weapons, and a built-in proton-axe. His armor was painted with hellfire motifs and his mask was shaped like a demon's. I couldn't help but wonder if he'd taken to wearing the outfit because toymakers were insisting because his old action figures weren't selling.

"Wow, this is some group," I said, looking around for Cindy.

That was when I heard Cindy cough and my attention immediately darted to her. Cindy was crawling out from between the ruined remains of two mecha that had been smashed together, holding her bloody fire-axe. Apparently, it had an ability to switch off its safety, as there were signs she'd gone axe-happy on several Darklight troopers nearby.

Cindy put down the axe and brushed off her cape. "Okay, which of you assholes smashed the mecha into each other without looking to see if a hot girl was between them? I know it's not any of the straight men or Black Witch. Come on, who's at fault?"

Bronze Medalist coughed. "To be fair, really, you were kind of unnoticeable in all of the chaos."

"I am always noticeable!" Cindy snapped. "I'm ridiculously awesome!"

That was when I wrapped my arms around Cindy and gave her a tight hug.

"It had better be if we are to overthrow the president of the United States and his army of misguided superheroes," Diabloman said.

"Then this group really isn't big enough," I said. "I don't suppose you know where we can get an inexhaustible source of super-robots."

"Actually, yes, but I'm hoping we can avoid casualties in the millions," Diabloman said.

Then I saw Mandy.

She was crouched behind the others, blocking the sunlight from her face with a hoodie and her leather coat hiked up above her shoulders. Yet, it was unmistakable. Mandy, the vampire who had been my wife, had come to help me.

I wasn't sure how to react.

"Okay, this is awkward on multiple levels. Nice, but awkward." Cindy looked up into the sky. "Oh, hey, Gabri...err, Ultragoddess! You're alive! Which is good because we came out here to help prevent you from dying!"

Gabrielle descended from the sky, looking down at Cindy and me with a sad look on her face before facing the others. "I appreciate all you guys have done for me. Certainly, I now know who the face of my enemy is. I didn't want you all involved, though, because of how dangerous this is going to be."

"Yes, because the first thing any superhero is going to be intimidated by is the prospect of *danger*," the Golden Scarab said. "Also, it's a wonderful thing to be kept in the dark about the president planning to murder your loved ones with his army of kill-bots and Nazi cyborgs. That will certainly protect us."

I was starting to like this guy. "Well, in my brief conversation with President Omega, it seems pretty clear he's taking his final days in office advice from Caligula. If we're going to stop this guy, it's got to be soon because it's not going to take long for him to spin this into something that even further paints us as bad guys."

"Surely, the Society of Superheroes can't be that stupid," Bronze Medalist said. "They'll have to know how dangerous President Omega is after all this mayhem and if you stop to explain things—"

Gabrielle shook her head, looking among us all. "Now that I know who the imposter Ultragod is, it all makes sense. Ultradevil has ultra-mesmerism the same way I and my father do. It's the ultimate power of suggestion and if he's able to plausibly frame his ideas to the Society of Superheroes, like, say, that I'm the villain and he's the hero then he's very likely got them eating out of his hand. We might be able to break that control but it's very likely we'll be running into trouble with them soon."

"Wait, you never used that on us, right?" Bronze Medalist said.

"No," the Black Witch said. "We're her friends. She'd never betray us like that."

"No, of course not," I muttered, remembering when she wiped my memory of her secret identity and our relationship *when I was her fiancé*.

"There's more going on than you know," Mandy said, still clinging to the almost non-existent shadows of the noonday sun. "I need to talk to you and Gary alone."

"Like hell you do, Vampirella!" Cindy snapped. "Go find a teenager to sparkle on and stay away from the man you've already ruined the life of."

"Okay, first of all my life isn't exactly ruined," I said, breaking away from my hug. "Second, I think we can safely let go of the Twilight jokes."

"Fuck that," Cindy said. "I've still got a bunch of things to say to Carmilla over here."

"Hey!" Selena said. "Carmilla is a feminist icon!"

"Carmilla is a serial killer of women!" Nightgirl said. "What are you talking about?"

"Well, technically—" The Golden Scarab started talking about the historical origins and subtext of the character.

Gabrielle then conjured an Ultra-Force starter pistol and fired it in the air. "Guys, we have to decide what our next move is and now. I think, against all my better judgment, it's best if we go directly after President Omega. There's no telling just how far he's prepared to go."

"I know," Mandy said. "Which is what I'm trying to tell you."

Diabloman, however, talked over. "Señorita Anders, we must strike at this monster directly but let it be those of us who are already monsters in the eyes of the public."

"I don't let other people take the fall for my actions," Gabrielle said. "Good or bad."

Mandy started growling.

"Okay, I think we should listen to Vamp-Mandy," I said.

"Vamp Mandy?" Cindy echoed.

"Well, I don't want to call her Mandy-Mandy," I said.

"How about just Blood-Sucking Murder Skank?" Cindy said. "That's a good name."

I honestly didn't know how to respond to that.

Gabrielle waved her hand. "Everyone, be quiet. What are you trying to tell us, Mandy. You can be honest with all of us. Not just me and Gary."

"It's too late," Mandy said. "The others are coming. I just have to get Gary to safety now."

"What?" Gabrielle said, confused.

Unfortunately, we got our answer when a twenty-yard-long teleportation rift appeared thirty feet away.

President Omega's voice carried through the air from the rift. "I would have loved to have teleported a nuclear bomb into the city, killed ten million people, and then blamed it all on Supers, but I've got something better planned. So instead, I'm going to introduce you to some of my new friends. Enjoy."

"What an asshole," Cindy muttered.

"I heard that!" Omega said. "Just for that, I'm totally mind-controlling the United States to think pale redheaded girls are ugly."

"I'd like to see you try!" Cindy shouted back then turned to me. "Wait, he can't do that, can he?"

I shrugged. "Maybe it's dark-haired bronze girls' turn."

"They're already hot!" Cindy said. "Look at the Hawaiian Huntress!"

We didn't have time to discuss Cindy's bizarre digression into looks when a small army of anti-heroes stepped through the rift. Some of them I recognized as people I'd killed, resurrected by Omega's technology like Colonel Disaster, but others were some of the worst "heroes" of all time. People who had been touted by a bloodthirsty populace during the nineties and early 2000s as the "answer" to supervillain crime, only to inflict massive collateral damage and display a disgusting lack of every virtue that made superheroes great.

There was the Third Reich-themed armored soldier Iron Cross, the swimsuit-wearing katana-wielding Ninjess, the wild-haired bloody-jawed Bloodscream the Retributive, the chain-smoking magnetically-powered Jane Union, Soulflayer the Living Ghost Which Kills, a group of gun-wielding Ex-Tomorrow Society teen heroes whom I only vaguely recognized, Homicide the Serial-Killer-Killer, the Black Scarab, Ares, Bloodwalker, and a guy who suspiciously resembled me in an all-white version of the Reaper's Cloak.

"Great Caesar's Ghost!" Adonis said, staring at them. "They've restored the Extreme."

"And worse!" Icarus said.

"Come my *eromenos*, we must put an end to this band of miscreants!"

Icarus looked embarrassed. "Could you not call me that in public?"

Before the rift closed, Omega gave some parting words. "Now, I fully don't expect my guys to win but I do think they'll slow you all down for the real heroes to arrive to arrest you all for all the collateral damage. I've got a lovely little set of cells for you all lined up in an anti-matter universe. I call it Omegatanamo Bay because, well, I was trying to make a pun and gave up after about ten minutes."

Battle was joined before he finished his little spiel. Everyone fighting but me.

Not that I didn't want to.

But Cloak gave voice to what I was already feeling as I turned insubstantial and found cover. "*We can't allow ourselves to be distracted by this pointless brawl, Gary. President Omega is just trying to slow us down to further consolidate his position against us and prevent him from stopping his greater plans—whatever they may be.*"

"Brilliant case of detective work," I said. "What with him having said all that not five seconds ago."

"*Sorry, but it's been awhile since we've dealt with villains willing to share their plans openly. I'm a bit out of practice.*"

"I'd say it's stupid of him but given Omega has been consistently *kicking our asses*, I can't really fault his methods."

Soulflayer, who looked like an empty black and white superhero costume that distorted in bizarre and horrific directions, proceeded to descend on my position. His voice was an unearthly hissing wail. "I sense the blood of the guilty and not-so-innocent on you. I will devour your spirit and use it to—"

I stuck my hand between the folds of the ghost's costume and sent him onto the afterlife with a blast of magical flame. Reality seemed to shake as a scream and thunder echoed from whatever distant dimension swallowed him up. Screams and wails followed before the echoes stopped.

"I'm guessing that wasn't heaven," I said, looking over my shoulder at the massive supervillain brawl tearing up the streets around me. "Seriously, you'd think a ghost would know better than to attack the guy Death sends to do her dirty work."

"I never liked Soulflayer. He and his gang of ruffians always seemed more interested in punishing the so-called guilty more than protecting the innocent."

"Oh, you're just noticing this now?" I snapped.

"The Society made many compromises with heroes we...perhaps shouldn't have. Law and order became more important than mercy."

Cloak's epiphany speech was interrupted by Ninjess slamming against the side of the spot where I was located as Mandy plopped herself in front of me. "Okay, Gary, our last conversation didn't exactly go very well."

"You think!?" I snapped.

"Come with me if you want to live!" Mandy said.

"Wait, what?"

Mandy growled, baring her fangs. "It's a *Terminator* reference!"

"I know that!"

"Gary, I won't let you die!" Mandy said, grabbing my arm. There was none of the viciousness that had been there last night. Instead, she was acting almost... human. "Not again."

"What?"

I reluctantly turned tangible and took it.

Then I saw Colonel Disaster come up behind her with his rifle and fire into us both. The bullets passed through her vampire form.

One of them went right into my chest and out the other side. I fell back against the ground, bleeding out and falling into oblivion.

Crap.

Chapter Sixteen

My Last Conversation with Dad (Nothing Funny Here)

As I bled out on the street, I dreamt of the night my father had his heart attack. It was strange the places your mind went when you were dying, but since it happened so often, I'd learned to just go with it. Besides, this was a memory appropriate to the situation. It was a memory about coming to terms with death.

I was really bad at that.

My parents and I had never really repaired our relationship after my brother's death. Both of them agreed, at least on some level, that Keith's supervillain lifestyle had led him to his death, while I lionized him as a martyr who could do no wrong.

By the time I was eighteen, I didn't want anything to do with them, and they went back to New Angeles. I paid my way through college with student loans and two jobs, later working as Doctor Thule's teacher's assistant. Mandy eventually convinced me to make a token effort at reconciliation, though we'd never really breached the rift over Keith.

Then they'd recognized me on television as Merciless.

Oiye.

This would be the third conversation I'd had with them since.

I was presently standing in the hallway of the Falconcrest City Hospital Cardiac Wing, getting berated by my short, blonde, sixty-three-year-old mother who was wearing a pink sweatshirt and long plaid dress.

My bald, sixty-four-year-old father, was sitting in the hospital bed in his room twelve feet to my left, looking horribly embarrassed.

"You're a disgrace, Gary," Linda Karkofsky said, staring at me through her red glasses. "I didn't raise you to be a criminal and here you are, making a mockery of our family name. Is it not enough that we had to endure your brother's ways? You had to do it to us too?"

I looked at her, trying to keep my temper. "Yes, because your family name is so much more damned important than my brother, *your son.*"

"Why?" Linda shook her hands as if wanting to strangle me. "You had a good life. You had a wife, even if she was THAT way, and a job. You could have been somebody and now you're...THIS!"

I narrowed my eyes. "*That* way?"

"No wonder she left you. I would have too!" Linda said, practically spitting in my face.

I took a moment to mentally count to ten. "Can I see my father?"

"We don't—"

"Come on in, Gary," Joel Karkofsky said, sighing. "Linda, go get some ice."

"I don't need any..." Linda trailed off before shooting my father a look then shaking her head. "I don't believe this."

She then stomped off.

I walked into my father's room. A nurse was checking his vitals. She looked like she would rather be anywhere in the world than here. I just let her finish her business and watched her rush out the door. Joel watched her too, seemingly amused by her reaction to his son, the terrifying supervillain in a black hoodie.

I suspected the hospital had called security, who had probably called the police who were probably calling on someone higher up. That gave me plenty of time to have my conversation with my dad before moving on. In retrospect, I should have just come after visiting hours when my mother wasn't shouting my identity to the four winds.

Joel looked at me. "Well, I may have been forced to skip Monday Night Football tonight, but at least I got dinner and a show." He looked down at the plate of Jello in front of him. "Such as it is."

"Sorry," I said, looking over at several bouquets of flowers nearby. One set was from my sister Kerri, another was from my niece Lisa, a couple were from coworkers, and a final was from the Silver Lightning. The Silver Lightning had been my brother's archnemesis for years but had watched out for the family after his death. "That's nice of John Volt."

Joel said, "He's an okay guy for one of those people."

I sighed. "Those people?"

I assumed he, like my mother, meant John Volt's divergent sexuality. My mother had never accepted Mandy's bisexuality.

Or her Wiccan faith.

Or being a Gentile.

Or being married to me.

At least until she was gone.

"A hippie!" Joel said, growling. "Those damn Volts are nothing but a bunch of pot-smoking superpowered peacenik tree-huggers."

Joel smiled, letting me know he was joking.

I smiled back. "It's good to see you're alive."

"Eh, for now," Joel said, more seriously. "I made my peace with God in Vietnam 2, fighting those damn P.H.A.N.T.O.M pseudo-Nazis with the Foundation for World Harmony. Every day since getting back has been a blessing."

I sighed, walking over and taking a seat across from him. "I'm sorry for disappointing you."

"Unlike your mother, I'm reserving judgment until I've heard your side of the story," Joel said, sighing. "Your brother became a supervillain because he got kicked out of the Navy Seals for a couple of blunts, plus the fact he was dead broke. He had bad friends who encouraged him to make stupid decisions."

I clenched my fists, trying to hold back my anger.

"That doesn't mean I didn't love him, Gary," Joel said, sighing. "What is family for if not to call you on your bullshit?"

He had me there. "Okay, what do you want to know?"

Joel stared at me. "Why be a supervillain? You could have been a hero."

I shrugged. "I hate the entire superhero and supervillain dynamic. One side good, the other evil, and never the twain shall meet. I guess I wanted to show my contempt for the world and exactly what I thought about it in a big and obvious way."

Joel drank a bit of water from his paper cup. "I saw you kill those Extreme people on television."

I frowned. "I'm sorry you had to see that."

"They killed a lot of innocent people," Joel said, surprising me.

"Yeah, they did," I said.

"I also saw Ultragod arrest you a few minutes later," Joel said, shaking his head. "Except, you were free not a few weeks later without any warrants. The FBI and Foundation websites say you're wanted but you're not on any pursuit lists."

"I kind of saved the world. People who agreed with the Extreme's methods come in every few months to try and take me out, but otherwise, I'm fairly low priority. I think Gabrielle is protecting me, too, which I didn't want."

The fact that I'd killed dozens of supervillains, destroyed the majority of zombies in Falconcrest City, and helped the city rebuild hadn't gone unnoticed. I was a multiple murderer and guilty of countless criminal offenses, but the country had degenerated to the point that no one cared as long as I kept my targets restricted to assholes.

In that respect, I was not so different from Shoot-Em-Up.

Joel looked at me, shaking his head. "So, Ultragoddess is still sweet on you?"

I blinked. "You knew she was Ultragoddess?"

"You didn't?" Joel said, staring. "I mean, her father was Ultragod in a hat and glasses. Then again, I still have my anti-hypnotism implant from the war. Your mom still thinks of her as that nice colored girl you let slip away."

I rubbed my temples, wishing my parents were less racist. *A lot* less racist. "Yeah, I suppose she did slip away."

"What happened to Mandy?" Joel asked. "Because I know that girl would never abandon you."

I answered without thinking. "She died."

"Your fault?" Joel asked, plain and without malice.

I was glad I could answer, "No. She died because of the whole zombie plague thing. Mandy was a hero to the end."

"Good," Joel said, taking another sip. "That should make it easier."

"Not really."

Joel looked down. "I'm sorry, son. No one in the world should have to outlive their spouse. Someone has to but there's only one worse pain in the world."

"Yeah," I said, looking away from him. "I thought when I became a supervillain, I'd have the opportunity to do whatever I wanted. I'd be able to change the world's rules to whatever I wanted them to be. For the past seven months, I've been doing nothing but looking for a way to find a way to bring her back. To spit in the face of reality and say I didn't have to deal with the consequences of my actions. With the consequences of life. That I could fix things the way I wanted them to be just by willing it hard enough."

"That's not being a supervillain, Gary. That's being God."

"I'm starting to get that."

"Are you going to keep doing it?" Joel asked, not sounding condemnatory or angry. Just curious.

"No," I answered him, bluntly. "It's not fun anymore and I've done whatever good I can do as the bad guy in Falconcrest City. It's finally out of the hole the Omega Corporation and the Brotherhood of Infamy dug for it. I also have no interest in being a drug dealer or pimp. I think people should be able to do what they want but consent is a kind of negotiable concept to the majority of people involved in those businesses."

"Will your supervillain friends object to your leaving?" Joel asked. "That was always a problem for it."

"Some will," I said, shrugging. "I'm not afraid of them."

"Maybe you should be," Joel said, finishing off his drink. "Did I ever tell you why we moved to Falconcrest City from New Angeles?"

"You mean after Keith died?"

"Did we move some other time?" my father asked, looking at me like I was a moron.

I stared at my dad. "Really? You want to take me to task over grammar?"

"Hey, you get your sarcasm from me."

"I always assumed you just wanted to get away from the media circus following Keith's death."

Theodore Whitman, the aforementioned Shoot-Em-Up, had lucked out by killing my brother and two other supervillains the day he did. It had been a perfect storm of timing as not only was it a slow news day, but it had also followed a series of particularly heinous crimes by repeat offender supervillains.

The media had embraced Theodore Whitman, as had his lawyers and the New Angeles PD, as a hero. The fact that Whitman was a cop had also gone a long way to getting him on their side as a man doing "necessary" vigilante justice. He had triggered hundreds of copycats, some successful and most not, who believed killing supervillains was the solution to them.

It had taken massive collateral damage, supervillains deciding there was no reason not to kill superheroes (or their families), and the general nihilistic scumbags the "Nineties Antihero" tended to attract to convince the public they'd made a mistake in embracing him.

By then he'd already been dead for a few years.

Killed by me at age fourteen.

"No," Joel said. "It wasn't that, though I was pretty damned disgusted when reporters asked me whether or not I thought my son deserved it outside of Keith's funeral. It was because of the Nefarious Nine."

I blinked. "My brother's old gang?"

"Why do you keep asking stupid questions? Yes, your brother's gang!"

"Excuse me all to hell."

The Nefarious Nine was a club, for lack of a better term, of supervillains who operated in the New Angeles area. They were primarily mid-card supervillains, no one exceptionally powerful but no one particularly weak either, who preferred nonviolent crimes over the bloody messes some left behind. They were theatrical bank robbers, jewelry-store thieves, technology bandits, and hold-up men. People died when they attempted to mess with the gang but they avoided killing cops or civilians. At least, until they took over Atlantis and hundreds died in the resulting civil war.

That had been ugly.

"I remember 'em," I said. "Most of the original crew is dead, retired, or in hiding. One turned into a hero around the time of their gender-reassignment."

"I blame them for ruining your brother's career," Joel said, sighing. "Keith was an adult, he made his choices, but he wanted to be somebody, and they convinced him the best path in life was to become a criminal. Your brother didn't want to be Stingray the Underwater Assassin when he died—he was trying get out of the life."

"I know," I said, thinking back to my meeting with his spirit. "He told me."

"How is he?" Joel asked. My powers freaked out a lot of people. Much the same as Kerri's. They didn't freak out my father.

"Happy," I said.

"Good," Joel said. "The thing was, what I'm trying to tell you is when Shoot-Em-Up killed your brother, the Nefarious Nine wanted to initiate you."

"Excuse me?"

"Your brother struggled for money between prison stays. For both his daughter and his wife. Yet the moment he died, money came pouring in with an offer to send you to special schooling with P.H.A.N.T.O.M or some weird cult of ninjas in the Himalayas. They saw in you a potential replacement five or six years down the road. I didn't want that for you, so I took you to Falconcrest City and prayed they wouldn't care enough to follow." Joel paused. "They didn't."

I'd never heard any of this and a part of me, I'm sorry to say, grew mad at my father. It had taken me until my thirties to become a supervillain because of a freak stroke of luck. As much as it had become a bitter pill, I'd yearned to be one from the time of my brother's death until I'd slipped the Reaper's Cloak on for the first time.

Knowing I could have had ten more years of being a supervillain, even if it involved something as reprehensible as P.H.A.N.T.O.M, filled me with a sense of missed opportunity. The rest of me knew exactly what my father had done. He'd given me a chance. A chance I'd squandered.

I took a deep breath. "Thank you. I mean that."

"You're welcome."

I tried to choose my next words carefully. "I'm sorry I've disappointed you, Dad."

"You haven't." Joel surprised me. "You saved Falconcrest City from zombies. You steal from real assholes. You also killed Magog the Biblical giant."

"You heard about that, huh?"

"Also, a bunch of other bad people. I'm not saying I approve of what you've done but you were true to yourself. Be who you are, son, even if it's a villain. At the end of the day, you only have to answer to yourself and those you love."

I stared at him. "Would you be telling me any of this if you weren't worried about dying?"

"No way in hell," Joel said. "Your mom is waiting outside the day, ready to give you another earful. Give me a hug, Gary."

"Alright," I said, doing so. "See you soon."

"You bet."

I was glad we had this conversation. I didn't believe for a second my father approved of my becoming a supervillain but it allowed me a sense of peace with my life path. I couldn't just stop being a criminal but I decided to re-direct my efforts to those especially deserving, at least until I was ready to leave. Not as a hero but as a better sort of bad guy. Because I didn't deserve to be a hero. I'd thrown that away by letting my wife die.

My father passed away two days later.

I remembered that as I found myself standing in an endless nothingness. It was the Nothing Beyond, the complete emptiness that existed beyond Heaven, Hell, and everything else past the physical universe.

"But what if he didn't have to?" a voice spoke behind me. "What if we could make all this better?"

It took me a second to realize it was my voice speaking.

Chapter Seventeen

Talking to Myself

I turned around and looked into the face of my doppelganger. I'd caught a glimpse of him for just a brief moment during the fight at the hospital and hadn't really got a chance to appreciate what he looked like. The first thing that struck me about him was, oddly, the fact that he was much better looking than me.

I'm an extremely handsome guy, don't get me wrong, but all of my features had completely smoothed out to a superhuman beauty similar to Adonis's. He had porcelain-white skin, platinum-white hair, and crystal blue eyes. The nose was nicely more Semitic than mine as well.

My doppelganger was wearing a silken, brilliant white hooded cloak that seemed to shine with its own inner light. He wasn't wearing one of the Reaper's Cloaks but a magical reproduction, like the kind the Nightmaster wore during our final confrontation during the Fall. It made me wonder what had happened to his version of Cloak before I decided I didn't want to know.

"Hello, Gary," my doppelganger said, standing in the middle of the endless void.

"Hello, Other Gary," I said, thinking up a name for him. "The last time I faced my exact duplicate in the middle of a big nothing didn't turn out so well."

"Believe me, I know," Other Gary said, extending his hand. "A pleasure to meet you, I am the Pre-Great Cataclysm Gary."

I, reluctantly, reached out and shook his hand. "Pre-Great Cataclysm?"

Cloak, as always, was a source of information. *"The Great Cataclysm,"* Cloak said, his voice low. *"The greatest failure of the Society of Superheroes. A gigantic war against the Great Beasts and an endless army of demons summoned by Diabloman. No one but the inner circle of the Society—Ultragod, Guinevere, and I—remembered it. We weren't able to save reality but we successfully rebooted it. We were told by the Cosmic Monitor there were other survivors but—"*

"So you're a Gary from a previous universe," I said, uninterested in the details. "Got it."

Other Gary smirked. "You're surprisingly accepting of this fact."

"I've long since given up on logic and sanity."

Other Gary chuckled. "That's probably for the best."

I decided to ditch the faux-pleasantness of this. "Why the hell are you working for Omega, you psychotic prick?"

Other Gary was surprisingly forthcoming. "Because your universe sucks."

"And how does working for President Looney Tunes help that?"

"Perhaps I should clarify I don't work for him," Other Gary said, clasping his hands together. "He works for me."

I paused. "Somehow, I doubt he's the most stable subordinate. Also, the question still applies. Why?"

Other Gary closed his eyes. "Perhaps it is better to show you."

He snapped his fingers and we were suddenly no longer surrounded by emptiness but in the middle of Downtown Falconcrest City. It was unlike any time I'd ever seen the metropolis, though. It was beautiful, with shining skyscrapers, clean streets, and air that didn't choke your lungs. Gone were the dark and somber faces of a people traumatized by a zombie apocalypse; instead was a sense of joy. Across the street from us was the Falconcrest City Bank, the one blown up by the Extreme during my second day out as Merciless. Here, it was still intact and open for business.

I was more than a little unnerved. "It looks like Atlas City."

"It is 1966," Other Gary said, sighing. "The height of superheroism. Except, in the Pre-Cataclysm world, we were already alive and adults. You were Ultragod's plucky cub reporter friend, or as to say I was, and we were part of the Teen Heroes who helped the Society of Superheroes solve crimes."

I paused. "Okay, that makes even less sense than time-travel usually does. How the hell would I be born three-and-a-half-decades earlier?"

"Abandoning logic in the face of superhero-related events is a good policy for a reason," Other Gary said, giving a dismissive wave of his hand. "Keep watching."

The alarm went off at the bank and two of my old foes—the Ice Cream Man and Big Ben—ran out carrying bags of loot while their costumed henchmen dragged out a pair of hostages. I hadn't known either of them very long because, well, I'd killed them both. They were a pair of psychopaths who'd had their deaths coming; I say that with full awareness of the hypocrisy.

These two looked different from the ones I remembered, lacking some of the inherent viciousness and malice I remembered oozing off the originals. This Ice Cream Man, for example, was dressed in a paper hat and white suit with a pair of earmuffs and a heavy overcoat while sporting a harmless freezing ray in his right hand. The one I'd known had filed down his teeth into shark-like incisors and cut off his own lips. Big Ben, by contrast, was a dwarf in a bowler hat and a Union Jack-themed suit carrying an umbrella.

The henchmen were both wearing black and white prison jumpsuits with shoe polish around their eyes and berets. They looked like the kind of comical crooks that menaced Scrooge McDuck and his nephews. I did a double take, though, when I saw the two hostages were a pair of sexy girls in bellbottoms and tie-dye shirts. It was a teenaged Mandy and Cindy, both wearing headbands, and ineffectually struggling.

"You're not going to get away with this!" Mandy said, without irony. "Merciful: The Hero of Mercy is going to save us."

"Yeah, you rats are going to get what's coming to him!" Cindy shouted. "Our boyfriend is going to whoop you!"

"Is this supposed to convince me the world is better?" I asked, looking over to Other Gary. "Because all this is showing is your world is completely sexist. Also curiously devoid of swearing."

"There's no shame in not being a fighter," Other Gary said, defensively. "Cindy is studying to be a doctor and Mandy an investigative journalist."

"Mandy *is* a fighter, though," I said. "So is Cindy. Besides, the sixties had Emma Peel. Not to mention there were plenty of female superheroes during this time as well—Guinevere, the Heroes of Tomorrow, and so on."

"True," Other Gary said. "Eventually, Mandy was so sick of being kidnapped that she went to study with her people in the Lost City of Shambhala."

"Her people?" I said, doing a double take after I realized he was referring to Mandy's Korean heritage. "You mean Californians? Seriously, your defense is it's not sexist because it's racist?"

Other Gary sighed. "Just watch."

Seconds later, a glowing white cloaked figure levitated down in front of them. It was a younger version of Other Gary who promptly pointed at the ne'er do wells and shouted, "Halt, evil-doers!"

"Got any popcorn?" I asked.

Other Gary conjured a bag and handed it over.

I took a handful of its contents and started crunching.

Mmmm.

Other Gary also conjured me a cola with a straw in it.

"Thanks."

Younger Other Gary then proceeded to punch out the Ice Cream Man with a resounding *whoomp* sound, followed by a wham sound as he punched the first of the henchmen. Big Men fired an energy blast from his umbrella which Younger Other Gary ducked, then delivered a kick to his jaw. A huge *boomph* noise came, followed by yet another wham noise as Younger Other Gary knocked out the last of the henchmen.

"Oh thank you!" Mandy said, kissing my second doppelganger, followed by Cindy. He then embraced both.

"Are they in like a threesome?" I asked, handing the popcorn bag back to Other Gary and taking a sip of my Coca-Cola. It was the kind of really good classic Coke which was only available before the eighties and had more calories than God.

"No, we don't really do that sort of thing," Other Gary said. "I was just caught in a perpetual love triangle. Quartet whenever Gabrielle broke up with her space boyfriends."

"Again, you have a really sanitized view of the sixties," I said, slurping on my straw. "Archie was totally hitting both Betty and Veronica while the two of them were with each other. Jughead pined for Archie, but eventually ended up with hamburgers and the occasional moment of solace with bisexual Reggie."

"That's completely not how that series went."

"Well, its how I read it. It was the era of Free Love, man. I much prefer the hippie part of the sixties to the sexist douchebag *Mad Men* version."

Other Gary smiled, then waved away the universe about it, returning us to the emptiness where we were before. "The thing is, I come from a more innocent time. A place where good and evil were absolutes. Heroes were heroes, villains were villains, and the former always triumphed over the latter. This world you live in is a mistake, full of complexities and cruelties that have no place in a world of flying jetpacks and talking apes."

"Yeah, but gay people can serve in the military and blacks can sit in the front of the bus. I consider that a pretty good trade-off."

Other Gary gave a wry smile. "Touché. But what if I could tell you it was possible to have the best of both worlds? Literally. All of the social progress of the last fifty years mixed with a complete absence of the worst excesses of superhero mythology. An idealistic world where we believe people with superpowers make the world a better place rather than one where we fear they're going to destroy it."

"You mean a place where the president isn't trying to put every Super in death camps?" I asked. "Which, again, brings us to the fact you're allied with the psycho guy who tried to kill my family."

Other Gary frowned. "You keep coming back to that."

"Blowing up my house and allying with the guy who killed my ex-girlfriend's father isn't the best way to start a relationship."

"Omega didn't kill Ultragod," Other Gary said, lowering his gaze. "I did."

I threw the Coke in his face and pulled out my pistols to shoot him during the distraction. Before I could respond, though, he had levitated underneath and then behind me and had wrapped his arm around my neck.

"Be at peace!" Other Gary shouted.

"Fuck you!" I shouted, furious. "You son of a bitch! You murdered the greatest superhero in the world!"

"Yes, I did," Other Gary said, his voice low. I've discovered we have a gift, my younger self. We have the ability to do whatever it is necessary to achieve the ends we require no matter how horrible or monstrous they may be. I'd make a pithy remark or pop culture reference to illustrate what I mean, but honestly, I don't remember any of Earth's films or books. It's been too long."

"For the love of God, why!?" I snapped, struggling against my doppelganger's grip but was unable to turn insubstantial or overcome it while he had his arm around my throat. I even bit into his arm, but it didn't seem to do any good.

"To bring back my Mandy," Other Gary said.

I stopped struggling. "What?"

Other Gary then looked up into the nothingness above us as if still seeing Falconcrest City's skyline. "This was the heyday of the good times, but not the end. Reality took Mandy from us, Gary. We had ten beautiful years of marriage in my timeline before she ended up dying. This was before Diabloman destroyed the universe during his days as a supervillain and the Society of Superheroes had to recreate it. I was within inches of resurrecting her and starting our life together over when the universe exploded around me. I survived, though, because I was already at one with Death. I woke up in a universe that was similar, but different from the one I'd come from. All of the superheroes were here, but nastier, meaner, and less able to save the day. The villains were crueler and more prone to being psychotic monsters. The government was awful and plotting Nazi-like genocides against Supers. There was also a new Gary and a new Mandy."

"Why kill Ultragod?" I growled, filled with a murderous fury toward the man who had quite possibly ruined my world.

"Because we can fix it," Other Gary said, letting go. "*I* can fix it. Gary, this is the future without my intervention."

Our surroundings changed again but what they turned into was a far cry from the campy city we'd left behind. . The sight that greeted us on the other side was the blasted ruins of Falconcrest City. Most of the city's skyline was rubble, reduced to nothing more than hollowed-out metal girders, the bones of the buildings I'd grown up beside.

Most of the suburbs had been replaced with half-mile-tall black concrete factories that poured out massive amounts of black smoke, making the stars impossible to see. A single skyscraper remained, twice as tall as the factories, with an obelisk shape and the P.H.A.N.T.O.M symbol emblazoned across its front. As if the scene wasn't frightening enough. the lights inside the obelisk were an ominous shade of red.

Looking to my side, I saw we were in the half-collapsed ruins of an elementary school with child-sized skeletons scattered across the ground along with the broken stone. The walls were covered in freshly-applied posters extolling the virtues of Supreme Leader Omega, wanted posters for various superheroes (most stamped "Terminated"), and various art deco artwork which Stalin would have been proud of. One displayed a board with a nail in its end being held over a tied-up man in a cape, saying, "Resist the Supers who have ruined the world."

I didn't know what was more disturbing, that they'd bothered to paper up the ruins of a school massacre or that they hadn't bothered to clean up the children's corpses. I suppose both were equally horrifying in their own way.

"James Cameron takes over the world?" I said, looking around for Arnold and Linda Hamilton.

"Not funny," Other Gary said, breathing in the smoggy, ash-filled air. "Your universe was broken from the time it was rebuilt following Diabloman's destruction of it. The conflicts between superheroes and supervillains got more and more destructive until the public turned against them both. Unfortunately, they hadn't counted on so much of the population siding with the Supers, even if it was a minority. Humanity destroyed itself in an apocalyptic war. That was before I got President Omega to go back in time and replace the bastard who was going to be elected instead."

"So, your solution to the coming genocide of all superhumans is to kill the world's greatest superhero and replace him with a guy who wants to commit genocide against all superhumans. This is a worse plan than I usually come up with. Where did I go wrong? Literally?"

Other Gary said, "To remake the universe, Gary, I needed necromantic energy. *A lot* of necromantic energy. The best way to get that energy is death. Massive amounts on a global scale. So, I figured the only way to achieve my goals was to absorb the energy of the world's destruction. Which I did when Omega destroyed it for me—the first time."

I paused. "The first time."

"After I absorbed the destruction of the world the first time at Omega's hands and his subsequent mismanagement, we reversed time and proceeded to conquer the world again so I could gain it again. One hundred years of death, followed by another hundred years of death. I only need to do it again and I'll have all of the energy I need to rewrite reality forever."

Other Gary waved his hand and I saw my sorcerer doppelganger supervising a century of warfare following the release of the Nanoplague. All of those individuals who hated Supers rejoiced at their destruction only to be exterminated themselves.

Other Gary, Ultradevil, and President Omega together annihilated everyone in the world who could resist, and when they were done, Other Gary betrayed them and gave Omega's time-travel technology to the resistance so they could go back and just barely fail to prevent events from happening again. Allowing Other Gary to do it over again. This would be the third time he helped destroy the world.

I stared at him. "Wow, I never thought I'd say this about anyone, least of all me, but you are *worse than Hitler.*"

Other Gary just laughed. It was the bitter humorless laugh of someone who'd forgotten how to. "Aren't you the one who said he'd do anything to bring Mandy back?"

"There are limits. Limits she would never want me to cross."

Other Gary looked down. "Like I said, we can cross any line we want to save our loved ones. For example, right now, I'm happy to restore your Mandy to you in exchange for you walking away."

Chapter Eighteen

Where I Deal with the Devil (Me)

My mouth went dry at Other Gary's offer. "You could do that?"

"*Gary*," Cloak said, his voice low. "*Don't.*"

"Just let me handle this," I whispered, not knowing how to react.

Other Gary dismissed the post-apocalyptic future we'd just visited and started pacing around. "I want to resurrect my world, my wife, and my family. That's a concept I'm sure you can appreciate even if you disapprove of the means."

"I think murdering literally billions of people, resurrecting them, and then murdering them again goes a little beyond disapproving of the means."

Other Gary gave a dismissive shrug. "If you say so. The simple fact is I have more than enough necromantic energy to re-arrange events in your reality so that Mandy gets her soul back. The moment you come back to reality, she'll be exactly as you planned to make her. A vampire with your wife's soul."

I closed my eyes, trying to control my emotion. "If you could do that, why not resurrect your own Mandy?"

"I don't want her to see *this* world," Other Gary said, balling his fists. "I want her to be in one she'll recognize. A better one without all the toxicity the past few decades have built up. Besides, I don't want my wife to see me like this. I want her to know me only as I was, will be, once I have settled all of this."

"No harm, no foul because everyone you will have murdered will be alive again?" I asked, trying to understand his mindset.

"Who would be the wiser?" Other Gary joked.

I wasn't in a joking mood anymore. "God."

"What has he ever done for us?" Other Gary said, the bitterness in his voice almost palpable.

"So, you just bring back Mandy and I let you go to go on and murder everyone, including me and Mandy. This doesn't seem like a very good deal."

Other Gary didn't seem to be listening. Instead, he was looking off into the distance at the great vast nothingness about us. "I am the original.

The first one to bear the name Gary Karkofsky who started this insane cycle of temporal manipulation and murder. I am you as the timeline originally intended."

"So, that's a yes."

"*Gary,*" Cloak said. "*For the longest time I have believed the timeline's integrity should be preserved and your casual messing around with it was foolish.*"

"Yeah?" I said back to him.

"*Forget it. If it helps you stop this madman, go ahead and knock it to pieces.*"

"Thanks," I said, shaking my head. "Not that I believe any of this. I'm the original, O.G, Gary Karkofsky."

"You don't believe me?" Other Gary said.

"Let's say I retain a healthy amount of skepticism when alternate reality versions of me show up and explain why multiple planetary genocide is necessary," I said, reminding myself this guy was insane. "How did you kill Ultragod anyway?"

"With a gun," Other Gary said, sighing. "The problem with so many other supervillains is they are projecting their anger onto the world to the point they need to draw out the act of murder. I didn't hate Ultragod so I was able to get close enough to him to kill him with a gold ultranium bullet. The mundanity is what allowed it to succeed."

"If it was that easy, he would have died years ago."

"Ultanium is not exactly a commonly known weakness. You, me, Ultragod, Ultragoddess, the Nightwalker, Tom Terror, and Guinevere are the only ones who were familiar with it. It's also a rare element only extractable from certain places—like, say, the spot I knew the Nightwalker kept his sample in the Old Clock Tower. There is also the fact that I have a face he could trust."

I wanted to punch the living shit out of him right then and there. "You used his trust of me to kill him."

"Yes," Other Gary said. "He, too, will come back in this New World I'm creating. The Nightwalker, Ultragod, our father, and others will all be restored. You'll be alive and so will your Mandy."

"The world can't be frozen," I said, pitying my doppelganger more than hating him. "All the heroes of the world can't be stuck in a cycle of nothing ever changing and only the good things happening. Change is necessary for the world to move on. Sometimes, that requires us to make sacrifices we don't want to make."

I felt like such an enormous hypocrite saying that.

Other Gary snorted. "People don't want to see Ultragod and the Nightwalker retire or die. They don't want to see their heroes grow old, marry, and have kids. No, they want them stuck in place with an eternity of pointless villain and hero fights. Characters in a grand story acting out a pantomime of good versus evil that prevents real growth or critical analysis."

"Which you want to return to."

"Give the people what they want, I always say." Other Gary sighed. "It's why I was able to persuade Omega to work for me. Despite having a freaking time machine, the idiot had been defeated hundreds of times by the Society of Superheroes and various costumed champions over the ages. All I had to do was promise him a chance to win and win again to get him on my side. As much as I'm doing this for noble and understandable reasons, Omega is just a dick and happy to be always going forward to a dystopian future that will never come."

"And Ultradevil?"

"Ultradevil is different," Other Gary said. "Ultradevil and his world were created by Entropicus as a way to analyze the nature of human morality. On that world, everyone who is good is evil and vice versa. Imagine being born as nothing more than an inversion of a real person. A fictional character created for the sole purpose of being the villain in another man's drama. Ultradevil went mad when he learned the nature of his world and spent years trying to kill Ultragod out of a sense of outrage that he was not a real person at all. All I had to promise him was the chance he would be able to replace Ultragod in this reality. In truth, I'm going to remake him when I fix the world and give him the chance to be the hero he always wanted to be."

"Versus, you know, just being a hero."

Other Gary frowned. "I take it I'm not convincing you to go along with my plan?"

"Your attempts would be a lot more persuasive if you weren't a bag full of crazy containing another bag full of crazy."

"You realize, that's still just one bag full of crazy, correct?"

I blinked. "Huh, you're right. That's a terrible phrase."

"Well, I suppose I'll have to kill you then," Other Gary said, frowning. "Unfortunate."

"Yeah, I bet you have severe regrets about that, what with having already sent President Omega to kill me once."

"He's not exactly the most loyal ally, what with being a homicidal lunatic and all."

"And you have so much in common," I said, faking shock. "I'm going to have to kill you, Other Me. Sorry. I understand what you're feeling better than anyone, but I also understand your Mandy would prefer to be dead than let you do that."

"We'll see about that. I suppose talk is cheap and actions speak louder than words." Other Gary snapped his fingers.

I felt an immense sense of necromantic power radiate outwards and wash over me before spreading out in every direction. There was a strange sense of reality being restructured all about me, and it was like no magic I'd ever witnessed.

I took a step back, stumbling in the process. "What have you done?"

"Restored your Mandy, of course," Other Gary replied. "I may have to kill you because, quite literally, you're the only person who knows how to get around my sort of plans but I'm not a complete monster. You should have some time to spend with her before events go completely out of control."

"That's impossible."

"Not at all. I've not only arranged for her to be healed, but have also given her plenty of involvement in our current little struggle. She, alone, can now tell you exactly what's going on and what needs to be done. It required a bit of finagling with the timeline, smashing a few realities back together, and rebooting portions of the universe but it's all better now. She's as good as new. Better even. Don't worry, though, I didn't directly make any improvements. They just naturally flowed from her personality."

I stared at him, unsure how to respond. "You're lying."

"Am I?" Other Gary said, smiling. "You've struggled for the past year to resurrect Mandy, so why would it surprise you to know that I, who have had centuries of experience, am able to do what you have been working toward?"

I opened my mouth then closed it.

"Unless, of course, you want me to reverse it?"

"No!" I shouted, raising my hands up. I hated owing my doppelganger anything but the prospect he'd done just what he'd claimed paralyzed me from making any hostile moves.

Other Gary chuckled. "I thought not. Who knows, perhaps you will be smart enough to realize it is better to enjoy what precious little time remains with your wife than attempt to fix what cannot, should not, be fixed."

"Leave me alone," I said, looking away.

"As you wish," Other Gary said. "The simple fact is I've accounted for every eventuality and have already eliminated all those who stand in my way. You should be grateful, in a way, since this means you really were this world's greatest supervillain."

With that, Other Gary vanished, and I was left alone in the empty void. I didn't know if I was alive or dead in the real world, though I suspected I was fine if my doppelganger was so certain I was still a threat to him. He wouldn't raise my wife from the dead to screw with me unless he assumed I needed screwing with in the first place.

"You can't actually be thinking of trusting him," Cloak said, sounding utterly appalled.

"In what universe did you think I would?" I said, honestly offended he'd think I'd go along with this joker.

"Sorry, I never quite know what you're going to do."

"I don't have many standards but I kind of draw the line at genocide. Actually, I draw the line significantly further back. Like in New Jersey."

"I shouldn't have doubted you even for a second."

"No, you shouldn't have." I needed a second to collect my thoughts. "Is it possible he's telling the truth?"

"At least as far as he thinks he is, probably. I've encountered many evil doppelgangers over the years."

"That's a statement that should never be uttered."

"It also explains a number of things I've been wondering about for some time. How Ultragod was able to be killed, how Omega was able to get so powerful so quickly, and what their peculiar obsession with you is."

I took a deep breath. "Cloak, you've got to believe I would never do anything to hurt Moses. I mean, even if I didn't like the guy, and I did, I would never hurt Gabrielle."

"Gary, I'm aware you're not a monster. The fact your Mandy is dead and you didn't become someone like your doppelganger is proof positive of that. There're an infinite number of variations on the same basic person spread throughout the universe. You're no more responsible for his actions than the cannibal pimp Gary's."

"We keep coming back to that guy with a disturbing regularity."

"Alternate pasts."

"Yeah-yeah," I said. "Well, at least as long as we're agreed I'm nothing like him."

"I wouldn't say that."

I narrowed my eyes. "*Nothing* alike."

"Don't take that as an insult," Cloak responded, surprising me. *"You are a criminal mind who is of remarkable acuity and unpredictability. You seem to know how heroes and villains will react before they happen as well as how to respond*

appropriately. I believe this version of you is responsible for what has happened because of that ability. It also means we need to play against his ability to defeat him."

"You're saying my evil doppelganger is dangerous because he has my genre savvy nature."

"*Yes, I suppose I am.*"

"Great." I closed my eyes. "What about that whole Mandy business?"

"*It's possible*," Cloak said. "*You do not have the pedigree or natural aptitude for truly powerful magic, but that sort of thing can be compensated for. This version of you possesses an immense amount of innate magical power. His plan to remake reality and create his own version of the Earth is probably impossible but such plans have been tried before. The Brotherhood of Infamy planned something similar, if you recall.*"

"Great, three major adventures and we're already recycling story beats."

"*Think of remaking reality as your villains' motif.*"

"I want it to be true," I said, trying to get a handle on my emotions. "But I can't bring myself to believe it. Reality is never this kind."

"Well, if it's any consolation, you won't be living to enjoy it," President Omega's voice spoke behind me.

"Ah crap," I said, turning around.

There, behind me in the endless void was President Omega in some sort of red and gold mechanical armor with a helmet covered in a translucent face plate. Both his hands glowed with strange energies which I could feel from several feet away. An omega symbol was on his chest plate and he looked sort of like an evil cybernetic Transformer.

Levitating beside President Omega, his arms crossed and his feet pressed together like M. Bison, was Ultradevil. His eyes were a glowing shade of red and he was looking down at me with a look of complete disdain.

"Oh, were you looking for Other Gary?" I asked, pointing behind me. "You just missed him."

"Actually, we're here to kill you," Ultradevil said, chuckling. "Frankly, after having to listen to that moron's prattle nonstop for the past few months, it'll be quite therapeutic."

I was fairly sure I was outmatched here. "Actually, having known him for five minutes, I now know why men hate me and women tolerate me. He has amazing looks and a horrible personality. Wait, aren't you guys supposed to be working for him?"

"With him," Omega said, frowning. "Even then, only until he manages to finish his plan to accumulate universe-changing levels of necromantic energy. Then, I plan to kill him and use it for myself. After all, why spend centuries or even millennia conquering this universe when I can just do it all at once? I mean, there are so many other universes to conquer."

"And what about you?" I said, hoping to delay my imminent death. "Didn't he say you were all obsessed with the fact that you're a bad guy and want to be a hero instead?"

"I do want to be a hero," Ultradevil said. "I wasn't handed my heroism on a silver platter like my alternate in this universe. After the universe is remade, I intend to launch a crusade across the Multiverse, exterminating all nonhumans and bringing peace as well as order to alternate Earths throughout the space-time continuum. I will be remembered as the greatest hero who ever lived."

"Well, I suppose you can take the villain out of the evil dimension but you can't take the evil dimension out of the villain," I said, taking a few steps back. "I don't suppose I could play the three of you against one another in hopes of defeating you all and saving the day?"

"I'm afraid not," Omega said, raising his glowing right hand. "I'm sorry, Gary, I really am. You're much more amusing than your doppelganger, and I would have enjoyed teaming up with you to butcher billions."

"What is with you three and genocide?" I said.

"It's fun," Omega said, smiling. 'That wonderful little feeling when you look down at the world, see it's full of dots, and then start removing thousands at a time."

"You realize Harry Lime was the villain in *The Third Man*, right?"

"Not much of a movie buff." That was when he fired an energy blast and I just barely managed to move my head out of the way.

"Ultradevil, kill him!" Omega shouted.

Ultradevil conjured a seventeen-foot-long Ultra-Force battle axe to cleave me in two.

Right before I woke up.

Denying my enemies their prize.

Chapter Nineteen

Where I Reconnect with My Wife

I became aware again and found myself breathing in humid air with the noise of water lapping against the side of stone. I didn't open my eyes immediately because they felt heavy. My chest hurt like hell and the rest of my body was like lead. I'd been shot through the heart. Partial-invulnerability or not, I was pretty sure that should have killed me.

"*It actually missed the heart by a few inches,*" Cloak said. "*Not that you didn't almost bleed out.*"

"Was I dreaming or did we meet with my crazy sixties doppelganger?" I asked. I was as stunned by his appearance as anyone.

"*You were dreaming and yes we did.*"

"Great, just when I think my world can't get any weirder after riding a cybernetic dinosaur, this happens," I said, stretching. "Now, I suppose we should go find out who is holding us prisoner. Why am I hearing Bon Jovi?" It was pretty vague but I could definitely hear "You Give Love a Bad Name" playing in the background.

"*I hear it too,*" Cloak said. "*I don't know who is holding us but I doubt its Darklight. They probably prefer metal.*"

"Hey, *I* like metal. Whatever the case, I think we can officially chalk up the United States government to be on the side of the bad guys this time. At least until we can remove President Omega from office." I'd deal with Other Gary afterward. How hard could it be to deal with someone who knew your every thought and motivation?

Oh right.

Cloak telepathically made a noise that sounded like a sigh. "*It seems we may actually have to revert to your plan to take out the false president and end his fascist reign over the country.*"

I smiled, which hurt. "So, what you're saying is, I'm right?"

It wasn't often I managed to get one over on one of the world's greatest superheroes.

"*Please stop acting like you're twelve years old,*" Cloak said.

"Oh hush, I'm acting like I'm fourteen at least."

Forcing my eyes open, I saw I was lying face down on a mattress in the middle of a circular brick chamber next to some sort of river. Clearing my head, I realized I was underground beside a storm sewer pumping station with access to the river. There was a black top-of-the-line speedboat nearby and a small armory of guns, armor, and grenades casually propped up against the wall.

A big steel door was drawn up over the entrance like a portcullis. The walls were covered in newspaper articles hammered up, posters of Mandy's favorite bands, and pictures stolen from my house. There was also a porcelain statue of a bull terrier stolen from a novelty shop. The Bon Jovi song was coming from a nearby boom box sitting on a metal chair. I shouldn't have been surprised that this was where she'd been hiding the entire time. Falconcrest City exceeded New York in terms of massive sewer size, and its storm tunnels were home to entire communities of people who didn't want to be found.

Including my wife, it seemed.

"And Mandy has kidnapped me and taken me to her secret lair," I said, shaking my head. "I would be upset, but..."

I reached up to touch my chest and saw it had been field-dressed and there was also blackish-red ichor on the wound.

Vampire blood.

Nature's unnatural cure-all.

"I guess we're going to find out if Other Gary was lying or not," I said, worried he was and worried he wasn't.

"*He might be telling the truth.*"

"Usually, you warn me to be cynical."

"*I am not that cruel, even if we both know you should be.*"

Standing up, I stretched my neck and headed down the side of the station to a metal door leading to the pumping station proper. The interior of the place was actually quite homey with furniture that resembled the kind we'd had at our house, a television set showing home movies from her childhood, and a variety of stuffed animals I'd put into storage so I didn't have to be reminded they belonged to my wife.

There was also a collection of television sets wired together with images of various hot spots around the city, a bookshelf-sized Foundation for World Harmony supercomputer processor attached to a million-dollar Aeon Inc. computer terminal, a police scanner, and a hundred open files on the coffee table describing P.H.A.N.T.O.M's operations for the past eighty years.

There was also a black and white photo of Charles Omega meeting with Adolf Hitler and Tom Terror for the formation of said organization. I also saw pictures of a hellish world of flames and industry that I recognized from Cloak's files as the planet Abaddon at the end of time. President Omega was meeting with the flamboyant space gods there and had taken selfies.

Apparently, Charles Omega had helped found P.H.A.N.T.O.M on behalf of Entropicus. Wow, he was an asshole.

I walked over to the photo and picked it up. "Okay, this is getting very *The Man in the High Castle*."

"*I should have realized Omega was a danger long before this,*" Cloak said. "*To think people used to call me Earth's Greatest Detective.*"

"Missing the fact that all of Falconcrest City's rich people and politicians were apocalypse-worshiping demon-cultists was kind of a failure on your part," I replied. "Just how much of time is fucked up by this guy, do you think?" I looked at the photos, which showed a history of President Omega throughout the past seventy years.

Kidnapping Patty Hearst, blowing up the Golden Gate Bridge, starting the Third Cuban Missile Crisis, and trying to assassinate Doctor Byrne during his talk with Martin Luther King about Superhuman rights.

"*It could be a stable time-loop and all of this was meant to happen,*" Cloak said.

"Do you think that's possible?"

"*No,*" Cloak said. "*No, your doppleganger's presence proves that. Either way, this is an outrage. History's natural flow being violated is monstrous.*"

"Is it? I've killed thirty-six Hitlers, remember?"

"*I try not to think of that. Those were all alternate pasts, though, so they don't count.*"

"This is why no one trusts superheroes. Your morality doesn't make any sense."

"*I generally don't think any interference in the time stream is a good idea.*"

"You must have hated *Quantum Leap*."

"*Unlike you, I try not to get my morality from pop culture.*"

"Says the guy who dressed up like the Shadow to fight crime."

"*Shut up, the Shadow was awesome.*"

I chuckled, recognizing Cloak's joke.

"*It's possible the world Omega has changed us from was a much better one.*" Cloak said, "*Take a look here. He killed Henry Ford and turned his company into Omega Automotive. Think about how that may have changed history for the worst.*"

"Versus the Jew-hating Nazi sympathizer?"

"*I can see I'm not going to make much headway here. We should find your wife and discuss why she's kidnapped you.*"

"Ex..." I started to correct him before shaking my head. I wasn't so sure anymore.

I heard the sound of a shower going in an adjacent room and walked through a nearby red door into a crude bathroom. There was a shower stall, a toilet, and a sink. The tile was yellow with age and there were three different sets of toothbrushes on the sink along with several different kinds of toothpaste and mouthwash. A white towel, the packaging in a trash can underneath it, was propped up on a nail hammered into the wall.

Mandy herself was taking a shower with her naked backside to me. The hot water was dribbling down her and she was shampooing her hair, an action I know she hadn't bothered with for almost a year due to the way she'd looked during our previous encounter. It was the same brand Mandy had used for the entirety of our marriage, a smelly verbena-scented one that was popular with the Renaissance Fair crowd.

For a moment, I was transported back to a happier time when I would have just taken my clothes off and joined her inside. It was times like this, every day now really, I regretted I'd ever decided to put on the Reaper's Cloak. I would have traded all my time as a supervillain, all the amazing adventures I'd had, even saving people's lives if it meant I could be with Mandy again. That was the reason why I wasn't, never could be, never would want to be, a hero.

"*Cloak, do me a favor and go back into my subconscious for a while, would you?*" I telepathically asked.

"*I'll leave you alone, Gary. Just….don't do anything stupid.*"

"*Please,*" I asked.

"*Alright.*"

With that, I was left alone with the vampire who had all of my wife's memories and personality. Who was possessed of a darkness that hadn't existed in my wife or had been so suppressed I'd never noticed it. Who theoretically had a soul or was missing part of hers. I didn't know the mechanics of it, but I could only watch her as she showered, lost in the memories of the past and how they contrasted with the present. Mandy didn't react to my voyeurism and finished washing before turning to me and stretching out her hand.

"Do you mind?" Mandy asked.

I took the white robe off its nail and handed it to her.

Mandy wrapped it around herself, this time deliberately giving me a good look at the body I'd held on countless occasions. The one I missed every time I went to sleep.

Tying the cloth belt, Mandy smiled. "You are my torment, Gary Karkofsky."

"Excuse me?" I said, blinking.

"Becoming a vampire freed me from the ambiguities of my existence. Fear, loneliness, mercy, compassion, and self-doubt. What was once a discordant painful world of colors became a perfect one of black and white. Mandy's desire for justice gave my life a purpose. A willingness to hunt down and destroy those who do not belong in this world. Yet, around you, I have explosions of those very emotions that confuse and muddle the issue. I've also had a long time to form new attachments to you even if you don't remember them."

"I'm sorry, what?"

"I'll get to that. I'm just explaining it's painful to be around you….the memories. Good and bad."

I wasn't sure how to respond to that. "I'm sorry I remind you of the person you used to be."

Mandy surprised me by saying, "I'm not."

"I...see."

"I did not feel as I did for you when I first awoke to this world," Mandy said. "Could not feel as I did. Yet your presence haunts my dreams. When the sun rises and I return to death, I dream of a time when I loved you and my heart still beat. I remember caring for you, our animals, friends, and a world where my purpose was not the only thing that drove me. It's a deeper worry than you know because there are places, people, and things I recall which will never be. I don't like feeling this way. Sometimes, I think it'd be better drive all these memories away and go back to the monster I was. A being who wouldn't care about what's to come."

My heart skipped a beat both from pain and longing. "Maybe you should try and give those feelings more of a shot."

"I have considered it," Mandy said, her voice low. "Even before I was reborn last night, I stalked you. I broke into your house to gaze upon you as you slept. I followed you on missions. I even lay beside you as you lay senseless, leaving before you awoke. So many times, I have wanted to return to you and pretend to be Mandy reborn. To adopt the guise of the woman whose form I wear and pretend—because in that pretending I might feel more happiness than I do drinking the life of my enemies."

"You say you wear Mandy's guise, but I think you are her," I said, saying what Cloak and Cindy as well as Death told me was not true. "Maybe not all of her, but enough of her to be someone I loved. You left me. You abandoned me. I would have given you all of my love if you'd simply been there when I woke up."

I didn't care how spectacularly creepy it was that Mandy had managed to be beside me all this time I was mourning her. Given she'd been just a hair's breadth away from killing me on multiple occasions since her transformation, it should have terrified me. It didn't. Instead, it told me there was more to Mandy than just the hunger. That my wife, some part of her, still lived on in the vampire before me. Not just physically either. Whether it was because of the magic used to resurrect her, Other Gary, or simply the power of true love, I didn't care. I had to believe this was her still.

Mandy stared at me. "I am a shadow of who I am. A woman out of time. Not—"

"Then why hunt criminals?" I asked, gesturing out the door. "Why have that radio to the Foundation for World Harmony? I bet you're working for them. You also look like you're investigating President Omega. That's not some monster created by the Book of Midnight's magic. That's Mandy. A woman who believed in justice and wanting to give back the world. Maybe all that's keeping you from being her is not letting that torment in. The pain of living, the pain of love, and the pain of loss."

Mandy looked down. "I'm sorry about your father, Gary."

I looked down then over my shoulder. "Yeah, well, everyone dies sometime."

"Including me."

"Not if I can help it," I said, softly. "I wanted to fix this."

"And if I don't want to be fixed? If I'm a new person now with a life much, much longer than the living Mandy's ever was?"

I turned around. "What *do* you want?"

Mandy was silent for a moment, then unexpectedly grabbed me by the shoulders and slammed me up against the wall. Her eyes turned an inhuman shade of blue and glowed. Her fangs extended and in that moment, she was once more the monster that inhabited my wife's body rather than my wife.

"What do you think!?" Mandy hissed. "I want you, dammit!"

I grabbed her by the side of her head and pressed my mouth against hers. She instantly dropped me as I bit her tongue hard enough to draw blood. She bit my tongue as well, the taste of fluids intermingling. I grabbed her by her behind and proceeded to slam her up against the side of the shower across the other end of the room.

Mandy let out a gasp of joy.

Mandy tore at my uniform, causing me to pull it back and reveal my naked form underneath. She clawed at my chest and bit my throat and wrist as well as the inner part of my thigh. She cut the side of her own throat, so I could drink of her blood in order to heal those wounds instantly.

Vampire bites were not like in the movies; they were painful and disfiguring, but the blood on the tips of her fangs gave the same narcotic effect as well as then some. Mandy wrapped her legs around me and what followed was a very destructive session of vampire sex.

Followed by another round.

By the time the two of us were done, much of Mandy's lair was completely trashed and only the fact I was partially invulnerable kept me from having killed myself. On the other hand, Mandy was snuggled up next to me on the floor with a surprisingly content look on her face. It was like the past. Too much like the past. We'd both changed greatly. I, not for the better. Still, if she had asked me in that moment to become a vampire like her, to abandon everything that I was, I would have said yes in a heartbeat. But then I might not love Mandy anymore. No, I needed to complete my mission for Death and avenge Ultragod. When I killed the parties responsible, then I would have her back.

I had to keep telling myself that.

"So, uh, how is everyone else?" I said, realizing I should have asked that question a few hours ago.

"They all escaped," Mandy said, a satisfied look on her face. "Ultragoddess generated a wormhole for some while the rest teleported out with the wizards. The media has branded them all traitors, though, and the Society has vowed to hunt down Ultragoddess' killer—which they continue to believe is you."

"That's good...kind of. What did you want to talk to us about?" I asked, finally ready to listen.

"I need your help, Gary," Mandy said, pressing her head against my shoulder.

"I take it has to do with President Omega's crazy-pants plan of crazy-pants?"

Mandy nodded, looking over to me. "It goes far beyond them, though, as well as you. President Omega is going to kill every single superhuman in the world."

I snorted. "Yeah, I heard the whole spiel from him while he monologued on a black and white television."

"I see I've missed quite a bit."

"Not that much, I've been kind of lost."

"I understand," Mandy said. "But we need to stop him now."

"Can't we just inform the Society? Fake Ultragod and all?"

"No," Mandy said. "Because in two days, he's going to release a nanite plague that will kill every superhuman in the world."

"We'll stop him."

"That's the problem, Gary. He's already succeeded. Twice."

Suddenly, things weren't quite so relaxing anymore. I also wondered if my actions here were betraying the other person I loved.

"*Yes*," Cloak said.

"Shut up," I muttered. "No one asked you."

Chapter Twenty

Where I Discover I'm John Connor

I pulled away from Mandy as we lay together on the bed. "Okay, you're going to have to pretend I'm a guy who doesn't understand what you mean by saying President Omega has already won twice. Is it a time-travel thing?"

"It's Omega the Time Ravager. It's always a time-travel thing."

I blinked. "Wow, that's a much cooler name than President Omega. He shouldn't have changed it."

"He only would have gotten Northern Kentucky to vote for him if he'd gone with that."

I smirked. "So, what happens?"

"He wins," Mandy said, taking an entirely cosmetic deep breath. "Out of all the supervillains in all of human history ranging from the beginning to the very end, he's the only one who successfully defeats them all. He destroys them all. The Society of Superheroes, the Tomorrow Society, and even his rivals in the Fraternity of Supervillains. The world's Supers are eradicated and he creates a new race of humanity to pour out as a plague of locusts on the rest of the universe until the very name 'humanity' becomes a foul word."

I sighed. "To think, there was a time when I thought *Warhammer 40K*'s humanity was actually kind of cool."

"Gary, this is no time for jokes."

"And yet when has that ever stopped me?"

Mandy paused. "Perhaps you're right. It is better to laugh than cry. I have shed enough bloody tears."

"Which is a song from the *Castlevania* games. You and your band did an awesome cover of it."

Mandy smiled. "The fact is, Gary, you're probably the only person in the world who President Omega fears."

"Excuse me? John Simms' Master with an American accent is afraid of me?"

"I actually have no idea what that reference means."

"Bad guy is afraid of me?" I offered, surprised at Mandy's lack of pop culture knowledge. Clearly, becoming one of the undead had affected her worse than I thought.

"Yes," Mandy said. "When he unleashes the Nanoplague on to Earth, it targets the Super gene. That string of DNA in every human being that, when active, bestows the ability to use magic or has a simple manifestation of magic in a single superpower. Millions die from mutants, mediums, psychics, and super-inventors to the famous names we've all come to know thanks to the crazy world we live in. The only people left are those who got their abilities from technology, training, and you."

I sighed. "Because I don't have an active supergene. Even with all the magic I use, it's all channeled through Cloak."

"Yes," Mandy said. "You organize what resistance there is and turn Omega's victory to ashes. For the next hundred years, you and your friends manage to thwart his efforts until Earth is finally destroyed by Entropicus for Omega's failure."

"Not really a heartwarming story of overcoming a dark apocalyptic future."

"I did say he wins. Though, I suppose it's better to say everyone loses under him."

"How do you know all this?" It wasn't like vampires and time-travel were particularly well known concepts.

"I lived it," Mandy said.

I blinked. "What now?"

"I lived through the destruction of the Earth—not once, but twice. The Nanoplague doesn't apparently recognize vampires as Supers due to the way the gene is mutated. Later, I was inoculated when he refined it. I learned a lot about controlling my dark side, helping others, and...falling in love with you again. When the world was about to be destroyed and you finally died, Death appeared to me and sent me mentally back in time."

"Oh that bitch," I said, growling.

Mandy blinked.

"Sorry," I said. "I don't normally use gendered language. I just am really pissed off right now. She knew this was going to happen."

"*Most certainly, being omniscient and all,*" Cloak muttered. "*Are you going to bring up Other Gary?*"

"Not yet." This all tracked with what Other Gary had said so far. "So, the heroes failed to stop Omega twice, huh?"

Mandy looked to one side. "It's not the first time I attempted to change history. I tried warning the Society of Superheroes and killing

Omega, and genuinely did my best to keep you out of danger. I didn't want to see you harmed."

"What happened?"

"He released the Nanoplague anyway, only he adjusted it to kill all non-Super humans. You managed to survive because of your recessive genes. Omega reincarnated himself as a machine and humanity became a war-torn mutated wasteland where the strong Supers dominated the weak while purging those deemed genetically inferior. You still rose up to be a major resistance fighter."

"Wow, future me is badass." I had to wonder if that's because my insane doppelganger was protecting me.

Mandy looked down. "And colder. In this reality, without Cindy, he proceeded to wipe out the ruling Supers of Earth and left nothing but the burning ruins of a world behind. Better humanity go extinct than super-powered Nazis rule it."

I paused. "The problem is, I agree with that sentiment."

Mandy closed her eyes. "Yeah, so do I. Either way, some force sent me back again."

I knew what that force was even if she didn't. Other Gary had lived up to his end of our 'bargain' even if I had no intention of letting him proceed with his plans. "How old are you?"

"You should never ask a girl her age."

"I just wanted to know how many birthday presents I owed you."

Mandy gazed into my eyes. "A lot. Centuries of coming to terms with worlds very different from this one and loving two very different Gary Karkofsky's."

"Can vampires love?"

"It seems so," Mandy said, unaware of the monster who had restored her soul. "Just not the way humans do. It's why the Gary's of both times loved others. Cindy in one reality, Gabrielle in another."

I took a deep breath. "I'm in love with Cindy."

"I know."

"You do?" I looked up. "Then why?"

"The heart wants what it wants."

Well, there was no use arguing with that logic. Stepping up out of the bed, I said, "Okay, well, I guess it's time to think about how to save the world. God, I hate this falling on me. I want to *conquer* the world, not save it."

"Doing the latter is necessary to achieve the former," Cloak pointed out.

"Details, details!" I snapped at Cloak.

Mandy wrapped her arms around her knees. "There's another option."

"Which is?"

"Go into space," Mandy said. "It's like *Star Trek* out there with millions of species, most of which look like human beings the various colors of Skittles. Earth, despite how much importance we put on it, just isn't that interesting. There are countless cultures, some better, some worse, just waiting to be visited, who don't have anything bad to say about humanity other than its superheroes keep interfering in state business. We could steal one of Doctor Aeon's hyperdrive-equipped rockets or the government's impounded spaceships to leave this place."

"So, you're telling me that after two tries, you just want to give up and let Omega conquer the Earth."

"Pretty much, yeah. Still a vampire."

I paused, thinking about that.

"*Gary...*" Cloak muttered.

"I'm not seriously considering that!" I snapped back at Cloak. "Well, I am, but not the way you're thinking. We should get one of those spaceships to get the people I care about into space and as a possible avenue for escape once we kill the president and stop his evil plan. I'm going to be a really unpopular guy after I kill him, even if I don't kill anyone who doesn't deserve it on the way to stopping him. It'd be nice to have a place where extradition treaties don't reach or black ops."

I envisioned myself finding a nice developing planet which hadn't yet reached the seventies, downloading a bunch of inventions of the galactic equivalent to the internet, settling down on said planet, and then proceeding to break the Prime Directive all to hell by selling them Google and bottled water to become the world's richest supervillain. Then I would parley my wealth into ruling that planet as their Benevolent Leader.

It wasn't Earth. Not even Australia.

But it was a plan.

"Gary, don't you think I've tried that?" Mandy said.

"Becoming a non-racist Ming the Merciless?" I said. "I dunno, you strike me more as a Princess Aura type."

"Gary, you had two-hundred years to try and figure out ways to defeat him. All you managed to do is stalemate him."

"I'll get the Venusians to invade."

"Ultradevil defeats them."

"I'll go to the forty-ninth century and kill him before he goes back in time."

"He already killed his younger self as a baby so he could live paradoxically."

I clenched my teeth. "I'll blow up the White House with a miniature-nuke."

"Emergency time-reverse microchip and teleportation unit."

"Voodoo curse!"

"Protection by a secret order of witches that deflect all magic worked against him."

I balled my fists together. "I'll figure something out."

"Gary, he's smarter than you!"

I closed my eyes. "Lots of people are smarter than me, Mandy. No one is a bigger magnificent bastard."

"That term was originally used to refer to General Rommel....who lost. Also, he was a big Nazi."

I opened my eyes and took a deep breath. "Mandy, and I do think of you as Mandy now, maybe not my Mandy but a Mandy, and one I care for—do you really think I would be the person you claim to love if you thought I would turn tail and abandon this planet? This planet full of Judaism, *Star Trek*, *Star Wars*, Captain Crunch Peanut Butter cereal, *The Lord of the Rings*, goth girls, *Mass Effect* 1 and 2 but not 3, *Monty Python and the Holy Grail*, dogs, tabletop role-playing games, sex, and *Blind Guardian*."

"Not *Game of Thrones*?"

I gave her a sad look. "It'll always be *A Song of Ice and Fire* to me. Also, it's kind of creepy how much Sophie Turner looks like a young Cindy. I sometimes wonder if HBO cloned her and put her duplicate onscreen."

"Uh-huh."

"Things may look tough, but it's always darkest before the dawn, because of solar orbiting patterns work that way, and they may take our lives but they'll never take our freedom. Which will still mean we're dead but that doesn't matter because friends, Romans, and countrymen will lend us their ears to always fight and never surrender like Corey Hart! Oh and something about Saint Crispin's Day!"

Mandy shook her head in disbelief.

I put my hands on my hips. "Okay, I'm not very good at making up speeches on the fly."

"No shit."

"Still, the sentiment remains." I stretched out my hand to her. "Will you help me save the world so we can rule it?"

Mandy smiled. "I'd be delighted."

It was the first real smile I'd seen from her in a long time.

"The third time's the charm, I suppose," I said, feeling the full weight of what we were about to embark on hitting me all at once.

Also, that we were still naked.

Well, at least no one was here to walk in on—

"Gary, you son of a bitch!" I heard Cindy's voice at the door.

God, are you screwing with me deliberately?

Seriously?

To quote Bill Watterson, someone is out to get you, Cloak said.

I turned around to see Cindy and Gabrielle, both in civilian clothes, who had somehow managed to track us down. Diabloman was present too, wearing a business suit and his luchador mask. Gabrielle and Diabloman mostly just looked embarrassed that they'd caught me naked with Mandy, but Cindy looked absolutely furious.

"How could you, Gary? With her!" Cindy snapped, turning and walking away from the door.

"Listen, she's not what you think she is." I got up and walked past the others, still not wearing any clothes.

"You can conjure me, you realize this, right?" Cloak said.

"I'd prefer something between us," I said back. "It doesn't make any sense but it's a preference."

"As you wish."

I cornered Cindy as she sat down on the mattress I woke up on. "I have never been madder at you! This is worse than that time you cheated on me with Christina Scabbia!"

I blinked. "That was actually Mandy, Cindy."

"Really?"

"Or the Black Witch," I said, trying to remember the details. "Admittedly, she's a lesbian, but we were both really drunk that night. It wouldn't be the first time people explored their bi-curious leani—err, all I remember is it was one of the Black Furies."

"The third one was Christina Scabbia's alternate universe counterpart from Htrae," Cindy pointed out.

"Really?" I said.

Cindy nodded. "That's what she claimed to me at the bar. Honestly, I think she was just an alien impersonating her. Our college was weird."

"Uh-huh."

"I mean, seriously. I was so furious with you after I found out. If I hadn't blown three other guys that week, I would have killed you."

"Sometimes, there are no words," Cloak said.

"You stay out of this," I whispered, wondering how I could make this right.

"It was me, by the way!" Mandy called from in her lair.

"Oh thank God," I said, breathing a sigh of relief.

"Do you love her?" Cindy asked, looking up, and I realized she was crying. "I could bear you never being with me because you were with your wife but not the...the..."

"I love you."

Cindy got up and kissed me.

"What is it about you?" Cloak muttered.

"I have no fucking idea," I thought back to him.

I kissed Cindy back and held her.

Chapter Twenty-One

Where We Draw Up Battle Plans

"So what does this mean?" Cindy said, burying her head into my shoulder.

"I don't know," I said, holding her. "I'll have the power to resurrect Mandy soon, but Other Mandy is in her body now and she's had centuries to become her own person. I can work around that, but—"

"Other Mandy?" Cindy interrupted. "Wow, she got to you fast."

"She's actually a two-hundred-year-old version of vampire Mandy who has survived two iterations of this universe by living through a century of dystopia, psychically travelling back in time to possess herself, then doing it again, failing to stop Omega again, then doing it again."

I wondered when all this insanity had become normal to me. It made me think I'd reached a milestone of some kind.

Cindy grasped the basics immediately. "So, *Quantum Leap* meets Terminator meets Dracula?"

"Yeah. I already blew my *Quantum Leap* reference, though, so I'm kicking myself. Either way, though, she's not the bad guy she used to be."

"And you learned this in between waking up and boning her?"

"Err...yes."

"Just checking."

I took a deep breath. "Whatever the case is, though, I'm willing to deal with the consequences, but actually willing to put that aside for once because of the imminent end of everything."

Cindy pulled away, still holding my hands. "How inconsiderate of the genocidal maniac to interfere with our personal crisis with his planned mass-murder on an epic scale."

"Just what I was thinking."

"Bloodthirsty Murder Skank isn't going to tear out my throat for interrupting her booty call, right?"

"Nope," Mandy said, causing both Cindy and me to jump as we noticed she was right beside us without having been noticed. It was one of the innate powers of vampires, at least from my research; they could sneak up on just about anything.

"Don't do that!" Cindy said, putting her hand over her heart. "At least play a scare chord or something."

Gabrielle and Diabloman, watching our entire encounter from the sidelines, looked amused.

Mandy, however, didn't take offense. "This may surprise you, Cindy, but I consider you a close friend. I think you'll feel the same toward me in time. As much as I love Gary I'm not threatened by you. Time is on my side as Mick Jagger would say and you've both been lengthy parts of my life."

"What, you intend to wait for me to die of old age?" Cindy said, not at all reassured by her statement.

"Pretty much, yeah," Mandy said, still smiling.

"And I'm back to hating you," Cindy said, glowering.

Mandy chuckled.

Cindy didn't look like she found it funny in the slightest.

Gabrielle, however, interrupted our little get-together. "As amusing as I find this—and believe me, I do find it amusing—we should get you some clothes on, Gary, and get back to thwarting the Nanoplague."

"You know about that?" Mandy asked.

Diabloman nodded. "*Si*. We took Colonel Disaster on our way out and interrogated him."

"Interrogated or tortured?" I asked.

"Interrogated," Gabrielle said, harshly. "My ultra-mesmerism got him to cough up a few details before he committed suicide with a cyanide pill, muttering something about being immortal."

"Pity," I said, not clarifying what I referred to.

"Colonel Disaster mentioned they were planning to unleash the Supers plague to wipe out millions of humans across the planet. He also said that the missiles that would carry the plague were being prepped in an underground base somewhere in Canada. It is part of the larger Project-Z Initiative."

"That creepy black ops thing where they cybernetically enhance Supers, brainwash them, and unleash them on the public?"

"*Si*," Diabloman said. "P.H.A.N.T.O.M was blamed for its existence but it appears to have been the United States all along."

"As much as I love blaming the Land of the Free and the Home of the Brave for everything wrong with the world since Reagan, I'm going to say that's probably more Omega's doing," I said, remembering Mandy's files. "The guy is the founder of P.H.A.N.T.O.M and has been manipulating events in this country since the early twentieth century. Who knows what kind of awful stuff he was involved in?"

"He's the reason the Beetles never got back together for a reunion tour after you saved John Lennon," Mandy said. "Nice job on that, by the way."

Man, I did a lot more time travel than I realized. All of it largely unrecorded too. My fans were going to be pissed.

"Time travel is fun," I said, going back to the bedroom to get dressed. I didn't have time to take a shower, which was a pity. I could really use one after all I'd been through. "Which is another reason this guy is ticking me off. I'm surprised he hasn't gone back in time to polish me off while I was on the toilet."

"Exposure to chronotonic energies is known to make interference with individual time-lines more difficult," Gabrielle said. "Given the amount of time-travelling my father did, it must have taken a massive amount of anti-time molecules to alter history enough to kill Ultragod. Given your little Hitler-killing jaunts, it's very likely you're immunized to retroactive assassination. I doubt there're enough anti-time molecules in the Multiverse to repeat what he did."

"What in the who now?" I asked.

Diabloman sighed. "Whenever time travel is involved, I find it best to just nod my head and go with it."

"Probably for the best," I admitted. "I don't really want to get into the who's and the what's of things. We'll need chalkboards and, graph paper, and we'd be here all day."

Cindy translated anyway. "She's saying Omega can't kill you anymore than you can kill him. Which is about our only advantage now."

"Another reason why we have to keep you safe, Gary," Mandy said.

"Yes, well, Danger is my middle name." I paused, walking out and restoring my costume around me. "It really is. My parents had issues. Since directly taking down President Omega isn't an option, we need to stop his Nanoplague. From what Mandy is saying, that's the key to the world going to hell."

"Unfortunately, we failed the previous two times," Mandy sighed. "Canada, it turns out, is a rather large place to search."

I paused a few seconds to think. "Okay, we got anything of the late Colonel Disaster?"

"His corpse is nearby," Diabloman said. "I could cut off his head and put it in a bowling bag."

"Or, maybe, cut some of his hair off?" I suggested. "Take his wallet or watch?"

"That would work too," Diabloman said.

"Cool," I said, remembering just how dangerous my henchmen were. "We take the head...err, samples, to my sister's safe house and have her talk to the late colonel's ghost. We find out where the base for Project-Z is and destroy the Nanoplague."

I wasn't happy about the prospect of involving my sister in all of this nonsense but given she was a Super and would be the first up against the wall when the revolution came; it seemed like a good time to break my policy of not involving family in superhero business.

"*That and she was almost bombed because of you,*" Cloak said. "*You know, when my family home was destroyed.*"

"*Are you still holding that against me?*" I thought back to him.

"*Yes, yes I am.*"

"*Bah, think of it as preventing me from defiling your home further.*"

"*There is that.*"

I wanted to tell everyone about Other Gary and his potential danger to everything. That a psychotic version of me from a dead universe was the one responsible for Gabrielle's dad's death and was serving as the quality control expert forcing Omega to read the Evil Overlord's List. I couldn't, though, because I didn't quite believe it myself. I didn't want to admit something of me, no matter how distantly removed, was responsible for all of this suffering.

Even if it had brought Mandy back to me.

And she felt like Mandy.

I was so confused.

"Your plan won't stop President Omega," Mandy said, bringing my attention back to the subject at hand. "It'll only slow him down."

"That's better than any other plan I've heard today," Gabrielle said, putting her hands on her hips. "Our situation is pretty grim. I've checked on the Society of Superheroes and they're all completely brainwashed now. They just announced a general kill order for Gary, me, and the other 'criminals' who helped me at the hospital."

"A general kill order?" I said, my attention once more on our situation. "You didn't kill Tom Terror and he was...Tom Terror!"

"It's only been used for alien warlords, gods, demons, undead, and robots."

Cindy looked at Gabrielle. "Oh, so it's a *racist* order."

The Afro-Hispanic Gabrielle raised an eyebrow.

"Okay, that was funnier in my head," Cindy said.

"Yeah," Gabrielle said.

"Shutting up now." Cindy made a zip-it gesture over her mouth.

"Good idea," Gabrielle said. "So, you three finish up your romantic whatzits and we'll get going to find out where the people we have to blow up are."

Gabrielle had regained much of her normal vigor. She had a target now, someone on whom she could focus all of the rage she'd felt from her father's murder. I understood that emotion all too well.

Hate, like grief, could keep you going a very long time.

Screw Jedi ethics.

"We'll discuss this," Cindy said. "At great length, don't you worry. We'll just do it when the world isn't ending."

"Oh, then it'll never happen," Mandy said. "The world is always ending."

"I personally don't even need to know what there is to discuss," Gabrielle said. "I'm in an open relationship with Jim Bernstein the Golden Scarab in this time period and Ultramind X in the forty-ninth century. It works well for us."

"Not with her," Cindy said, her voice low.

"I'm not giving up on my husband," Mandy said.

"He's not your—" Cindy started to say.

"Don't I get a say in this?" I asked.

"*No*," Cindy and Mandy said at once.

Diabloman pointed at my chest. "This will end in tears, mark my words. It is why I believe in the traditional marriage."

"This is all ridiculous," I muttered, my voice low. "I'm sorry I'm hurting you. I shouldn't have—"

"Gary—" Cindy started to say.

"Please."

I couldn't say if Cindy was more angry or concerned by her next look. Then again, I was being an asshole, so what else could I say?

"Sure," Cindy muttered. "Whatever you say."

I turned around and walked over to get into the boat docked at the side of Mandy's lair, uninterested in any further discussion. It felt like I was a cosmic chew toy, being gnawed on by God's dog. I'd been happy with Mandy, and if I could trade everything to get her back, I would. That just didn't seem to be an option, though, no matter how things progressed. I didn't want to be caught in some kind of crazy Archie love triangle (Veronica, by the way, always Veronica). I just wanted to be with one person I could love with all my heart and soul.

Forever.

"*Susan*," Cloak said.

"What?" I said, starting the boat.

Everyone in the group exchanged a look and reluctantly got on board. The boat pulled out seconds later, heading down the sewer tunnels to Lake Falconcrest. We could get pretty close to the woods where Kerri was staying with Lisa. I decided to focus on that, even though I already knew the answer to the question of whether I would be with Cindy or the faux Mandy if both would have me.

I shouldn't be with anyone.

"My wife's name was Susan," Cloak said. *"I don't think I've ever told you about her."*

"No, you didn't," I muttered.

"It's not exactly a subject I'm very comfortable talking about. You know the basics of the story. I was married to a woman, we had a young son, and they were gunned down in a drive-by shooting from the local mobsters. I was a mere cop then, influential because of my family but still just trying to make the city a better place one house at a time. Their deaths inspired me to use the family's wealth to study the occult arts, found the Brotherhood of Infamy, and do some terribly insipid things before my brother convinced me to do something useful with my powers."

"Believe me," I said. "I sympathize."

"I know you do. I've felt helpless throughout your year of hell because I know there's absolutely nothing anyone can say or do to make your kind of pain better. Our kind of pain. I did the exact same thing as you, seeking answers in the occult and mad science to try to bring back my loved ones. It drove me a little bit insane."

"You tried to destroy the world."

*"Okay, it drove me **a lot** insane."*

"How did you eventually get over it?" I said, ignoring the fact that I was talking aloud. Thankfully, everyone was used to it by now.

"Over it?" Cloak said, surprised I'd even ask. *"I didn't. There were a couple of women thereafter who were special to me but I let my love for Susan poison my relationship with them. I died alone, except for my brother, content in trying to help other people deal with their pain because I never could resolve my own."*

"Sounds like it wasn't your love for Susan driving you but your guilt."

"Don't try to psychoanalyze me, Gary," Cloak said. *"I've been analyzed by the best, even if you're right."*

"What was Susan like?"

"She was a wonderful woman. Funny and courageous. She worked at the local newspaper as an investigative reporter."

"Isn't that a bit cliché?"

"There were only so many professions back then for women to be in regular contact with people hanging around crime scenes."

"Ah."

"There were times, though, I made connections with people who might have made me enjoy the world again as a living man rather than a walking shadow. Queen Isis the Invincible, a stage magician I knew as a Marianne Nassar who was vibrant and joyful. Lady Larceny, the Queen of Crime who might have been willing to set aside that if I could set aside my pain. Madame Molotov the Communist Agent, Princess Eternia of the Light Dimension and Daughter of Entropicus, even Guinevere and I might have had a chance if only I'd let us."

"It's starting to sound like bragging now."

"The thing is, Gary that we are all searching for someone to ease the inherent loneliness of being human. We create rules about romance, fidelity, and love because we're afraid without them that we're even more likely to be hurt. I pushed aside all of that potential comfort because I didn't want to dishonor the memory of the life I shared with my wife."

"Admirable."

"The dead make no judgments. They ask for nothing. Those who return from it are forever changed but all agree—the petty habits and desires of humans are of little consequence to the greater universe. You, as Death's Chosen, should know this."

"Death is curable in this world."

"Perhaps," Cloak said. "But when I finally spoke to my wife after I became a hero, the thing I learned was she'd rather I have been happy than torture myself with her image. I also tortured those I had come to love and call friend out of the sake of immortalizing my grief. You love Cindy. Don't screw that up."

I closed my eyes as we hit the open water. "I do."

Chapter Twenty-Two

The Long Creepy Boat Ride

There was a long silence as the speedboat passed Lake Falconcrest's black waters. It was the sixth Great Lake and was the reason Falconcrest City had grown to become the third largest city in America as well as the heart of Michigan.

It was also cold, perpetually gloomy, and filled with all manner of islands used by everyone from smugglers to supervillains. The city was no stranger to ghost stories, but the worst were always about the islands. My grandfather used to tell me a particularly eerie one about a haunted leper colony that had been murdered by Falconcrest City's settlers so they could steal the lepers' gold. These lepers then rose from the grave a century later to wreak their revenge on the murderers' descendants. Only as an adult did I realize he'd stolen the premise from John Carpenter's *The Fog*.

Today, though, I could believe it.

Although it was mid-afternoon, storm clouds had rolled in, and the lake's surface was covered in a massive cloud that was almost assuredly unnatural. Unnatural and my hometown went together like peanut butter and jelly, though, so I didn't pay much attention to it. There was very little light and I was tempted to turn on the speedboat's spotlights before deciding it was better to move along unnoticed.

Gabrielle and Mandy sat on one side of the speedboat's side while Diabloman and Cindy sat on the other. It was an awkward situation and I had no one to blame but myself. The worst part was, as much as I loved Cindy, I didn't entirely regret doing what I'd done. There was a part of me, a deeply buried part at least, which believed Mandy was somehow inside the vampire walking around. Certainly, she acted a hell of a lot more like my wife than she had yesterday but even that just made it more confusing.

No, I'd made my choice.

Forward.

Not back.

I just hope Cindy could forgive me.

"So how is everyone else?" I asked, desperate to break the silence I'd unwittingly imposed. "Did anyone, uh, die?"

"Aside from Colonel Disaster, no," Diabloman said, looking up to me. "We had some close calls with the Extreme's complete disregard for life but the Black Witch was extremely good at protecting us with her spells. Angel Eyes healed those individuals who suffered grievous injuries as well."

"Everyone was good to me, coming to rescue me like that."

"Nicky and the Fruitbat expect to be paid in five figures. Your assets seized or not."

"I covered that up, though," I said. "Hid the money with Kerri who gets freaked out by parking tickets."

"It may surprise you but President Omega doesn't seem to mind the occasional bit of illegality," Diabloman said. "I'm sorry, Gary, but you're flat broke."

I sighed. "Oh well. It's not like I didn't keep funds hidden away."

"I checked, those are gone too."

"Well...crap."

Cindy gave a half-chuckle. "It's okay, Gary. You can sleep on my couch until we get you sanitized and checked for Bloodsucking Murder Skank-related STDs."

"I keep forgetting you really don't like me now," Mandy said. "I'm not the woman you remember."

"That's the problem," Cindy said. "You're not who I remember. Only three people have done anything for me in my entire life. Not my parents, not my pimp, not my teachers in school, not the guys and girls I've hooked up with. I've had two friends since the time I was in diapers, Gabrielle and Gary. Mandy, however, gave her life for me, and I'm not going to forget that. You...make a mockery of her sacrifice."

Mandy looked down. "You're right, I do."

Cindy's eyes widened.

"I can't explain all of the amazing things I've seen in the past two centuries," Mandy said, her voice sad and wistful. "That as terrible as the world becomes—and it will be terrible—it was bearable because of the family around me. I know so many people who you may never get to meet, may never even be born, because of what we're doing here. Even so, they were all willing to give their lives to make the world never have to experience what it does. You're a part of that, Cindy. You're better than you think you are and deserve a family."

Cindy stared at her. "That would mean a great deal more coming from someone with a pulse."

"Hey," I said, offended. "No bias against the dead."

"Sorry, Cloak," Cindy said. "You're totally the person I'm thinking of when I say some of my best friends are dead."

"Have you ever actually heard Cloak speak?" Gabrielle said.

"Nope," Cindy said. "But he's got Gary's back and that's enough."

"*I'm oddly touched*," Cloak said.

"Could someone turn on the radio?" Diabloman said. "Family drama is unsettling to me."

"Sure," I said, switching it on. The tail end of Sabaton's *Carolus Rex* was playing before it switched to an emergency broadcast. "Hail to the Chief" started playing and I got a bad feeling I was about to listen to a message from the president.

I was right.

President Omega spoke with an amused, self-satisfied tone. "My fellow Americans, you are perhaps wondering why in the past hour hordes of giant robots have seized control of every major city in America, why I have herded Congress to disintegration booths, and why I have outlawed the letter K. Actually, you're probably not wondering why this is because I have asserted my mind-control satellites over much of the United States so you're all drooling idiots now believing I'm just the best person on Earth."

In the sky above, I heard the sound of whooshing rocket boosters and saw the shadow of hundreds of humanoid-shaped Exterminator warbots sailing through the air to Falconcrest City.

"That's not good," I said, making sure to move myself further into the fog. I used a combination of my abilities to make it dense and thicker around our boat until we were all but invisible.

President Omega continued. "In the words of General Haig: I am in control. I control the horizontal and the vertical, and if this were television, I would be screwing with your reception right now just to show that I could. Already, time-portals are opening across the planet, unleashing hordes of my forth-ninth century death machines to secure the other nations of Earth. Very little of which will matter as soon as the rest of my satellites come online. The Society of Superheroes will not help you because they're completely trapped in a pleasant dream where everything is a fine and I'm their beloved leader. You may ask why I'm telling you all of this, my mouth-breathing audience, and the answer is because some of you will be immune to my mind-control satellites. Too strong-willed, magically protected, or too out-of-direct-line-of-fire to be brainwashed. You, my free-thinking friends, are why I do this. Solely so I can rejoice in your appreciation of how utterly fucked you are."

Cindy frowned. "Okay, now he's just being a dick."

"Imagine dealing with this for centuries," Mandy muttered, rolling her eyes. "It gets worse."

"How?" I asked, immediately wishing I hadn't tempted fate.

"Very soon I am going to cleanse this planet of aliens, sentient machines, Supers, straight-A students, martial artists, cooking show hosts, and people who could possibly pose a threat to me. Some of you may think I'm motivated by racism or prejudice. No, truth be told, I hate you all. I intend to make my reign a living hell for all of you until you beg for death and I have built an unstoppable army from your children's corpses. But I digress. I have a special message for Gary Karkofsky, Cindy Wakowski, Gabrielle Anders, that Mexican Satanist I forget the name of—"

"Hey!" Diabloman said. "At least remember the name."

"And Mandy," President Omega added the last bit with a little chuckle at the end. "I am coming for you." The words hung in the air before his tone became chipper and upbeat. "Now onto a collection of my top 100 favorite hits from the past ten-thousand years. Starting with Jefferson Starship's *We Built This City*!"

I blinked and turned off the radio.

"Is it wrong I'm starting to like this guy's style?" I suggested.

No one found it funny.

"Tough crowd," I muttered, going back to driving the boat.

"Seriously, dude needs therapy," Cindy said, "and that's me saying that. What are the mental health facilities like in the forty-ninth century?"

"Therapy in the future has a 99.999999 percent success rate for producing amiable decent pacifists," Gabrielle said. "So you can't blame the system really for one outlier."

She was being sarcastic.

Mostly.

"How much time do we have?" I asked. If we prevented the Nanoplague, would we still end up having a world that was completely wrecked?

Mandy said, "By my reckoning, a little under forty hours. President Omega isn't exactly big on restraint—"

"Oh, I hadn't noticed!" I said, faking shock.

"Don't be a smartass," Mandy said. "As soon as he gets the weapons ready and loaded, he's going to launch them."

"How the fuck did this guy impersonate someone rationale for decades?" Cindy said.

"Robots," Mandy said. "Human Duplicate Units to handle all of his politicking while he butchered people and destroyed lives."

Cindy blinked. "Okay. That's...that doesn't really speak well for our ability to find and deal with infiltrators."

"He always turned back time whenever exposed."

"Damn save-scumming," Cindy muttered. "Takes the fun out of the game."

"Well, let's work quickly," I said. "Diabloman, did you get my mother to safety?"

"And did you not get my mother out?" Cindy asked. "Because, if you didn't, I'll be very grateful."

Diabloman sighed. "My teams have been prepared to get all of our loved ones to safety in the event of Operation: Kingslayer. I know that some of my teams were intercepted, though, and everyone involved was killed. I don't know if the people who were being protected were harmed in any way. I also haven't been able to get in contact with my wife and daughter, though I have always been circumspect about their location so it is unlikely they are in any danger. At least, that is what I pray, to whatever god or demon will listen."

Wow.

It made me wonder what I could possibly say to make things better. Diabloman was, despite his past, the single most devoted family man I'd ever known. His wife and daughter had brought him back from the brink of suicide when his powers turned against him. They'd given him a reason to live when he was ready to lie down and die in guilt over his previous actions. If his family was gone then Diabloman as I knew him would end.

I whispered. "God, if you owe me any favors, look after him. Even if he does work for the opposition."

I got no response. Only one god listened to me and I hadn't yet delivered Ultragod's killer to her.

"They'll be all right, D." I didn't know if it was true, but sometimes a comforting lie was better than the truth.

"I believe so," Diabloman said. "If not, then I will kill Omega and there will be one final act to ask from you, Boss."

I had no doubt what that would be. "Yeah, well, let's hope it doesn't come to that."

Seconds later, the fog parted and I slowed down the speedboat since we were approaching the island on which Diabloman had set up his safe house. We'd been extra careful in renting this one out, not using any known associates or money transfers, with no visits that could be tracked.

It was also a cellphone and internet dead zone thanks to some weird magnetic stuff which, again, was filed under "Falconcrest City weird stuff."

The island itself didn't even look like the kind of place you'd want to rent out to anyone, with its tall pine trees and soft cover of frost—in the middle of summer. There was only a single roof-covered pier leading up to a dirt road, and I couldn't help but think my sister would be happy here while Lisa would be willing murder me for my satellite phone. Which I didn't have— otherwise, the government would have tracked me down and killed me with a missile by now.

"What did you say this place was called again?"

"Mist Island," Diabloman said.

"Huh, well let's hope Sirrus and Achenar aren't around."

Not a peep from anyone.

"*Myst*? The steampunk magic book game? There's no real graphics but a bunch of still pictures that...you know, never mind, it's a dated reference."

"They can't all be winners, Gary," Cindy said.

"Yeah."

We docked the boat on the side of Mist Island before setting out. Gabrielle zipped up to do a search of the island from the air, flying very low, and so far didn't seem to think anything was wrong. Which was good. Still, I had a sense something was wrong.

As we started up the dirt road to the cabin, I hung back from the others, following up the rear and trying to make sense of all this. In the end, I realized I couldn't just leave them all ignorant of Other Gary's role. If my doppelganger really were me, then he would probably try to come after me through those I loved, and I wasn't about to let that happen. Even so, I needed them to be warned in case they had to take me out.

Putting my fingers in my mouth, I whistled. "Guys, come here a moment."

Mandy, Diabloman, and Cindy all turned their heads back to me.

"Yes?" Mandy said.

"It's time you learned who, exactly, killed Ultragod."

All of them stared.

I clasped my hands together. "Okay, this is going to be a long story."

"Your evil doppelganger murdered him and planned to frame you for it," Cindy said.

"Yeah." I did a double-take. "Wait, what?"

Chapter Twenty-Three

Last Minute Revelations

"What now?" I said, stunned that Cindy had already figured out the highly improbable series of events we were dealing with.

"I've been puzzling over what President Omega said during our meeting together and why he was so pissed at you," Cindy said, ignoring the fact everyone around her was completely gobsmacked. "He said a lot of this was your plan and that he was really going to enjoy killing you for how annoying you were."

"Do you just figured an evil(er) version of me was responsible?" I said, surprised she'd made that leap of logic.

"Not quite," Cindy continued. "When Ultradevil showed up, it started to make sense to me that there might be more doppelgangers out there. President Omega claimed he intended to nuke Falconcrest City but backed away at the last second, a most uncharacteristic behavior of him. That was soon followed by the arrival of the Extreme, one of which—"

"Resembled me," I said, genuinely impressed. "Honestly, I was a little surprised when we didn't have a mirror match. You think when your doppelganger arrives, you're supposed to fight. I mean, that's the way we always handled it in *Streetfighter 2* tournaments."

"I hated you always picked Chun-Li," Cindy muttered. "It's not your fault, Gary, it's his."

"Believe me, I know," I said. "Merciful Moses, people, I *liked* Ultragod. Sort of."

"I do not believe there is any force on Earth that could compel you to hurt the women you love," Diabloman said.

"Except being a complete dumbass," Cindy said, glaring at Mandy.

"That's not going to end anytime soon, is it?" Mandy asked.

"You think?" Cindy asked.

"How are we going to tell Ms. Gabrielle?" Diabloman asked, clearly wondering how my ex was going to react to such a horrifying revelation. She needed us right now, and I didn't want to take away some of her few friends in this trying time. I could never forgive someone for something like this, even if it wasn't their fault. Other Gary was me—a twisted reflection of me, but me nonetheless. It was like the *Infamous* series before it got ruined by the ending of the second game.

"How are we going to tell Gabrielle what?" Gabrielle said, flying down and landing beside us.

"Uh..." I muttered.

Cindy looked down at her feet.

Mandy stuck her hands in her pockets.

Diabloman said, "We're debating whether or not Gary has an evil doppelganger which might have killed Ultragod. In all likelihood, he does, and it's responsible. We are now thinking it's going to come and kill us."

Gabrielle blinked. "Really?"

"Thanks, D, really," I said, sighing. "I really needed that."

Gabrielle rolled her eyes. "Gary, I'm not going to blame you for the actions of your double. That's like blaming my father for Ultradevil's actions."

"You aren't?" I said, surprised.

"Nega-Goddess, Ultrademoness, Ultradummy, Evil Goddess—" Ultragoddess said.

"You have a lot of evil counterparts," I observed.

"Occupational hazard," Gabrielle said.

"Ultranatrix," Cindy said.

"We don't talk about her," Gabrielle said.

"What if it's like, Gary from a fake past gone insane with grief and plotting against all his former loved ones?" Cindy asked.

"Okay, someone told you about this," I muttered.

"No, I'm just a lucky guesser!" Cindy raised her hands in fake surrender. "Honest!"

"Then I'd be mad," Gabrielle said, not reacting at all. "The island is free from any reinforcements. There're also four life-signs inside the house."

"That would be Fruitbat and Nicky Tesla," Diabloman said. "They will be guarding your sibling and niece."

"Well, let's go talk to them," I said, continuing up the dirt road. "I'm honestly sick of this conversation."

Walking up the dirt road, I heard the earth crunch beneath my feet as the cabin eventually came into view. "Cabin" was actually a poor term for it because it looked more like someone had constructed a mansion from logs. It was two stories tall and possessed of its own shack-sized generator, and all of the windows had thick curtains over them.

The canopy of trees noticeably blocked any direct view of us or our path. I was put in mind of the building Osama Bin Laden was hiding in before Super Agent X put a bullet in his head. There was no television inside or signals, but the place had a bomb shelter underneath stocked with decades of movies, books, and material to keep one's mind occupied.

It was also a place that had been stocked with an equivalent amount of supplies. If we wanted to leave the speedboat under the pier's roof, we could probably stay here unmolested for however long we wanted. We could get Diabloman's family here, cover the place in a spell to disguise it, and let the world take care of itself. An alternative to leaving for space or trying to save the world. A few minutes ago, I wouldn't have contemplated something similar to Mandy's plan, but that was before I'd discovered I'd potentially killed the world's greatest hero. Who knew what I was capable of now.

"*You're not going to abandon humanity*," Cloak said.

"It's never about humanity," I said, sighing. "That's one of the things you've never learned. It's about the people I care about. No more, no less."

"*I don't believe that.*"

"Believe what you want," I said. "The world sucks, and if it was better, then people like Omega wouldn't be in charge. Hell, we wouldn't need people like Gabrielle and the Society to take care of things because we'd all be pitching in together. Instead, superheroes are those poor bastards bailing out a sinking lifeboat while the majority of passengers are just sitting on their asses watching."

We reached the front door and I turned the doorknob.

It was unlocked.

That wasn't a good sign.

As the door creaked open, I saw the interior. The first thing I noticed was blood on the ground. A lot of blood. Nicky Tesla and the Fruitbat were lying on the ground with their throats slit and their eyes rolled back into their heads. I hadn't known the Fruitbat long, but he was one of my people, and that pissed me off.

Nicky, by contrast, filled me with a sense of surprise. I wondered about all of her relatives I'd have to contact now since she'd come from a large family of German-American scientists, people who had fled to the United States to escape persecution from P.H.A.N.T.O.M during World War 2. I once argued it would have been better to call herself Lady Einstein since Tesla had been Croatian, but she'd hit me with a bathroom-ray and told me to piss off. The rest of the room made me feel even worse.

Sitting on the leather couch to the right of the room, their arms and legs bound together with Ultra-Force manacles, were Kerri and Lisa. Kerri was looking remarkably sedate despite the atmosphere, perhaps because she wasn't particularly afraid of death. Lisa, by contrast, looked pissed off, and if not for the fact that she needed her hands to use her powers, she would have been blasting away at her jailer—suicidal move or not.

There were two other occupants in the chamber. The first was, of course, Ultradevil. His right eye was covered in an eye patch from where Ultragoddess had either smashed it in or straight up knocked it out. His face was a bruised mess, with several scars that had been sewed up with super-steel thread and staples. From the way he carried himself, I suspected he also had taped ribs underneath the red and black version of the Ultragod costume he'd cloaked himself with. Ultradevil wasn't in charge, though. I could tell by the way his eyes were focused on the man beside him, sitting in a rocking chair over the corpses.

"Hello, Ga—" Other Gary didn't get a chance to say anything else because I was blasting him with a column of flames so powerful they should have incinerated him outright, but instead smashed him through the wall behind him, the room behind that, and out its window into the forest beyond. I then turned insubstantial and ran through a surprised Ultradevil, going after him. Pulling out my pistols, I immediately started firing them over and over again.

I didn't care what my doppelganger had to say. He'd murdered two of my people, one a friend, as well as endangered my family. Keith's daughter, my niece. My sister. He'd murdered Ultragod. I honestly didn't care at this point. Fuck, he was responsible for two centuries of Mandy living through a dystopian future. All I knew was I wanted to kill the man, torch his remains, and scatter the ashes.

That was when he blasted me with a freezing ray of ice that hit me despite my intangibility. I felt like I was being burned. Dropping my guns, I struck back with my fire powers, and the two of us started dueling with the air around us, becoming a massive collection of steam. He had gotten up, a dozen bullet holes in his chest healing before my eyes, and was now pouring out an attack of great mystical potency. It was the kind of chilling ray that would freeze people in blocks of ice, and proved to be a lot more lethal than television would have you believe.

"Not today," I grunted, channeling the same white-hot rage that had created the first column of fire and gradually pushing back Other Gary's assault. The frost against my skin was painful, but it didn't distract me from my singular desire to put my doppelganger in the ground. Slowly but surely, I forced back his icy attack and the flames came within inches of his hands. I was going to kill him.

I was stronger.

Then a gigantic pillar of ice shot up from the ground under my feet, sending me flying through the air before I landed with a thud. Other Gary hadn't been beaten back; he'd just been diverting his power for something else. Above my head, I saw Gabrielle and Ultradevil battling it out again.

This time, despite his injuries, Ultradevil seemed to have the advantage as I saw two Ultra-Force doppelgangers joining the fight alongside him. It took me a second to realize they were ghosts of dead Ultra-Family members. Copies of Ultragod and Ultragodling. My doppelganger had summoned Gabrielle's dead father and half-brother to fight against her.

"Bastard," I muttered, climbing to my feet. "What the hell is wrong with you?"

"A lot of things," Other Gary said. "I told you I was going to kill you. I hope you enjoyed your time with your wife. It was the final cigarette before your execution."

"I don't smoke!" I said, blasting at him again.

Again, Other Gary effortlessly knocked away the blast. "Which is another thing I hate about this timeline."

"Smoking kills!" I said, too angry to give any decent rejoinders.

"Oh shut up!" Other Gary shouted back, meeting me blow for blow.

Diabloman, Cindy, and Mandy ran out to join the fight against my doppelganger. Lisa, much to my irritation, was present as well, while Kerri hung back. Other Gary didn't pay them any attention and made a half-hearted circle with his hand. Ghosts of my enemies: the Ice Cream Man, the Typewriter, Ganglord Gorilla, and even Sunlight appeared. They promptly charged my henchmen and family, leaving me alone with my duplicate.

"Stay the hell away from my family!" I said, picking my pistols up off the ground and unloading with them.

All of Other Gary's bullet wounds had healed by this point, and each of the bullets I fired struck a piece of ice he conjured in the air. The ice pieces exploded one by one in rapid succession, creating dozens of sparkling detonations in the air without my doppelganger even looking like he was exerting himself.

"I'm sorry," Other Gary said. "I can't do that."

"Why the hell not!?" I shouted, realizing that my duplicate had access to powers way, way above my level.

Maybe even Nightwalker levels.

Other Gary let out a sigh. "Because, Gary, I've come too far and done too much to ever stop now. You need to die, and I'm sorry, but I'm going to have to kill your Mandy as well along with all of your friends. So sorry."

That was when I felt him reach out and grab my throat with his mind.

He'd mastered the Darth Vader choke trick.

Chapter Twenty-Four

Mirror Match

"Asshole," I choked out, clutching my throat and gasping for air.

I had never been more furious. I wanted to take my doppelganger by the throat and strangle him to death with my bare hands. Everything around me seemed to become less real as I focused on that single thought: survive.

I wasn't much of a magician. In fact, I was a really awful one. In Harry Potter terms, I was one notch above a Squib, but I had a lot of anger to fuel sorcery, and nothing was more powerful than anger. Giving into the proverbial dark side, I pushed back against my doppelganger's attack with all of my might and telekinetically forced oxygen into my lungs before knocking him back three steps. It took just about everything I had, but it meant I wasn't out of the fight.

Not yet.

"You stand in the way of a superior age's restoration," Other Gary said, shaking his head. He clearly hadn't expected me to push him back.

"Yeah yeah," I said, breathing out once more. "You're from a shiny happy utopia. Except, of course, Mandy died in your reality. So maybe it's not as nice and friendly as you remember. I understand your pain, literally I do, but how the hell does that justify any of this?"

Other Gary closed his eyes. "I tried to fix this world, I really did. I tried to be happy for you and Mandy. But you were ruining the life you were meant to live, just like everyone else in this stinking timeline is a perversion of what should be. You weren't happy being a normal man, you wanted to be a supervillain. A *supervillain* for fudge's sake."

Apparently, there wasn't any swearing on Pre-Catastrophe Earth.

Other Gary continued. "I traveled through time, back and forth, looking for solutions, but the answers were always the same. Superheroes always served as agents of the status quo. They propped up conservative corrupt regimes that deserved to be brought down by reform or revolution. They focused all of their attention on stopping supervillains instead, even when they were right. Then Mandy died, saving a friend heroically, but you brought her back as a twisted parody of herself—"

"Screw you, psycho!" Mandy said, throwing the ghost of Sunlight through a tree where it splattered into ectoplasm.

Other Gary sighed. "I knew what I had to do. I am going to *fix this*."

Hearing him speak like that, I burst out laughing.

"What?" Other Gary said.

"You actually have no idea what you're doing, do you?" I said. "I've said those words before and I know they're spoken when you're out of ideas."

"I know exactly what I'm doing, thank you. I eliminated Ultragod, I convinced Omega to ally with Ultradevil, I formulated the plan that will save us all."

"This entire plot is a rehash of what the Brotherhood of Infamy tried to do and what Diabloman *did* do. You're so burned out on your own worthlessness, you can't even come up with an original plan for world domination."

Other Gary clenched his teeth. "That is *not* what is happening here."

I stared at him, my voice dripping with venom. "If you're anything like me, you spent your entire life defining yourself through others. Keith, Mandy, and everyone else. Which is a good thing because they gave you strength, but they were gone you didn't know what the hell to do with yourself. You couldn't join the dating scene, adopt a kid, or anything worthwhile. You decided to stew in your own misery instead. Mandy has been dead for a year and I never became the psycho you did. I've also lived with this crappy world my entire life. Sometimes, I even make it better, and I was never tempted to murder any of my loved one's parents!"

"You little *punk*."

"Not since high school," I said, disgusted with my doppelganger. "You know what's really sad? Mandy and I would have *welcomed* you into our home. You didn't have to be alone. We could have been superbuddies. We could have worked out a way to get your Mandy back or, God forbid, let you die so you could be with her? This is a cosmic temper tantrum and it is the most pathetic thing I have ever seen. You can tell a supervillain by the quality of their henchmen, and Omega as well as Ultradevil? Big on power, short on brains. You, Other Gary, suck."

Other Gary trembled in rage.

It was time for the crowning moment of glory to my hastily-concocted plan. "And for the piece de la resistance, the fact you can summon ghosts means *I* can summon ghosts too."

"*Gary, what are you doing?*" Cloak asked.

"Something really stupid," I said.

"*I see*," Cloak said.

"Other Mandy," I said simply. "Please come forth."

I snapped my fingers for dramatic effect and hoped this worked, because otherwise I was screwed. We all were. Feeling a rush of power, a sense of strange satisfaction, and the presence of an otherworldly energy, I knew it had worked. I reached back to the universe that had been and found the soul of my doppelganger's lover.

I don't think I could have actually pulled it off on my own without Death's permission, but being her chosen came with its advantages, and knowing this guy was part of the conspiracy that killed Ultragod put into perspective just why Death was interested in avenging him. I imagined this Gary had once been in her good graces but was now officially on her shit list.

Reality folded in my mind, and I got a glimpse of the universe that Other Gary came from. It was from this reality that I drew forth Other Mandy's ghost. In the brief moment I touched her spirit, I felt a good and decent person who had been worth saving even if her world was a repressive den of conservatism. She appeared in front of Other Gary, still looking like she was in her twenties, with a headband, a long skirt, and a sweater that looked straight from a period-appropriate TV show.

"Hey tiger," Other Mandy said, her voice echoing as she spoke.

Other Gary proceeded to lose his shit. Covering his face, he turned away from her, tears in his eyes. "No! No! No! Please don't look at me! They've ruined me! This world! This place! I'm sorry, I'm sorry!"

"Not as much as you're going to be," I said, my voice dull.

I then lifted up a single pistol and shot him through Other Mandy's ghost.

Right through the eyes.

Other Mandy's ghost vanished.

I then shot him again.

And again.

And again.

After about the sixth shot to the head, he stopped regenerating and all of the ghosts around the forest vanished.

Other Gary was dead.

"Yay," I said, my voice empty. I'd killed a lot of supervillains and antiheroes in my time, but this is the first time I felt bad about it.

What a waste.

"May he find peace in whatever afterlife awaits him," Cloak said. *"The Primals watch over and keep him."*

"I don't care what happens to him," I said, looking away. "He endangered my family. Doppelganger or not."

It felt hollow, though.

My introspection was interrupted by Gabrielle being slammed into the ground behind me at two hundred miles per hour. It generated an impact crater eight feet in every direction and threw burning dirt in the air. Defeating Other Gary had destroyed the other Ultra-Force ghosts, but it had still weakened her enough that Ultradevil had been able to rally around her. He looked about ready to collapse, though, standing above her, and Gabrielle didn't look completely out of it.

"Fools," Ultradevil said, between heavy breaths. "Do you really think killing Merciful is going to stop anything? He was *always* going to die. We were going to kill him after he killed you. We barely will lose any necromantic power from his death. He didn't use Omega and me. We used him, and now there is one less place to divide the Earth among our triumvirate. The Society of Superheroes may have overthrown my reign on Htrae, but I will—"

Ultradevil didn't have time to say anything else because Lisa unleashed a sparkling collection of fireworks-like energy blasts in his face. The blast blinded him and sent him back a few paces toward me.

I lifted up my gun behind his head and pulled the trigger. The hellfire bullet passed out the front of his temple and he fell face-forward into the ground beside Ultragoddess. Gabrielle was already getting up by this point and just barely managed to pull her cape out of the way before Ultradevil landed on it.

"Dodge this?" Cloak suggested.

I tossed my gun on the ground, not at all interested in it anymore. "Yeah, I'm not really in the mood for quips now."

Gabrielle looked down at Ultradevil. "I'm not a killer, Gary. I thought I might be but it turns out I don't have it in me. I won't lie to you, though, I'm not at all sorry these people are dead. Both of them."

"No judgments from me," I said, looking over at Mandy. "Do you think we've changed the future?"

"I never saw Merciful in the future. Ultradevil's death is new too," Mandy said. "You weren't supposed to kill him for a few decades."

"Whee," I said, waving a dismissive hand. "Yay us. Maybe the Society of Superheroes will no longer be crazy and we can fix all this."

"Ultra-mesmerism doesn't work like that, I'm afraid," Ultragoddess said. "I might be able to reverse the process on them, but only one at a time, and we don't have time to try that on the Society's literal hundreds of members."

I called over to Kerri. "You okay?"

Kerri popped her head out from behind one of the cabin walls. "Oh, yes. Can we not do this again? Ever?"

"I'll try," I said.

"Super!" Kerri said.

"Lisa?" I asked.

Lisa punched the air. "That was awesome! Did you see that? I totally beat Ultragod! Err, Evil Ultragod! I'm like in the world-class now! Everyone in the world is going to know my superhero codename, which I've decided—"

"My niece is named Sparkler, by the way," I addressed everyone. "You know, the lamest of all fireworks."

"What!?" Lisa said.

"I like sparklers," Cindy said, plopping her butt on the ground. "Ugh. Do we still have to save the world?"

"I'm afraid so," I said. "This has just made it a great deal easier. I'm hoping, at least."

"I am not Sparkler!" Lisa shouted.

"You are totally Sparkler," Cindy said, looking over at her. "Diabloman."

"Sparkler indeed," Diabloman said, cracking his knuckles. "If you don't mind, Gary, could you check on my family?"

It was a grim prospect, but I nodded. "Sure."

"They're fine," came a female voice filled the air.

A whoosh of wind sent pine needles flying around us before we were joined by my boss and the person who dispatched me to solve Ultragod's murder.

Death.

Oh boy.

Chapter Twenty-Five

Where I Try to Pass the Buck

Death appeared in a goth punk outfit that would have been at home in Mandy's closet during the late nineties. Today she was wearing a black leather bustier, leather pants, and a pair of Doc Martens. She had blood-red hair, braids, and skin as white as porcelain. Her irises were a deep shade of yellow and she was sucking on a lollipop.

"Gary, why does Death look like a hotter version of you with black angel wings?" Cindy asked, positively drooling.

I looked over at Death, confused.

"Santa Muerte looks like my dead sister," Diabloman said, looking down. "Spellbinder deserved better than death at my hands."

"I see nothing," Mandy said, confused. "Nothing at all. Just hear a voice."

"Skeletal man with a scythe here," Gabrielle said. "Weird."

"Principal Withers?" Lisa said.

"Your relationship with the end of life determines how I appear," Death said. "Beloved, hated, or accepted."

"Hi!" Kerri waved. "Long time no see."

"Hello, Kerri." Death waved back. "My other favorite person in the whole world."

"Should I be bothered you love my family so much?" I asked, not sure how to react to that one.

Of course, right now I was on an emotional roller coaster. Merciful was dead, Ultradevil was dead, two of my henchmen were gone, my family was safe, the world was about to end, and we were still short the world's greatest superhero. I wasn't sure I could take much more of this.

"Don't be bothered I love the Karkofskys," Death said and sang the opening to *The Addams Family*.

"Okay, Death is quoting *The Addams Family* theme," Mandy said, shaking her head. "Now my unlife is complete."

"Life is strange when you're a time-traveling girl," Cindy said, taking a deep breath. "So this is Samael, huh? Nice to meet you. Please don't damn me horribly, unless Hell is actually kind of cool."

"Sorry, it's not."

"Dammit!" Cindy said. "Points for Chosen People?"

"Sure, why not," Death said, moving the lollipop to the other side of her mouth. "Congratulations on accomplishing two-thirds of your mission to avenge Ultragod."

"Is that why you're here?" I asked. With all the chaos, I'd almost forgotten about the deal I'd made with Death.

"*No you didn't,*" Cloak said.

"*You're right,*" I said back, telepathically. "*I've been thinking about bringing Mandy back only every other second.*"

"Yes," Death said. "I made a deal and I never back down from one."

There was an ominous tone to her voice that I wasn't entirely happy with. Then again, I had more or less blackmailed her into resurrecting Mandy. As I understood it, most of her minions reacted to her orders with "Yes, mistress" and "Absolutely, mistress." I was the first to take the time-honored Torah approach of arguing with God over every little important detail.

Still, I was surprised she was showing up now. "Don't I have to kill Omega first?"

"I have even odds you'll die horribly," Death said, surprising me. "So, I thought I'd be nice and give you your reward now. Besides, Merciful was the one who actually pulled the trigger."

I shot a glance over at Gabrielle, unsure how to react. Ultragoddess had always thought my being involved in her life would get me killed, but it turned out it had gotten her father killed instead. If Gary hadn't known all of her family's secrets, then there was no chance he would have caught Moses Anders off-guard like that.

"*Don't blame yourself,*" Cloak reassured me.

"Even though I myself am to blame?" I pointed out.

"*Err, yes,*" Cloak said. "*I think.*"

Gabrielle didn't comment on any of that, instead focusing on the fact that her father was avenged. "I wish I could say that made me feel better, but all I can think about is the millions of people who are going to die if we stop Omega. I don't suppose you could—"

"No," Death said, interrupting her plea for aid. "I exert unimaginable influence across a myriad of dimensions, but I only work through intermediaries by ancient decree. Billions of people across countless galaxies die every second, so the consequences of Omega exterminating the people of Earth don't matter from my perspective. They do, however, matter enough to those I care for to say I hope you succeed."

"Those you care for?" I asked.

"You're pals with the end-of-all-things." Death smiled. "Don't let it go to your head."

"Thanks." I sucked in my breath, ready to get this over with. "Well, you know what I want."

I was honestly surprised this was going to happen. I had been waiting for the other shoe to drop since my pact with Death had been struck. After the disaster in resurrecting her with *The Book of Midnight*, I'd fully expected the world to end before I managed to get Mandy back. It would be an awkward series of conversations, what to do about Cindy and all, but I didn't care. I loved Mandy and would have her back in my life. I loved Cindy too, and if Mandy wasn't all right with that, well, then at least she'd be safe. Still, I steeled myself, because it was almost too much to hope for that this was really going to happen.

"Yeah, about that." Death scratched the side of her head. It was an embarrassed gesture that looked inappropriate on someone so regal. "You do realize Mandy already has her soul back, right?"

"Yes," I said. "I know. I just didn't know if Other Gary was lying his ass off."

"What?" Mandy said. "I do?"

"He wasn't," Death said to me. "Your predecessor was driven mad by the destruction of his world, isolation, and self-hatred he felt over failing to protect his wife. He didn't allow himself to love again, and it rotted him from the inside until he wanted to lash out against everyone and everything. Even so, he was still capable of feeling, loving, and caring. Enough to try and give you back something he had suffered the loss of."

"He's still a dick," I said. "Also, one assuredly consigned to hell."

Death closed her eyes. "Hell is what he was living before. Now he will have to experience that forever."

"The Evil Gary gave you your soul back," Diabloman explained. "Then he sent you back in time twice as part of an elaborate scheme, but I suspect he couldn't kill you like he could the rest of the world. It seems simple enough to me."

"Your definition of simple leaves a lot to be desired," I said, completely flabbergasted by that revelation.

"I'm me again?" Mandy said. "Not just a vampire who learned some impulse control?"

"You never wondered why you weren't a rampaging psychopath anymore?" Death asked Mandy, letting out an amused chuckle.

She was enjoying this far too much.

"No, I didn't wonder why I wasn't psychopathic anymore," Mandy said, furious. "I spent decades wondering if I was just a copy and you don't bother to—"

"Mandy, don't taunt the eldritch abomination," I said.

Death glared at me.

All of the grass underneath my feet died.

"Who is not in this room," I said, quickly correcting myself. "You should also be polite to this much-beloved force of nature who is our dear, dear friend."

Cindy proceeded to wrap Mandy in a hug and squeeze her, almost causing the vampiress to fall over. "I'm sorry I called you a Bloodsucking Murder Skank! I promise to only do that affectionately from now on."

I was too stunned to react and wished I could fall over. I couldn't even go over to hug my wife. "So this entire time you knew Mandy was going to come back with your weird time-reincarnation thing?"

"Yes," Death said. "I am omniscient."

"Then don't you know how the whole Omega thing is going to turn out?"

Death didn't even shrug. "Yes, but I don't want to be impolite and say I'm not going to tell you."

Point to her. "Then why make me go through all this song and dance? You could have just told me."

"Death is not kind," Death said, simply. "Also, you needed to undergo this painful journey to strengthen yourself for the coming struggle."

"This reminds me very much of Glinda telling Dorothy that the ruby slippers would take her home," Kerri said, walking up beside Lisa. "I always thought that was very rude of her."

"Glinda was totally in cahoots with the Wizard to take out the Wicked Witch of the West," I said, before deciding I was still not in the mood for quips. "Never mind, forget I said anything about that. Well, thank you anyway, Death. You've done something for me which I will be forever grateful for."

It was hard to be thankful under the circumstances. Still, I tried.

Death didn't depart, though. Instead, she just stood there as if judging me from head to toe. "I owe you a favor, or at least two-thirds of one, Gary. Anyone you want brought back to life or anyone you want killed."

I stared at her. "What's your game, Death?"

Death gave a half-smile. "No game. I just always pay my debts."

"Like a Lannister!" Cindy said, still hugging Mandy.

Mandy looked over at me, starting to look uncomfortable. "Gary, may I point out what happened last time you made a deal with a godlike super being? I became what I am."

"Death isn't like Zul-Barbas. We all meet her eventually." I took a deep breath. "Anyone?"

"Within reason," Death said.

"Like Gabrielle's father?" I asked, very careful about what she was saying.

"Or your brother," Death said, walking up to me and putting her arm around me. "Or your henchwoman back there, or even yourself, to give you an extra life, like in video games."

"Actually, they just do checkpoints and save files in video games now."

"Pity."

This wasn't something I'd expected and it made me wonder what exactly Death was planning. People bargained with death all the time, and for the most part, Death gave them exactly squat for their trouble. The fact she was an unreasonable, uncompromising, completely arbitrary force of nature was one of her more charming qualities. It didn't matter if you were rich, poor, a king, or a peasant—Death treated you all the same. The fact she was changing that policy should have, and did, scare the hell out of me. But I wasn't going to let this opportunity slip by either.

"My brother is happy where he is," I said, remembering my conversation with him. "How about Lancel Warren?"

Death removed her arm. "He still has to pay for his crimes."

"*Thank you, Gary,*" Cloak said, sounding touched. "*It's the thought that counts.*"

"I've never thought that statement made any sense," I said, looking over to Gabrielle. "What do you think?"

Gabrielle looked torn before making a decision that surprised us all. "You should use Death's power to kill Omega. We need to stop him, no matter the cost. Don't worry about my father."

"Wow, even I think that's cold," Cindy said.

Gabrielle didn't respond, just looked over at me.

I didn't look back, instead mulling the idea over in my head. "This isn't going to be a 'Monkey's Paw' situation where I make the death and they come back wrong? Because that sucked the first time."

"No funny business," Death said, making a little Star of David over her heart.

"You should bring back Ultragod," I said, finally making my decision.

"Really?" Gabrielle said, looking up. "Gary—"

"Are you sure?" Death asked, taking a step back. "What Merciful said wasn't entirely untrue. Ultragod does serve as a force that stifles change. Superheroes prop up the status quo and keep it from falling to chaos. It has been a long time since he was a champion for social justice and reform like his daughter is now. Gabrielle is entirely capable of taking up the mantle of the world's greatest hero, just as you have taken up the Nightwalker's role alongside your wife."

"Oh God forbid," I said, horrified at the idea. "I am entirely not doing that."

Death didn't react to that. "He has also earned his rest."

"Well, give him a choice of coming back or not," I said calmly. "The fact is that in my old pre-superhero life, Death was pretty damn permanent. You just had to suck it up and deal with it. People talk about the drama of life and maturity of dealing with tragedy, but I became a super-person to get away from all that. It was my escape into a world where things could be made better. It gives me a warm comforting feeling to believe this planet has someone like Ultragod looking out for it. Even if, you know, I intend to eventually take it from him."

Death nodded. "You realize if he turns down the offer of being resurrected; it will still cancel any debt I owe to you."

"Is he likely to?" I asked.

"He's been saving the world for a very long time," Death said, her voice low. "His wife passed away three months ago when her longevity treatments finally gave way."

I looked over at Gabrielle. "Your mom's dead?"

"I couldn't get in touch to tell," Gabrielle said. "We were keeping from the media while we sorted through things."

"I see."

"*Poor Polly,*" Cloak said. "*She never wore a cape but the world's greatest civil rights attorney was a hero in her own right.*"

It seemed a lot of the world's oldest stalwarts were passing away these days. Sunlight, Ultragod, Polly Pratchett, the Nightwalker, Ultragodling, and more. Getting Mandy back made the world a great deal brighter for me, but I wondered how darker it had to seem for the rest of us.

"*There will always be more heroes,*" Cloak said.

"Not the same," I said, taking a deep breath. "Ask Ultragod anyway."

Death vanished.

"Thank you," Gabrielle said. "But you shouldn't have done that."

"Your dad did more good than Omega will ever be able to do evil," I said. "Besides, he's probably far better equipped to deal with something like this than I am."

The truth was, I was hoping Ultragod would pop back from the dead and deal with President Omega so I could go back to being a self-entitled bastard ripping off corporations for millions. I wanted to spend the next few years on an island somewhere with Mandy and Cindy, provided they were willing, and relax. I wanted them to be happy because that made me happy. I dreaded Death's answer, though, because I suspected what it would be before she returned. When she did, the sympathetic expression on her face spoke volumes.

"He's not coming, is he?" I asked.

"No," Death said. "He told me to tell you that he believes you will keep the world safe, but he's...spent."

"Is he happy? With mom?" Gabrielle asked.

"Yes."

"Then I'm okay with that," Gabrielle said. "Thank you."

Death pressed a finger to my forehead and I knew, instantly, where President Omega's underground base was located along with all of the information Colonel Disaster had about its defenses. It was a fortress even the Society of Superheroes would have difficulty breaching the interior of.

"Good luck," Death said. "I mean that."

And she was gone.

Mandy walked over, practically dragging Cindy with her before the latter reluctantly let go and placed her hand on my shoulder.

I embraced her back.

I was so happy; I didn't notice Other Gary's body had gone missing for five whole minutes.

***

Fear not! Merciless will return in *The Science of Supervillainy*. Coming in late 2016 or early 2017!

About the Author

C.T. Phipps is a lifelong student of horror, science fiction, and fantasy. An avid tabletop gamer, he discovered this passion led him to write and turned him into a lifelong geek. He is the author of The Rules of Supervillainy, the Red Room series, the forthcoming Wraith Knight, as well as the soon to be released Agent G series. C.T. lives in Ashland, Ky with his wife and their four dogs. You can find out more about him and his work by reading his blog, The United Federation of Charles, (http://unitedfederationofcharles.blogspot.com//)

Made in the USA
Lexington, KY
22 September 2016